Dear Reader,

Imagine that one of A
bachelors has been fou
luxurious penthouse.
the victim died in a bo
the evidence indicates the
engaged in something downright scandalous—a
crime that could most definitely lead to murder!
Sound like a delicious premise? We thought so. And
so did bestselling authors Jackie Merritt, Justine
Davis and Joan Elliott Pickart. In this intriguing
anthology, the three romantic tales not only follow
the crime investigation to its stunning verdict but
also show that love is the ultimate reward for the
individuals assigned to the case!

In Jackie Merritt's "Premeditated Passion," veteran
detective Joshua Benton and medical examiner
Maggie Sutter are called in to gather forensic
evidence to investigate the crime. Though Josh
remembers Maggie as being his best friend's little
sister, Maggie is determined to show this man who'd
once played a starring role in all her adolescent
fantasies that he's met his match!

Detective Colin Waters isn't happy about being
partnered with new hire Darien Wilson in Justine
Davis's "Behind the Badge." But when Darien turns
up evidence that the victim led a double life, Waters
finds it virtually impossible to resist her charms.

And finally, in Joan Elliott Pickart's "Verdict:
Marriage," DA Evan Stone gets more than he
bargained for when a judge orders him to spend
an evening with documentary filmmaker Jennifer
Anderson. The two quickly discover that there's a
fine line between love and hate…And Evan is in for
his own shocking surprise when Jennifer shows up to
film the trial.

We hope you enjoy these three romantic tales.

Happy reading!

The Editors
M&B Books

MTW . MM

JOAN ELLIOTT PICKART

is the author of over eighty-five novels. When she isn't writing, she has tea parties, reads stories, plays dress up—and the list goes on—with her young daughter, Autumn. Joan also has three grown daughters and three wonderful little grandchildren. Joan and Autumn live in a small town in the high pine country of Arizona.

JUSTINE DAVIS

sold her first book in 1989 and followed that up with the sale of nineteen novels in less than two years. Justine accomplished this while maintaining her full-time job at a city police department until she retired to write full-time. She now lives with her husband and the perfect dog—plus a family of eagles—on Puget Sound in Washington State.

JACKIE MERRITT

is a bestselling author of fifty romances. She and her husband are living in southern Nevada again, falling back on old habits of loving the long warm or slightly cool winters and trying almost desperately to head north for the months of July and August, when the fiery sun bakes people and cacti alike.

BODY OF EVIDENCE

JOAN ELLIOTT PICKART
JUSTINE DAVIS
JACKIE MERRITT

M&B

*M&B™ and M&B™ with the Rose Device
are trademarks of the publisher.*

*First published in Great Britain 2006
by Harlequin Mills & Boon Limited, Eton House,
18-24 Paradise Road, Richmond, Surrey TW9 1SR*

BODY OF EVIDENCE © by Harlequin Books SA 2003

The publisher acknowledges the copyright holders of the
individual works as follows:

Premeditated Passion © Carolyn Joyner 2003
Behind the Badge © Janice Davis Smith 2003
Verdict: Marriage © Joan Elliott Pickart 2003

ISBN 0 373 21829 X

109-0306

*Printed and bound in Spain
by Litografía Rosés S.A., Barcelona*

CONTENTS

PREMEDITATED PASSION

Jackie Merritt

Dear Reader,

When my M&B editors asked me to write about a crime, I became quite excited. I'm a big fan of the forensic science shows on television, which depict the modern-day methods of bringing criminals to justice. With such incredible technology at the fingertips of criminologists and law enforcement in general, the percentage of unsolved crimes has to be dropping.

Of course this book isn't just about murder, investigation and justice. Romance blossoms among the clues and hard work of the Chicago police department, and I'm sure you will enjoy reading Josh and Maggie's story as much as I enjoyed writing it.

Jackie Merritt

Chapter 1

Maggie Sutter's heart seemed to be beating much faster than was healthy. She knew she had to pull herself together, as she needed every one of her five senses and every cell in her brain functioning on the highest plane for her to properly and thoroughly investigate the scene of a homicide. But the idea of talking to Josh Benton, and working closely with him, simply wouldn't leave her thoughts.

Maggie rode the elevator to the Gardner penthouse on the thirty-fifth floor of one of the luxury residential apartment buildings on Chicago's Gold Coast. Taking off her heavy jacket during the rise, she concluded that this was not your everyday street crime. The Gardner name was known to anyone who paid attention to the business section of Chicago's newspapers, or to the society pages. The family had clout and immense wealth. Old money, Maggie was certain, and the kind of lifestyle only others of the same class could grasp. Maggie had never longed for great wealth, and she was much more affected by working this case with Josh Benton than hearing that the victim was a Gardner.

The elevator doors opened with barely a whisper and Maggie stepped through them and into a different world, a huge foyer with marble floors and walls, and a few pieces of elegant furniture that had probably cost more than she made in a year. Two uniformed cops were on elevator duty in the foyer, and one of them checked her ID and compared the photo on it with her face.

"Has anyone checked this area for prints?" she asked him.

"Not yet. The photographer's been at it for about a half hour. He took some shots in here."

Maggie's gaze went over the frame of the elevator. Places of entrance and exit sometimes yielded all sorts of evidence. "Make sure anyone using the elevators keeps their hands in their pockets," she said. "And the stairs as well," she added, eyeing a door to the left that had to lead to a stairwell. She walked away from the two men and entered the penthouse apartment.

In the most incredibly beautiful room she'd ever

seen—counting magazines and movies—Maggie saw a woman sitting on a plush, ivory-colored sofa and crying into a handful of tissues. Changing direction, Maggie walked over to her and the cop seated next to her.

Maggie arched her eyebrow inquisitively at the officer, and he promptly introduced the woman as Miriam Hobart. He explained, "She's been a housekeeper in this apartment for ten years. She found Franklin Gardner's body. Something woke her…a sound…and she got up to try to locate its source." That information prompted another gush of tears from the woman and some loud sobs.

Maggie thought for a moment then decided not to question the woman. First of all, Miriam Hobart was still in shock—or appeared to be—and in the weeping stage of grief. Second, this was Detective Josh Benton's case, and he might not appreciate her questioning anyone without a direct order from him. As primary detective on the case, he would orchestrate the investigation.

The elegant living room was immaculate and obviously not the scene of the crime. The sofa was already contaminated, so Maggie laid her jacket on the far end of it.

"Which room?" she asked.

"The study. Just follow the trail of uniforms," the officer said.

Maggie did exactly that and wound through large,

elegantly decorated rooms until she found the study. The police photographer was still working, and Maggie stayed in the doorway. She could see the victim on the carpet. He was wearing a white terry robe that reminded Maggie of the ones passed out in posh health clubs.

"How much longer will you be in here, Jack?" she asked.

The photographer looked her way. "I'm done. You and whoever else works this case are going to have so many shots of this place…and of the victim…that you'll despise me."

"I doubt that." Jack began gathering his equipment. "Could you hang around for another thirty or so minutes?" she asked him. "I need photographs of the carpet under the body, but it can't be moved until I do some prelim work."

"Guess so. I'll be down in the lobby. Here's my cell number," he said, handing her his card. "Just give me a ring and I'll come back up, but I don't want to wait in here. After twenty years on the job, I still can't take the smell of a murder scene."

"Seen anything of Detective Benton?" she asked, making sure not to sound as though she gave a damn.

"Yeah, he's around. I saw him last in the master bedroom. Well, like I said, I don't like murder scenes. Call down when you're ready for me."

Maggie nodded and then frowned over Jack's second reference to a "murder scene," which this probably was, even though she hadn't yet found proof of that. Someone thought it was, however. Criminalists were not called out for heart attack victims.

Knowing nothing of Josh's methods of investigation—maybe he always checked every room of a crime scene domicile before he did anything else—Maggie walked closer to the body and spotted the blood under the head. It wasn't a huge puddle, which pretty much ruled out an arterial wound. There were also spots of blood on the white robe, about six or seven of them. Mr. Gardner's legs were bare and a white slipper hung on his right foot while the other slipper resided about a yard from his left foot.

Setting down her bag, Maggie opened it and took out a fresh pair of latex gloves, which she pulled onto her hands. She laid some white paper on the carpet next to Franklin Gardner's body and used it to kneel on.

The victim's eyes were open—blank and staring. He appeared lifeless but Maggie checked for a pulse anyway. Finding none, she reached into the bag again for the little recorder she used at crime scenes and attached the microphone so she could record with her hands free. After switching it on, she began speaking. "Victim has been identified by housekeeper Miriam Hobart as Franklin Gardner. No family verification at this point. Victim is male, Caucasian, approximately fifty years of age and appears physically fit. Victim has blue eyes, black hair and darkly tanned skin. No physical exam yet, but there are…'' Maggie stopped to count, ''seven spots of blood on the front of his robe in the chest area. I'm now going to open the robe.''

She was just beginning to untie the knotted sash that kept the robe closed when she heard Josh Benton's voice in the doorway.

''So how's it going?'' he asked, and walked over to her and the victim.

Maggie gulped and turned off the recorder. She lifted her face and looked at Detective Benton. ''I'm really just getting started.''

Detective Josh Benton's gray eyes rested on the face of the woman examining the dead body of the man lying on the carpet, dropped to her photo ID and then returned to her face. He could hardly believe his own eyes.

''My God, Maggie Sutter! What are you doing here? Wait, erase that. It's obvious what you're doing here, but how come…I mean, how long…how come you never contacted me and let me know you were in the department?''

Maggie felt her face get warm. ''We passed each other once in a hallway and you…you didn't recognize me.''

''Well, hell, why didn't you yell at me, or trip

me, or something?'' Josh kept looking at her, seeing small differences between the Maggie Sutter he'd known years ago and the extremely attractive woman she was today.

"I could hardly do that," Maggie murmured, almost feverish from the thorough inspection she was getting.

"Didn't your hair used to be redder?"

"It got darker over the years."

"So, is Tim still living in California?"

His question about Maggie's older brother startled her. They had a corpse on their hands—a suspected homicide victim—and Benton was choosing this morning to talk about her family? No way, she thought, and ignored the question completely.

"I was just beginning a prelim on the victim," she repeated flatly. "Shall I continue or do you want to take over?" She would accede to his wishes. He was her superior in the department, if not her boss. And, of course, for this case he *would* be her boss. It grated that he wasn't even embarrassed about not recognizing her that day. Obviously he'd been a more sensitive person ten years ago when he and Tim had been best friends.

"Go ahead with what you were doing. I want to take a look around the room. It hasn't yet been dusted for prints, so everyone needs to be extremely cautious about touching anything without gloves." He glanced at her hands. "I see you're up to speed."

Maggie lowered her eyes and wondered cynically if he even trusted her to investigate a crime scene at all. To be honest, he just barely resembled the earnest young cop he'd been when she'd had that painful crush on him ten years ago. Not in looks. He was still outrageously handsome, maybe even better looking, but that was about it. Back then she had seen him as the most wonderful, the handsomest, greatest guy ever born. She remembered him as being kind and sweet and nice to everyone. Obviously her opinion had been severely distorted by teenage idol worship.

Wearing latex gloves, Josh strolled around the room peering at various objects while keeping an eye on Maggie. He still could hardly believe that she was here, at a crime scene and working on his team. It just seemed so off-the-wall to him. When, exactly, had she become interested in investigative law enforcement?

Maggie opened Gardner's robe and talked into the miniature microphone near her mouth about the wounds on his chest.

"Seven small…very small puncture wounds. An ice pick perhaps. Do people still use ice picks in their homes, considering the variety of ice-makers on the market? Note. Check the bar."

Josh heard her and walked over to the elegantly carved wood bar with its six leather-covered stools, went behind it and took a rather admiring inventory of the many bottles of expensive liquor that were displayed on lighted shelves. He located a built-in refrigerator, another one strictly for bottles of wine and also a large automatic ice-maker. He was about to give up on Maggie's ice pick theory—at least for the moment—when he opened a door and saw a collection of antique ice picks in a glass case. Each one was held in place by a small leather strap, and there were no empty spaces, no empty straps.

Maggie was examining the back of the victim's head, which bore a serious scalp depression and possible skull split that had to be the cause of the blood on the carpet.

She looked over to Benton who asked dryly, "Was he killed twice?"

Maggie gasped. "What?"

Josh could tell that he'd shocked her. "Maggie, when you've done this for twelve years, like I have, that soft heart of yours will be considerably harder."

"I hope not," she said passionately. "I'm done with my prelim. Do you want to check the body before I call down to the lobby for the photographer? I'd like some photos of the carpet under the body."

"Yes, I want a look at him."

Maggie got to her feet and Josh took her place. He looked at the victim's hands and fingernails. "Good manicure," he remarked. Then he checked the man's feet, legs and groin area. "He has some bruising...rather odd shapes...on his face. Also some signs of struggle, defensive bruises, on his forearms and hands. The medical examiner will have to determine cause of death in an autopsy, 'cause from where I sit, it could have been caused by the chest wounds or the crushing blow to his head when he fell and hit that coffee table."

"What?" Maggie easily found the culprit table and flushed to the roots of her hair. She should have seen the blood on the corner of that table the minute she entered the study. Benton hadn't missed it and she had. Damn! Was she so discombobulated over working with him that her brain wasn't functioning with its usual efficiency?

Josh got up. "Call down for Jack and also the fingerprint team. I want everything in this room dusted for prints, especially the bar area. Also, there's a collection of antique ice picks in a special cabinet behind the bar. I want them individually bagged and tested for evidence. You can handle that at the crime lab. You stay with the body until I say it's ready for the morgue. I've checked out most of the apartment, and I'm going to finish that before leaving."

Maggie tried to hide the humiliation she felt over missing something so obvious as blood on the sharp corner of that coffee table. She lifted her chin and said, "I would estimate his death to have occurred around four hours ago. Do you agree?"

"Agreed," Josh stated and strode from the room.

Maggie dug out her cell phone and dialed Jack's number. "I'm ready for those photos, Jack. And if the lab people are down there to do the prints, ask them to come up with you. Orders from Benton."

"Will do."

The body had been taken away and most of the police officers had gone. The sun was up, weak and pale, not even warming the area enough to create fog. Maggie stood at a wall of windows in a gorgeous sitting room and looked out at an incredible view of Lake Michigan. Her own body ached; she hadn't slept enough and she had a full day of work ahead of her.

She was so tired she didn't even hear Josh enter the room until he spoke.

"How about a cup of coffee?" Josh asked, making Maggie jump because she hadn't heard him behind her. "There's a little place a few blocks from here that serves mighty fine coffee and a good breakfast, as well, if you're hungry."

"I'm not a bit hungry, but I could definitely use some coffee. We're not through here, though, are we? Shouldn't one of us talk to the housekeeper?"

"I'm not sure who's going to handle interviews yet, but don't worry, the housekeeper's not going anywhere. Neither are the other residents of this building. We'll get around to each and every one of them, but we still need to have that coffee. Let's go.''

"Let me get my things," Maggie said.

The Coffeehouse Café was small and trendy. Josh and Maggie found an empty table and sat down. Josh mentioned breakfast again, but Maggie told him she wasn't ready to eat, which she wasn't. When hot, delicious-smelling coffee was brought to their table, though, she reached for her cup immediately.

"You're right," she said after a satisfying sip. "This is terrific coffee."

Josh had ordered some bacon and toast, and he ate as well as enjoyed his coffee. He sent Maggie a glance. "Spend enough time with me and you'll find out that I'm right most of the time."

"Oh, really? When did that metamorphosis come about? I don't recall your being Mr. Perfect when you and Tim hung together." It was a lie. In those days she'd thought of him as nothing but perfect.

"You didn't? Hmm. That surprises me. How is ol' Tim doing these days?"

"Ol' Tim is doing great. You do know he got married, don't you?"

"Yeah, I knew that."

"Well, he also has two little boys. Did you know that?"

"No. Two sons, huh? Got any pictures of them?"

"Not with me."

"So, how'd you end up like me instead of like Tim? He's still into computers, I suppose."

Maggie arched her eyebrows. "Yes, he is, and doing extremely well financially. But I don't see any similarities between you and me, other than both of us being cops."

"I was a cop when you were still in kindergarten."

"Hardly. You're only ten years older than I am. I'm twenty-six. And the two of us being cops doesn't make us think and act alike."

"Do I detect disapproval in your voice?"

"Well, you're certainly not right all the damned time. No one is."

"Hey, I said most of the time, and I was only kidding anyway. Can't you take a joke anymore? If I remember right, you used to laugh at jokes."

"The last time we talked I was sixteen and naive. I'm neither of those now."

Josh had finished eating. Holding his cup with both hands, his elbows on the table, he gave her a long look. "You're all grown up, I can't deny that."

Was that admiration and lechery in his stunning gray eyes? Maggie wondered. A shiver went up her spine. He was even more handsome now than he'd been when she'd suffered that torturous crush. And he'd treated her like a kid, never once suspecting that he was the star player in all of her teenage fantasies.

Well, wouldn't he have a laugh if she suddenly blurted that she was no more experienced with men now than she'd been ten years ago? She wasn't overly proud of being a virgin at her age, but she had never met a guy who had affected her in a sexual way. Of course, she'd had her nose stuck in a book almost constantly in college, and since graduation she had worked darned hard to get where she was in the Chicago Police Department.

But Josh affected her. He had when she was a teenager and he possessed the same powerful magnetism today. She felt all sorts of things just from looking at him, from having him look at her, and the last thing she wanted was a quickie affair with the only man she might have grown up to love, given half a chance.

"Maybe we should talk about the case," she said.

Josh's lips turned up in a knowing little half grin. She was pretty and she was also sharp enough to know how to keep a hot-blooded predator at arm's length. Besides, she was Tim's sister, and Maggie might not know it, but that meant something to Josh. He might kid around with Maggie Sutter, but that was as far as it would ever go for him.

"There's very little to talk about at this point," he said. "You know the drill…the autopsy and med-

ical examiner's report on cause of death…the endless interviews…the lab reports…and on and on.''

"Okay, fine. You're giving the orders, so I'd like
to hear mine.''

"You've got bags of possible evidence to examine and test. Spend the day at the crime lab. As for
me, I intend to talk to the M.E. The question hound-
ing me is what came first, the stab wounds or the
blow to his head. I think that's going to be a key
issue in this case.''

Maggie was impressed with Josh's logic, which
sort of saddened her because he seemed to see things
more clearly than she did. His years of experience
undoubtedly accounted for such acuity, but she
couldn't help envying it.

"All right," she agreed. "Drop me off at the
Gardner building so I can pick up my car. Would
you like me to contact you any time today?''

"If you find anything I should know about, yes.''
Josh reached into his inside coat pocket and brought
out a business card. "All my phone numbers are on
that.''

Maggie handed him her card. "In case you need
to talk to me," she said.

"Good. We're in sync.''

Much more than you could ever imagine. Maggie
hated thinking those words and surely her expression or voice gave no clues to her thoughts, but
Josh's good looks, his intelligence and macho male-

ness were again burrowing under her skin and setting up residence in the vicinity of her heart. She
would have to be careful around him or he would
catch on, and if he ever realized that he had the
upper hand where her emotions were concerned,
there was no predicting what might happen.

Or maybe there was. Maggie's stomach sank clear
to her toes, but she rose and left the café with Josh
as though he meant no more to her than any other
cop she had worked with.

It was scary that he did…already…after only one
time together.

Chapter 2

One of the jobs of a criminalist was to reconstruct the crime under investigation. Sketches of the murder scene, photographs and physical evidence all came into play. Maggie thought about the process while analyzing and testing the samples of everything from carpet fibers to fingernail scrapings that she had taken from Franklin Gardner's study. As always, she was careful to keep very close tabs on even the smallest item, as it just might prove invaluable in bringing a killer to justice.

Around two that afternoon the growling of Maggie's stomach was a strong reminder that she hadn't eaten since last night. But because she wanted to finish her tests so she could log the evidence before leaving the premises, she settled for an energy bar from a vending machine. It helped, and by seven that evening she had completed everything that could be completed in one day, and then carried it all to the evidence room.

"Each bag is tagged," she told the person in charge, even though nothing that *wasn't* tagged could be logged in. "I'll be picking up several of the bags during the next few days for further testing." Maggie was mostly referring to Franklin Gardner's collection of ice picks. They were suspiciously lacking in fingerprints—possibly wiped clean by Franklin's attacker—and two had trace amounts of blood. She needed more time on them.

She was walking out to her car when it dawned on her that Josh Benton hadn't called. Feeling slighted personally was one thing, but professionally? No way, she thought. Her work today had accomplished a great deal, and she fully intended on staying right in the middle of this investigation. Instead of going home, she drove to the Detective Bureau, parked her car and walked in. Sometimes the place was pure bedlam. This evening, it was merely busy.

Maggie collected her written messages on her way past the duty officer, gave them a quick look and saw nothing that couldn't wait, then proceeded to the desk she had been assigned two months ago. It was in a room crammed with file cabinets and about twenty other desks. The only items on hers were a telephone and a silent, blank-faced computer.

Passing up her desk, Maggie went in search of Detective Benton. His desk, she had discovered, was in a different room, one that was divided into tiny cubicles. It wasn't the Ritz, by any stretch of the imagination, but it was something Maggie aspired to herself one day. It wouldn't happen for years, she knew, but it gave her pleasure to think of that far-off event.

The door of Josh's private space was open. Maggie peered in and saw Josh talking on the phone. He saw her, as well, and waved her in. She chose a chair and waited for him to finish.

He finally did, and while putting down the phone he asked her, "How'd it go at the lab?"

"Routinely," she replied. She laid some papers on his desk. "Reports of my preliminary exam of the victim in situ. I haven't finished with the ice picks, but there are no prints on them, not even a smudge. Wiped clean would be my guess, but two of them show trace amounts of blood. Type O-positive on one, animal blood on the other. Another guess is that that one was used to pry frozen steaks apart, or some kind of meat. If it becomes important, I can, of course, run further tests and identify the specie of animal. As for the other, do we know Franklin Gardner's blood type?"

"O-positive," Josh said calmly.

Maggie's gaze locked with Josh's. "Then that ice pick could be the murder weapon."

"Could be," Josh concurred. "On first look, the M.E. agreed that cause of death could be the head wound, the chest wounds or both, which we already surmised. But we won't know anything for sure until we get his autopsy report, which he hasn't yet faxed over. I asked for a rush job, but you know how that goes."

"Did you mention the media interest in the case?"

"Pulled every string I could. But *our* most recent murder victim isn't the only one in Chicago whose name makes the general population genuflect," Josh said dryly. "Anyhow, the report could come in anytime."

"How about fingerprint analysis of the apartment? Those guys lifted dozens of specimens from doorways, tables, the bar and on and on. Do we have anything in writing from that direction yet?"

"No. They said they would have some results by tomorrow. I was told that two captains drove out to the Gardner mansion to inform Franklin's mother of his death."

Maggie raised her eyebrows. "Captains? I thought you would go, so you could see her reaction. Were you told how she took the news?"

"Are you thinking that Franklin's mother might have something to do with his premature demise?"

"Don't look so skeptical. Anything's possible. Everyone Franklin knew is a suspect until *we* know otherwise. There was no sign of forced entry into either the building, the private elevator or the penthouse. Franklin admitted his killer himself, so it had to be someone he knew...or hoped to know. What about his love life? Did he have a girlfriend...or more than one? Maybe the reason he was killed twice, as you so delicately put it earlier today, was because it was a crime of passion. You know, where the killer is so emotionally wound up that he or she doesn't know when to quit."

"You have a good imagination."

"Can't be an investigative cop without one."

"It helps...but it can also hinder. We do our best work with provable facts."

"When they're available, yes, but when they're not we had better be able to connect the dots...or the circumstantial evidence...all on our own. How about the housekeeper? Did anyone interrogate her yet, and is she being permitted to stay at the apartment? Nothing should be disturbed...or cleaned...in that place."

"Really?" Josh drawled. "Gosh, I didn't know that."

Maggie's face reddened. "Sorry, I didn't mean to patronize. But what did you do with Miriam Hobart?"

"Threw her into the deepest, darkest dungeon in

Chicago. What else would I do with the housekeeper of a murder victim?''

''Are you making fun of me?''

''You're way too serious, Maggie. Lighten up.''

Maggie got to her feet. ''I don't think it's possible to be 'too serious' about a homicide. I'm going home.''

Josh rose. ''How about us eating dinner together first?''

Maggie's pulse quickened, although the way she looked couldn't possibly be sparking any foolish ideas in Josh Benton's head. She'd gotten up in the middle of last night and come to work without a speck of makeup on her face and barely a hairdo. Even so, she looked worse now than she had then, because the wear and tear of the day had to show on her face.

''Sorry, but if you're through with me, I'd like to go home.''

''I'm not through with you, Maggie,'' Josh said quietly. ''Don't even think it.''

His tone of voice threw Maggie much more than the words he'd said. Odder still was the strange look on his face, as though he hadn't meant to sound like the big bad hunter after the little red fox. But surprised or not, they both knew exactly how he had sounded, and Maggie narrowed her eyes at him while he proceeded to put on a tough, almost belligerent expression. It was, Maggie decided, an I-dare-you-to-make-something-out-of-it expression. A cop's expression, distant and challenging.

She was too tired to take on another challenge today, not even a personal one that she would have loved to pursue at various times during the past ten years.

Deciding to ignore the sexual innuendo she'd just heard in his voice—for the time being, at least—she spoke rather coolly. "If there's anything else we should discuss this evening, I will, of course, sit down again. If not...?"

Josh wondered what in hell had come over him. This was Maggie, Tim's kid sister.

"Yeah, go on home. There's nothing more we have to do tonight. Unless you're handling other cases that need attention."

"I have several in process, but I'm up to speed on them. They're not nearly as urgent as the Gardner homicide, anyway. Well, if that's it for the day, I'll say good-night."

"Oh, there is one thing. Have you worked with Colin Waters?"

Maggie had started to leave, but she turned at the door, wearily leaned her shoulder against the frame and shook her head. "No, but I know who he is. Why?"

"I've brought him in on the case. Orders from the powers-that-be are to get this one done fast. Colin is one of the best investigators we have. I talked to him earlier today, and he and his partner, Darien Wilson, are already working on it. Just thought you should know the latest. I'm sure they'll be glad to read your prelim report.''

"Fine. Do you want me to check in here in the morning, or should I go directly to the lab?''

"Check in here first. Whether I'm here or not, take a look at the Gardner file, just in case some new report has come in.''

"I should be adding several more reports to the file tomorrow. Okay, is that it?''

"That's it. See you tomorrow.''

"If you're here,'' Maggie reminded him.

Without another word, Maggie left Josh's office.

With Maggie gone, Josh let himself dwell on her. Something about her had gotten under his skin. True, he'd been without female companionship for a while, a good six months, actually, since he and Tasha, a model he had dated for over a year, had called it quits. But he hadn't noticed any unusual suffering because of a lack of regular sex. In fact, he realized with a frown that he really hadn't been thinking of sex at all since Tasha. And it wasn't because attractive women were scarce. He simply hadn't wanted any sort of relationship with a woman. With a wry twist of his lips, Josh wondered if he was getting old.

But he was thinking of relationships now, wasn't

he? All because of seeing Maggie Sutter again, who should represent nothing beyond some fine old memories. Ten years ago he and Tim Sutter had been good friends, and often when Josh had dropped in on Tim, there would be Maggie, cute as any teenage girl could ever be, sassy, giggly and looking at him with her gorgeous violet-blue eyes.

She didn't look at him in the same way now, Josh thought with a bit of a wince. In fact, if there was any expression at all in her eyes when she looked at him, it was cool disdain. Was that because he hadn't shown recognition during the accidental meeting that she claimed had occurred between them? He'd been startled as hell to see her as a cop and on duty smack-dab in the middle of his arena, to be exact, and he still wasn't sure he liked it, particularly since she was making him think some pretty off-the-wall thoughts. And her being Tim's sister somehow made her seem to be off-limits.

Josh had lost track of Tim, but Tim had done the same with him. They lived different lives, Tim in California with his computers, his wife and kids, and he, Josh, sticking close to home, never even considering marriage or leaving Chicago, working hard and advancing in the police department. In truth, he and Tim couldn't be more different from each other, they always had been, but still, during their twenties, they had hit it off.

Josh sighed quietly. If Tim had stayed in the Chicago area, they'd probably still be friends. In the next heartbeat another thought, a question, gave Josh a start. What about Tim and Maggie's mother? Josh remembered Lottie Sutter almost as well as he did her kids. Was Lottie alive and thriving? He hoped she was. They used to have some really good discussions.

He sat there for another ten minutes thinking about the Sutter family, then, rather abruptly, the long day got the better of him and he realized that he was almost too tired to get out of his chair and go home. But if he didn't do it soon he would probably fall asleep right where he sat.

He forced himself to his feet—for the last time that day, he hoped.

Maggie slept like the dead that night. Her alarm clock jarred her awake at 6:00 a.m., and she shoved aside the covers and walked to the shower with her eyes only half-open. The shower finished what the buzzing of the clock's alarm had started—got her brain and body functioning on normal. She turned on the TV in her bedroom to catch the weather report and made a face when she heard it. "High today of thirty-five degrees and snow flurries by late afternoon. Current temperature is twenty-six degrees."

"Great," Maggie muttered, wishing her life away by wishing for spring and some decent weather. Almost every winter was the same. By March she was so ready for sunshine and warmth that she fantasized herself living in a southern state, where the sun shone brightly nearly every day of the year. She could always find a job in law enforcement, couldn't she? With her education and training? Of course she could.

The television program went from the weather report to local news stories. Maggie only partially listened until she heard, "Franklin Gardner, international businessman and lifelong resident of Chicago, was found dead in his penthouse apartment early yesterday morning. Police are investigating his death as a possible homicide."

The "possible homicide" comment surprised Maggie, because had Franklin Gardner's entire family been notified already? Occasionally the cart got out before the horse in breaking newscasts, but surely Benton was controlling all information passed to the media.

Maggie told herself to stay out of that part of the investigation. Josh hadn't gotten where he was in the department by talking out of turn. He knew the rules, probably better than she did.

This morning Maggie put on a little makeup and didn't even try to kid herself that it wasn't because of Josh Benton. Dressed in charcoal, almost-black wool slacks and turtleneck sweater, she bundled herself into her heavy outside jacket, scarf and gloves and left her apartment.

Entering the garage was like bucking a wave of Arctic air. Her breath fogged in front of her face and she thought about how great it would be if the garage were heated. Of course, when she found this apartment, she'd been thrilled it had a parking garage and she could still afford the rent!

Mumbling to herself that living through scorching Arizona summers was probably just as bad as freezing Illinois temperatures in March, Maggie hurried to her car, unlocked it and got in.

She inserted the key in the ignition and turned it. Nothing happened. Startled, she did it again and again. Nothing happened. Her car was dead. Groaning, she put her head on the steering wheel.

But it was too cold to sit there and feel sorry for herself for long. Raising her head, she got out her cell phone and the card Josh had given her yesterday. She dialed his cell number. He answered on the second ring with a gruff-sounding "Detective Benton."

"This is Maggie. My car is dead. I'm going to call a mechanic, and there's no telling how long that will take. Obviously I'm going to be coming in late. Thought you should know."

"Where do you live?"

"Pardon?"

"Give me your address. Maybe it's just your battery. If it is, I'll give you a jump."

"You're going to fix my car?"

"Don't sound so doubtful. I know a *few* things about cars, and I've got a set of jumper cables. Unless you'd rather call that expensive mechanic than let me take a look at it."

"Um, no…no, of course not." Maggie reluctantly recited her address. "But I hate imposing on your time."

"If I felt it was an imposition, I wouldn't have offered to help out."

"Well…all right. It's freezing in this garage so I'll be waiting in my apartment. Just ring my bell."

Josh cleared his throat and squelched an impulse to tell her that he'd love to ring her bell. In fact, she just might love *having* her bell rung by him.

"I should be there in twenty minutes," he stated, *without* innuendo.

"Um…thank you." Maggie hit the button to break the call and stuffed the phone back into her bag. She tried the ignition again, got no response at all from the wayward engine, then shook her head disgustedly and got out. She locked the car and headed for the elevator, cursing under her breath.

Damn it, why hadn't he just let her call for a mechanic and be done with it? Or better still, when he'd made his intrusive offer of assistance, why hadn't she thought fast, refused with thanks, and told him she had *already* called for a mechanic?

Inside her apartment she yanked off her gloves and jacket and then ran around like a wild woman, frantically picking up things, such as the slippers she'd left by the sofa several nights back, and the Sunday newspapers that were still strewn across her little kitchen table three days later. She grabbed a stack of junk mail that she'd been intending to toss for days and dropped it in the trash can, and put the dirty dishes stacked in the sink into the apartment-size dishwasher she'd been almost as glad to see as the garage when she'd rented the place.

She suddenly needed coffee, and she put on a pot to brew. Hurrying to her bedroom, she made the bed and then ran into the bathroom to straighten things up in there, just in case Josh should ask to use it. She was horribly nervous and couldn't seem to calm her racing pulse, however many times she reminded herself that she had outgrown Josh Benton years and years ago.

Of course, if that was the truth, the whole truth and nothing but the truth, would she be nervous at all?

Maggie was on her second cup of coffee when the building's front door buzzer went off. She set her cup on the counter, went to her apartment's front door and pushed a button. ''Yes?''

"It's me. Buzz me in."

Maggie complied and then opened the door to watch for Josh to step out of the elevator down the hall. As usual, it seemed an eternity for the hydraulic lift to make its snail-like way from the first floor to the fourth, but finally Maggie heard it grind to a shuddering stop. The doors slowly opened and Josh began walking toward her.

"I should have taken the stairs. It would've been faster."

"Which is what I usually do. The only time I use the elevator is when I'm loaded down with groceries, or something else. Come on in."

Josh followed her in. "This building has a garage in the basement?"

"Yes. I'll get my jacket."

"Not so fast. Do I smell fresh coffee?"

"Uh…yes. Would you like some?"

"Sure would. I was going to stop at a coffeehouse, but then you called and I figured I'd better get over here right away."

Maggie led him to the kitchen and proceeded to fill a mug for him. "That's what I do on most mornings, stop somewhere for a large coffee to go." She handed the mug to Josh who took it and then set it on the table.

"I'm going to take my jacket off, sit down and enjoy this, if you don't mind. The first cup of the

day always tastes best to me. Come and join me at
the table.''

"In a minute. You go ahead and sit down. And I
don't mind if you enjoy your first cup of the day,''
she murmured, a lie if she'd ever told one. She
minded everything that was happening, minded him
being there at all, minded that he'd had the nerve to
ask for coffee and that he'd been nice enough to
offer to jump her car—if that was all it needed. But
mostly she minded his astonishing good looks,
which seemed a hundred times more striking this
morning than they had yesterday. Her stupid stomach was doing somersaults just from looking at him.

And he seemed so at home! Not at all uncomfortable or bashful or anything else that she could
detect and read as a negative reaction to being alone
in her apartment with her.

Maggie's thoughts turned cynical. Josh Benton
was probably so used to drinking morning coffee in
women's apartments, undoubtedly after spending
the night, that why on earth would this perfectly
innocent situation with her make him feel uneasy?

Well, he might be just fine with this…this togeth-
erness, but she was not. "I have my car keys right
here,'' Maggie said, holding them up so he could
see.

Josh grinned. "Trying to get rid of me already?''

"Of course not! Take your time. I'll finish my
own coffee.'' To prove that her second lie was the

unmitigated truth, Maggie took her cup to the table and sat across from him. "Were you at the Bureau when I called your cell?" she asked in an effort to keep any conversation between them on business.

"On my way." Josh got up, refilled his mug and resumed his seat. He took a sip and looked as satisfied as a frog in a rainfall. "I'm coming alive," he said. "I do love my coffee. I hope I never have to give it up. You probably don't even remember when almost everyone smoked, but I sure do. Went through hell quitting that habit, mostly because I enjoyed it so much. But it was getting so you couldn't find a building that permitted smoking, and standing outside in this kind of weather to light up got very old, very fast."

"I never did smoke, so I know very little about the trauma of quitting. I've heard horror stories about it, though."

"Believe every one of them." Josh locked his gaze with Maggie's. "You know, I don't think I've ever seen anyone else with eyes the color of yours."

Maggie felt her face get warm. He had switched gears so fast he'd caught her off guard. "I...I'm sure the color is not unique," she stammered.

"It's *very* unique, and you're very beautiful." Josh hadn't intended to say any of those things, and he was even more startled by them than Maggie was. But she *was* beautiful this morning, and maybe she'd been beautiful yesterday, as well, and he'd been too wrapped up in the Gardner case to see her clearly.

Maggie felt as stiff as a board—a board with red cheeks. "I wish you wouldn't say things like that," she said, her voice sounding thin and shaky. "We have to work together, and…and…"

Josh got to his feet and walked around the table to her. Tipping her chin with his forefinger he said softly, "And what, Maggie?"

She didn't move away from him, she couldn't. And when she saw his face coming closer to hers, she knew he was going to kiss her.

She parted her lips and sucked in a soft breath.

Breathless seconds passed in slow motion for Maggie. Fragmented thoughts drifted through her mind. *I know this man…it's not as though he's a stranger. I want to feel his kiss…his lips on mine. Have I waited all this time for Josh Benton to reenter my life?*

His scent seemed more familiar than her own. His body emanated exciting warmth. She felt things deep inside of her that were brand-new but instinctively recognizable.

But…why was he hesitating?

The answer to that question seemed written in neon in Josh's brain, and finally he muttered a curse and finished his remark of self-disgusted recrimination with, "What the hell am I doing?" He stepped away from Maggie and plucked the keys from her hand so quickly that she reeled. "Come on," he growled. "Take me to your car."

His abrupt change of heart was like a physical blow for Maggie. She had to battle both fury and tears, for she believed that showing either side of the pain he'd just caused her would make her look immature and foolish. And she would die before knowingly appearing as anything but strong and uncaring in front of Josh.

Chapter 3

Putting on her most indifferent expression, Maggie said a cold "Excuse me" and went around him to leave the kitchen ahead of him. Pulling on her warm clothing again, she led him from the apartment. In the hall she took a second to make sure the door was locked, then again took the lead. "We'll use the stairs," she said without inflection.

And with every step down to the basement garage, she asked herself why Josh had been so eager to kiss her one second and then so angry with himself...or with her...in practically the next. Only one possibility made complete and utter sense: he was involved with someone else.

Maggie nearly lost the control she'd been using

on her emotions over that conclusion, and anger began eating holes in her hard-eyed composure. Another woman—he was in love and committed—and he'd dared to lead *her* on! To make her think that something was beginning to coalesce, to happen for them. In that instant she hated the man he was now—the *great* Detective Benton—and even the handsome, outgoing, hopeful young cop he'd been when she'd known him before.

Once in the frigid basement, she handed him the keys. "My car's over there, the dark green sedan."

The tone of her voice said it all for Josh. He'd started something he shouldn't have, and she resented him now as only a woman perceiving herself scorned could resent a man. God help him, he thought, he hadn't meant to make Maggie feel scorned, or anything else, for that matter.

"Uh, maybe we should talk about it," he said without quite meeting her eyes. Damn it, he should have insisted on talking about it upstairs the minute he'd backed off.

Maggie's eyes flashed pure fire at him. "There's nothing to talk about. Are you going to try starting my car, or have you changed your mind about that, too?"

Josh knew when to quit. Forcing an issue with a furious woman not only wasn't smart; it might reasonably be classified as temporary insanity.

He walked away from her without another word, heading for her car.

Maggie worked at the lab all day, going as far with the ice picks as she could without specific instructions to cover the investigative spectrum with them, which would have included DNA analysis. DNA testing would have been imperative if any genetic material had shown up at the murder scene from a second person, ostensibly the killer. Since there was nothing except Franklin Gardner's own blood, there was no reason to analyze his DNA. Not yet, at any rate.

Maggie's stack of written reports grew as the morning passed. Around two, she made copies of everything to take with her for the case file, delivered the originals to the clerical department for permanent recording, then gathered her belongings and drove to the Detective Bureau.

The second she walked in someone drawled, "Heard you had car trouble this morning."

"My, how news does travel around here," Maggie said wryly. "It was no big deal, just a dead battery. Everything's fine now."

"Well, I heard that Benton raced to your rescue."

Maggie caught the teasing twinkle in the other officer's eyes. Personal relationships weren't encouraged between cops, but they happened, and when they did the gossip, the innuendo and the com-ical remarks—not all of them clean—went on until either the relationship fizzled out or it became old news and everyone got bored with it.

Maggie raised her eyebrows and widened her eyes. "D'ya think he's on the verge of popping the question? A guy fixing a girl's car is pretty serious stuff."

The detective walked off laughing, relieving most of Maggie's concern about a perfectly innocent incident feeding the gossip mill. True, the morning might *not* have turned out so innocently if Benton had followed through with that kiss, but he hadn't and that was the end of it.

At least that was what she'd been telling herself all day. *It began and ended all in a matter of thirty seconds, so for God's sake stop making a big deal out of it. Romance is a lost art, and if you're naive enough to think that an incomplete pass pertains to anything but a football play, you are living in the dark ages, my girl!*

It was sound advice but impossible to accept as the final word on this morning's episode. Just thinking of it again stirred Maggie's ire, and she slapped her copies of the lab reports down on her desk, shed her heavy coat and hung it on a nearby hook, all with a sour expression on her face. After shoving her gloves and scarf into her backpack, then leaving everything behind that she'd brought in with her, she went to the New Case file cabinet to get the Gardner file.

It wasn't there. Obviously one of the other detectives on the case was using it. If it was Josh...?

Frowning, Maggie returned to her desk and sat down. Avoiding Josh for any length of time was impossible, but she wished it weren't. In fact, she wished she never had to look into those gray eyes of his ever again. He'd humiliated her, not by making his desire to kiss her so obvious, but because he'd changed his mind while looking directly into her ridiculously love-struck eyes. Well, maybe not *love*, but certainly he must have sensed her weak-kneed acquiescence and anticipation of the big event. Damn him, would she ever live it down?

Sighing because she would rather be laughing than crying—if only to herself—she began thumbing through the reports in front of her. She knew them by heart, but it was something to do until she figured out a way to get hold of the Gardner case file without running into Benton.

Maggie narrowed her eyes in thought. Maybe Colin Waters had it. Actually anyone in the building with an investigative interest in the homicide could be looking through it.

If Maggie had lifted her gaze just a little, and then looked to the left, she would have seen Detective Benton watching her. Josh had called the crime lab, learned that Maggie had left for the day and then taken the case file and headed for the squad room and her assigned desk.

But upon entering the room and seeing her so intently studying the papers in front of her, obviously concentrating so deeply that she heard none of the noise around her, he had stopped dead in his tracks. He should not have made that move this morning, but he couldn't help wishing that he'd taken it to its logical conclusion. All day he had paid the ultimate price for behaving like a gentleman instead of the horny toad Maggie had turned him into. She drew him irresistibly, and he ached now just from looking at her. It was a shock of huge proportions; never could he have imagined himself getting all hot and bothered over Tim's kid sister.

Muttering under his breath, he began moving again, walking over to Maggie's desk. "You might want to see this," he said gruffly, and laid the case file near her right hand.

Maggie saw that it was the Gardner case file. "Yes, thank you," she said coolly, although it was a miracle that the sudden flash of heat all but melting her vital organs didn't show in her voice. She realized with a heavy heart that this could not go on. Her career was at stake, as well as her peace of mind. There had to be a way to bring this unbearable tension between her and Josh to a head and then quash it forever.

"I have these to add to the file," she said, indicating the reports in front of her.

"Did you run across anything unusual?"

"Actually, no. Whoever killed Franklin Gardner left no part of himself behind. He…or she…is either very lucky or very smart about forensic procedures."

"Yes, well, that happens. Take a look at the file and if you want to talk afterward, I'll be around." Abruptly, Josh turned and left.

Maggie watched him go, but instead of hating him as she had believed to be the case earlier that day, she felt so much yearning that tears pricked her eyes. Heaving a sigh of despair—what in heaven's name had she done that was so terrible she deserved to fall for a guy who had the ability to look right through her?—she reached for the case file and opened it.

The first thing she saw was the autopsy report and she quickly read that Franklin Gardner had died from a blow to the back of his skull. The ice pick wasn't meaningless, but it had not been the cause of Gardner's death!

But why on earth would anyone stab a dead man? Stab him over and over again? Hadn't Gardner appeared dead? Was it possible that Franklin Gardner had accidentally fallen and hit his head on the corner of the table? Then someone, the person who had been in the study with him, had used what he had thought was merely unconsciousness as an opportunity to stab the life out of the disabled man?

Frowning, Maggie read on: Bruising on victim's face appears to have been made by something the attacker was wearing, most likely a large ring. *My Lord, the poor man was also beaten?*

Maggie sat back, contemplating the conflicting information. After a few minutes she checked the other reports in the file. So far Detectives Waters and Wilson had interviewed the housekeeper and the building supervisor. Miriam Hobart merely repeated in her statement what Maggie had already been told. An unknown noise woke her, she got up to check on it and found Mr. Gardner on the floor in the study. Frightened, she rushed back to her room and called 9-1-1.

The super's statement didn't offer much more, except for his opinion that Gardner had been an arrogant, unfriendly man, but he also told the detectives that his wife had always despised the penthouse resident. In speaking directly to the wife, the detectives noticed her knitting bag and spotted some long, thin knitting needles in it.

Maggie caught the implication, but her report on the ice pick would inform Waters and Wilson that Gardner was not stabbed by knitting needles.

After inserting her own reports into the file, Maggie sat and speculated. Gardner had been beaten and stabbed. Had the beating come first, then his fall and after that the stabbing? It made a crazy sort of sense. Possibly dazed from being struck in the face, Gardner had fallen—maybe tripped over something—and hit his head on the table. The attacker, not realizing that his victim was already dead, ran to the bar, grabbed an ice pick and returned to Gardner's immobile body to repeatedly drive the sharp point of the pick into his chest.

Maggie's phone rang. Absently she picked it up and said, "Detective Sutter."

"Hi, got a minute?"

"Natalie, hi. Yes, I can talk. What's going on?"

"Just thought we might have a burger or pizza together tonight. How about it? Do you have to work late, or can we meet somewhere. I have something to tell you."

"Bet I can guess what it is," Maggie said teasingly. From the lilt in her friend's voice, her news had to be about a new man in her life.

"But don't guess, okay? I'm dying to tell you all about it. Can we meet around six-thirty?"

"I don't see why not. Where?"

"Do you want pizza or a burger?"

"Um…pizza. How about meeting at Tony's?"

"Great. See you at six-thirty."

After putting down the phone, Maggie checked the time. It was almost five. She had plenty of time to talk to Benton before she drove to Tony's Pizzeria.

Bracing herself for a face-to-face with Josh, Maggie took the case file and her cell phone—she rarely did anything without it—and went to his private cubicle. He was at his desk, on the phone, and exactly as he'd done the first time Maggie had come to his domain, he waved her in.

She lowered herself onto a chair, then realized to whom Josh was speaking—the head of the Bureau of Detectives! Instantly alert, Maggie didn't even pretend not to listen.

"It might be just a little too soon, sir," Josh said. He had swung his chair around so that he was sitting sideways to his desk and looking out a window. It was dark outside, Maggie saw. Early nightfall was another aspect of winter she didn't enjoy. "Doesn't the woman understand her son was murdered?" Josh asked into the phone.

And then, "Yes, I realize the importance of closure to a mother, and that Mrs. Gardner would like to hold the funeral right away, but is the M.E. a hundred percent certain the body has no more secrets to tell?"

After a silent minute, Josh said, "All right, fine. But I'm going over to the morgue and have one more look at the deceased before the body is released. When am I going? Right now. Talk to you later."

He put down the phone, swung his chair around

and looked at Maggie. She set the case file on his desk. "Could we discuss…?" she began.

Josh interrupted her by getting to his feet. "Right now I'm going to the morgue for a last look at Gardner's body. Maybe you should come along." He paused a moment, then added, "Yeah, no maybe about it. I *want* you with me. You might see something I don't. And we can talk on the way. Go get your coat."

"But…but…"

Josh stopped moving and frowned at her. "But what?"

"Nothing. I'll get my coat." She left in a rush and on the way back to her desk she used her cell phone and dialed Natalie's number. "Sorry, but I have to cancel," she said. "Something came up, boss's orders. Maybe tomorrow night, okay?"

"Oh, darn. All right, we'll do it tomorrow night."

"Bye, Nat."

Bundled up again, she joined Josh in the corridor leading to the parking area. They walked out together without talking. When they were in his car and underway, he said gruffly, as though greatly perturbed, "Mrs. Gardner is pestering the police commissioner for release of her son's body for burial. I think it's too soon, but I was just warned that it's probably going to happen, whatever I think about it."

"Are you thinking the M.E. missed something?

Is that why we're going to take another look at the body?''

''Sometimes there's room for differing interpretations of bodily wounds. I don't doubt the M.E.'s findings. Hell, I don't know if I doubt anything, but I need to satisfy whatever it is that keeps gnawing at my gut.''

''Oh, you have one of those gut feelings that's so prolific in detective novels.''

Josh slanted a startled look at her. ''You don't get 'em?''

''Only when I eat chili laced with loads of hot peppers.''

''You're really pissed off at me, aren't you?''

''Whatever gave you that idea?''

''Well, your frozen face *could* be a clue.''

He was using sarcasm on her, the jerk? ''A frozen face is small potatoes compared to a frozen heart.''

''What's that supposed to mean, that my heart is frozen? And just how the hell would you know if it was?''

''Clue upon clue upon clue, perhaps?''

''Because I didn't follow through with that pass this morning? I had my reasons,'' Josh said grimly.

''I'm sure you did.''

Josh let her have the last word and drove the rest of the way in silence. Maggie acted unconcerned, as though she couldn't possibly care less about anything he did or said, when, in actuality, the ache in her chest felt like a mortal wound. This whole thing might mean nothing to him, but it was destroying her professionalism as well as breaking her heart. She had to do something about it.

The question, of course, was what? What on earth could she do to jar Josh Benton as he had jarred her? Was *still* jarring her!

At the morgue Josh requested a viewing of Franklin Gardner's body. Ten minutes later he and Maggie were standing on opposite sides of the gurney on which Gardner's remains had been delivered from a refrigeration unit to a viewing room. Both Josh and Maggie wore latex gloves.

"He put up a fight," Josh murmured, concentrating on the blotchy discolored spots on the victim's arms and hands. "And the facial bruises have an odd pattern."

"The report mentioned the probability of a large ring worn by the attacker."

"I would think a diamond, for instance, would have broken the skin…leave cuts instead of impact bruises. Any large gemstone might cut the skin, for that matter."

Maggie frowned a bit, thinking. "Unless it didn't protrude above the overall design of the ring."

"There *is* a design, isn't there? Do you see it in the facial bruises?"

Maggie bent over to peer more closely at the facial bruises. "There's something," she said slowly.

"A pattern of some sort. But I can't make it out, can you?"

"No. Do you have your camera with you?"

"In my backpack. I'll get it." Maggie removed her gloves and tossed them in the appropriate waste receptacle, then went into her backpack, which she had left on the counter near the door. Returning to the gurney with her camera, she asked, "Haven't we received the photos Jack took at the scene yet?"

"They're in my office."

Maggie stiffened. "Why aren't they in the case file?"

"Because I've been studying them, trying to figure out which ones *should* be in the case file," Josh snapped. "You can examine them anytime you want. There are far too many to keep them all in the file, and…and didn't you see my note in the file when you went through it?"

"No, I did not."

"Well, it's there. Take some close-ups of those facial bruises."

Maggie's camera was hi-tech digital with automatic, immediate development. For more exacting detail, the photos could also be transferred to a computer, and from there the sky was the limit. Enlargements and an array of shadings that brought out various characteristics were often used on data.

Wondering how she could have missed seeing Josh's note about Jack's photos, she decided that she had missed nothing in that file. The great Benton might have intended to insert a note, but he hadn't done it. God, what an ego, she thought. Bring him down a peg? Her? Hardly.

She focused entirely on the facial bruises and the camera clicked, whirred and coughed out instant photos that Josh grabbed and studied. He finally said, "That's enough. Thanks."

"You're very welcome," she said icily and walked over to her backpack and put away the camera. Returning to the gurney, however, she couldn't resist saying, "I doubt that Jack overlooked the facial bruises in his numerous shots of the scene. But I must be wrong in that assumption, since you've been studying his photos. Jack would have to be at fault, not you."

Josh scowled at her for at least a full minute, then snarled, "Come on, let's get the hell out of here."

"Of course, anything you say." Maggie's mind whispered the word *master,* but she couldn't let herself say it out loud. That would be going too far.

It did tickle her, though, that she'd grated on Josh's nerves, and she rode back to district headquarters with a little half smile on her face.

Josh thought he saw her smiling when they passed under a bright streetlight, but he squelched the impulse to ask her what was funny and said instead, "It could be a signet ring."

"What? Sorry, I wasn't listening. What did you say?"

"I was referring to the attacker's ring. It could be a signet ring, one of those huge sports rings or a fraternity ring, or maybe just a college class ring. Some are really big, especially if it's in a large size because the killer has large hands."

"Sounds as though you're ruling out women in this homicide."

"Some women have large hands," Josh said as they reached his car.

"Few women wear college class rings. Fewer still own a sport ring, and I really have never personally known a woman who possessed a fraternity ring."

"Oh, really? How about the ones that are given frat rings from their boyfriends?"

"You mean our killer is a coed today? Now *that* theory surprises me."

Josh fell silent as he started the car's engine, then said quietly, "You know what surprises me, Maggie? You do. What do you want from me?"

Maggie couldn't believe her ears. Her pulse ran wild and she wished she could backtrack and steer this conversation in another direction. But it was too late. All she could do now was stand up for herself and show Josh Benton that he didn't scare her.

"I could ask you the same question," she said brazenly. "But I fear I'd hear a different answer at any given time of the day. Take this morning. I think we both know what you wanted from me this morning, although I do admit to not having a clue at the moment. Guess I'm not a mind reader after all. Maybe I was wrong about this morning, too.''

''You weren't wrong.''

''Pardon? What did you say?''

''You heard me. I said you weren't wrong.''

''Prove it,'' Maggie said before she could stop herself.

Josh had had enough. He wove through traffic and made a sharp right turn into a dark alley. Slamming on the brakes, he put the shifting gear in park, unhooked his seat belt and then slid as close to her as he could get, considering the elaborate console on the seat between them.

Maggie was staring at him wide-eyed, trying to make out his eyes in the dim dash lights. ''Wha-what're you doing?'' she stammered.

''Proving it,'' he growled, and unhooked her seat belt. He took her by the shoulders and pulled her toward him, close enough that he easily found her lips with his. His kiss was hot and hard, and she felt herself breaking apart, piece by piece.

When she could no longer breathe through her nose, she jerked her face to the side and whispered hoarsely, ''No more. You proved your point.''

''Not entirely.'' He took her hand and brought it to his lap.

She wanted to leave it there. She wanted to unzip

his pants and feel the heat of his arousal on the palm of her hand. Instead, she drew it back slowly and waited to see what he would do next.

He finally did it. "Is that what you want?" he asked harshly. "I didn't want to hurt Tim by messing with you, but I'm losing ground on that noble concept. If you want sex with me, I think I'm ready to crumble. But you have to remember something. The reason I'm not married is because I don't like the statistics. Everyone I know…practically everyone…has been married and divorced at least once. I won't live my life like that. There are usually kids, and they're the ones who really suffer, but so does at least one person in every destroyed marriage.

"Maggie, if you and I sleep together that's all it will ever be. Can you live with that? If you can, we'll go to my place right now and make love all night." He stopped talking and waited. "Don't you have an answer?"

"Not tonight I don't," she whispered, shaken to her very soul. "Please, let's go."

"Are you going to have an answer tomorrow?"

"I…don't know."

"I already know your answer, you don't have to say a word. You want marriage and kids, the same as everybody else does."

"Everybody but you."

Josh slid back behind the wheel. "Could be. I

won't argue about it. I'm who and what I am, and it's take me as I am or not at all.''

"I have the picture, loud and clear. You don't have to belabor the point.'' She fought tears all the way back to the Bureau and her car, but she also did a lot of deep thinking. And just before getting out of Josh's vehicle, she let him have it with both barrels. "I will never believe you haven't married and plan to remain a bachelor for life because of divorce statistics. You're conning yourself and I think you know it. Just don't insult me again by using that line of drivel with me!''

Chapter 4

Maggie's current workweeks ran Mondays through Fridays. In a few more weeks that would change, as everyone in the Detective Bureau, even forensic specialists, had to rotate their days off so that no one had a lock on the traditional weekend. It was an equitable arrangement, Maggie felt, fair to everyone. She willingly worked her weekends when necessary, but as she began work on Friday she actually prayed that no one heading up a case would request her services on Saturday or Sunday. She needed some time off, and two days away from Josh Benton should help her down-in-the-mouth mood immensely.

She couldn't stop thinking about the things he'd said to her.

What *she'd* said to him had been richly deserved, she told herself, and maybe she should have said more. Any woman stupid enough to get mixed up with a man of Josh's sentiments and outlook on the only things that really mattered in this grueling life—love, marriage, children—deserved all the pain she would suffer. That life wasn't for her, Maggie thought again and again, and if it were possible to rip every shred of feeling from her body until she truly got over the arrogant jerk, she would do it in a New York minute.

But that was where she was stymied. Her feelings were their own master, apparently, and uncontrollable. Her heart thumped much too frenetically whenever she caught sight of Benton, and when he talked to her about the Gardner case and she had to look him in the eye, she got weak in the knees and felt like a pot of molten lava was boiling her insides. It made her almost ill to acknowledge such a weak-willed thing about herself, but how could she deny something so obvious? She could tell herself a million times that she hated Josh, but it wasn't true. She had always considered herself so sane and sensible, but where was her sensibility now? *It's probably hiding behind your incredibly stupid heart that's just begging to be smashed to smithereens!*

Trying almost desperately to not drown in self-pity and not completely succeeding, Maggie studied photos for most of the day, those that Jack had snapped at the scene, those she had taken at the morgue. Especially provocative were the shots—both Jack's and hers—of the victim's facial bruises. A major step in the process for Maggie was booting up her computer, pulling up the photographic analysis program and then inserting the tiny digital disk from her camera.

For hours she studied the images on the monitor, enlarged pertinent areas of the photographs and used different screening and shading techniques to enhance vague features of the photos. Zooming in on the characteristics of one particularly harsh bruise, Maggie frowned and narrowed her eyes at the screen. There was a design of sorts in that bruise, but it still wasn't clear enough to identify.

"I'd like us to go over the case file together."

Maggie nearly jumped out of her skin. It was Josh's voice, and she had been so involved that she hadn't realized he'd been sneaking up on her.

Well, maybe the word *sneaking* was a bit harsh. He could hardly do much sneaking when there were other detectives all over the place.

Maggie looked at her watch. It was almost six, her shift was only minutes away from being over for the day. And then, thank goodness, she had a whole weekend to pull herself together.

"It shouldn't take that long," Josh said, fully comprehending the reason for Maggie checking the time.

"Fine," she said stiffly.

"We'll do it at my desk." He walked away.

"I have to print something, then turn off the computer," Maggie called to his retreating back.

He waved his right arm without looking back, an impersonal acknowledgment that grated on Maggie's nerves. All but gritting her teeth, she printed, saved her work and then followed proper procedure to safely shut down the computer.

She also picked up the photographs, which she had arranged in order of importance. One small stack remained on her desk when everything else had been cleared away. Along with the printed image of the vague design she had just started to digest, she brought those with her, and strode to Josh's office with an all-business look in her eyes. *This meeting is not getting personal! If he says one thing that's not related to the case, I'm going to let him have it again, and if he files a complaint with human resources about my bad attitude and conduct, I'll tell them exactly what he said to me yesterday. How would he like that, huh?*

He wouldn't like it, and she knew it. But there were things going on that she didn't like and still had to put up with.

For some unknown reason Maggie felt tears stinging the backs of her eyes. *God, am I going to start bawling every time Josh says something to me? What in heck is wrong with me?*

Josh looked up when she slipped into his little cubicle and took a chair. The case file was open in front of him, and he started the discussion with, "I don't see a report on the coffee table."

"It's there. I examined every inch of that table and wrote a detailed report on it. The table is in the evidence room at the crime lab and the report is in that file."

"Show me." Josh slid the folder toward her.

Maggie pursed her lips. Was he calling her a liar? Doubting her efficiency? She grabbed the folder, opened it and began thumbing through the reports. She pulled out the coffee table report and held it out to him, but barely noticed when he took it. Another one had caught her eye, one she hadn't yet read, and she stopped to scan it. Detectives Waters and Wilson had driven to the Gardner estate and talked to Mrs. Cecelia Gardner, Franklin's mother.

"Detective…let me see who signed this." Maggie looked for the signature and continued. "Detective Waters indicated that Cecelia Gardner was at a charity function the night her son was killed, among many witnesses." Maggie looked at Josh. "Do charity affairs last all night?"

"Time of death was set by the M.E. as having occurred before midnight."

Frowning slightly, recalling that she had judged Gardner's death to have occurred at around that same time after her preliminary examination at the crime scene, Maggie chewed on her lower lip and thought about this new development. Mrs. Gardner was almost eighty years old, which certainly didn't preclude an occasional late night. Maggie decided her imagination was going to extremes. She dropped her eyes to the report and read that Detective Waters and his partner, Detective Wilson, had made inquiries about Franklin's son, Stephen, age twenty-three, who wasn't at home when they called.

"I didn't know Franklin had a son," Maggie murmured.

"There's also a Lyle Gardner, Franklin's older brother. He lives at the Gardner estate, as well, but was home supposedly watching television that night."

Maggie raised an eyebrow, pondering the Gardner family. "Everyone lives with Cecelia Gardner, except for Franklin. Was he a bit of a bohemian?"

"Probably just a little more independent than the other men in his family. Could be he liked his privacy."

"He could have had reasons for liking his privacy."

"Such as?"

"Late-night visitors? Maybe people of questionable character? People his mother might have objected to?"

"There's still the chance the whole thing began as a burglary."

Maggie sniffed. "I never did buy into that theory, and since you haven't talked about it, either—not in my presence, at any rate—it appears to be pretty low on the motive totem pole."

"What do *you* think could be the motive?"

"I believe that Franklin knew his killer and some sort of disagreement evolved into violence."

Josh hesitated a few moments, then nodded. "I think the same thing. You're pretty sharp, Detective Sutter."

"Uh, thanks." Maggie's cheeks burned, not from the compliment but from what she'd just seen— again—in his eyes. Now, what was it she had been going to say if he became even remotely personal with her?

Josh leaned back and enjoyed the view. That glorious dark red hair of hers was a major temptation. She always wore it back from her face, and he would love to see it wild and free. Or tangled beneath her head on a pillow. Ah, yes, how could he deny the pleasure that would bring him?

Maggie's interest in the case file had waned dramatically. In fact, she could hardly make out the typewritten words on the reports. Benton kept giving off sexual vibes, saying things with his eyes that he wouldn't dare put into words. Not on the job, at least.

But how about in her apartment? Something had *almost* happened there. Could she make it happen again, only this time with her keeping things rolling along?

But what if he really was involved with someone? The last thing Maggie could ever see herself doing was carrying on a clandestine affair with a married or otherwise committed man.

How could she find out? An idea occurred to her. "This has nothing to do with the case, but I've been thinking about having a little dinner party. If I put you on the guest list, would you come or refuse?"

Josh couldn't quite conceal his surprise. Or his instantaneous curiosity. What was *really* going on behind those stunning violet eyes of hers? Had she decided that his little speech yesterday had been more of a compliment than an insult? After all, wasn't honesty always better than deceit, which was the game a lot of guys on the prowl practiced with women they wanted to bed? But considering the way she had bristled before getting out of his car, a dinner invitation was just about the last thing he could have imagined happening between them.

He regarded her for a long moment. "Are you and I becoming friends?"

Maggie knew she had perplexed him. "Does a dinner invitation indicate an offer of friendship to you?"

"Yes, but I was under the distinct impression you didn't like me. You *used* to like me, but that was a long time ago and people change."

"Yes, they certainly do," Maggie drawled dryly. "Back to that dinner idea, should I put your name on the guest list, or not? I would include your wife...or girlfriend...of course."

"My wife! Didn't I tell you just yesterday that I'm not the marrying kind?"

"And I told you what I thought of such obvious malarkey, didn't I? Why you still think that I'm backward enough to believe every word you say is beyond me. Do I really strike you as being a pickle short?"

Josh laughed. "A pickle short of what? Look, if you throw a dinner party and want me as a guest, I could probably scare up a date, just to keep your numbers even. That's assuming, of course, that you would have a date of your own at the table."

At that exact moment Maggie's cell phone rang. She looked at the caller ID and saw Natalie's name and number. "Oh, I forgot my promise," she groaned. "May I take this call?" she asked Josh.

He shrugged. "Go ahead."

"Thanks." Maggie pressed the talk button. "Nat, I'm sorry but I'm very busy and can't talk right now. You're calling about tonight, aren't you?"

"Yes, but it's not what you think. Tonight I'm the one who's canceling," Natalie said with a little giggle. "I've got a date with my new guy."

"Oh, good for you. Let's get together over the weekend, okay?"

"If I can. He's pretty hot stuff…or at least he *looks* like he is. I'll probably find out all about it tonight. I'll let you go. Just didn't want to leave you hanging on a Friday night."

"I appreciate the consideration. Bye for now."

Maggie broke the connection and saw the most peculiar look on Benton's face, a rather sour look, in fact. It struck her then that *Nat* was a non-gender name. She could have been talking to a man!

The damned dog in the manger. He didn't want the hay but neither did he want the horse to have it. Okay, she'd had enough of his lecherous looks and about-face attitudes. It was kill or cure time…and he sure deserved anything she might dream up to make him show his true colors.

"I have the weekend off," she said casually. "What's your day like tomorrow?"

Startled, Josh sat up straighter. "Um, I'll be here for most of it. Why?"

"That dinner party I mentioned."

"You can plan a party and invite people that fast?"

"My friends aren't at all uptight. If they're not busy, they'll be happy to come."

"Well…sure…I guess I could make it. About what time?"

Maggie could tell he wasn't thrilled about this. He seemed sort of squirmy to her, but since he'd already said he would come if invited, he would keep his word.

Good boy. "Seven should do it. Is seven okay for you?"

"It's…uh, fine."

"Good. Now, I have something I'd like you to take a look at." Maggie handed him the photo she had enhanced and printed.

Josh took it, studied it for several moments then looked at her. "You've brought up portions of a design. That's darn good computer work, Maggie. Do you think you could make this clearer still?"

"I fully intend to try. Maybe I should come in tomorrow and work on it," she added thoughtfully. Personal plans were secondary to solving a crime of this magnitude, especially when the plan was nothing more than a half-baked, undeveloped, completely aimless impulse in the back of her mind. It was all about putting Benton in his place, of course, but how did a sexual greenhorn accomplish such a feat with an obviously experienced man?

Shuddering and praying he wouldn't notice, she expanded her previous comment. "Tomorrow morning, at least. What do you think?"

Josh nodded. "Maybe you should. But would your working tomorrow morning…say until noon… ruin your dinner party plans?"

Maggie began gathering her things. "I don't think so. Is there anything else for now?"

"Well, we could talk all night about the case, but I doubt we would know any more at sunup than we do right now. Are you going to be here in the morning, then?"

"Yes."

Josh got to his feet. "Maybe I'll see you, maybe not. I plan to spend some time at the lab in the morning. I'd like another look at that coffee table, for one thing."

Maggie was immediately defensive. "I'm sure you'll find everything in order as far as the tests and analyses I did at the lab."

"Did I say I wouldn't? Did I even hint that you might not have handled everything as professionally as possible?"

"Well, no, but…"

"Go home, Maggie. I'll either see you here in the morning or at your apartment at seven tomorrow evening."

Cheeks on fire over being dismissed so abruptly, she hurried out.

All during the drive home she worried about her virginity. The only thing she knew about luring a man into either making love or an awful fool of himself was what she'd read in novels, or heard about from friends. Did she possess enough knowledge to behave as a worldly woman? She *had* to, she told herself. She simply had to! If he ever caught on that she was green as a gourd around men, he would probably laugh her into next week.

"Oh dear Lord," she whispered, almost afraid to get to the bottom of what was driving her into doing something so foreign to her nature.

The streets were dangerously icy in spots. Maggie drove with a tight grip on the steering wheel, an eye out for black ice and an agonizing sense of despair. The despair was a result of feeling so confused about tomorrow night. When Benton arrived at her door expecting to join other guests for her "dinner party" and discovered he was the *only* guest, would he bolt? Laugh at her?

At a red light Maggie watched for the green signal and realized that she had turned into an awful wimp since meeting Josh again. Other than her outburst last night, she had let him walk all over her. For heaven's sake, why? Had she been thinking that he was so far above her that he was better than she was? He wasn't a bit more intelligent. Yes, he had more experience with the CPD, but he was also ten years older, which meant that when he reached retirement age, she would still be going strong.

"Hmm," she murmured thoughtfully. The signal light turned green and she got the car moving again.

And that was when her plan—so vague and undefined before—became clear in her mind. Each and every step of it. She *wasn't* a wimp, she never had been, and tomorrow night she was going to knock Josh's socks off.

Still at his desk, Josh finally heaved a sigh and closed the Gardner case file. It was becoming thicker by the day—by the hour, actually. Colin Waters and his partner were doing an exemplary job of inter-rogating family, friends and business associates. There was a report in the file about Desmond Reicher, the COO for Gardner Corporation, which was intriguing because of its reference to Reicher, supposedly an upstanding citizen, possibly having an underworld connection. The report left Josh un-easy and wondering if Franklin had been aware of the corporation's chief operating officer's extracur-ricular activities. And, of course, the logical question to follow that one could only be, was Gardner him-self involved in Reicher's unlawful schemes, if they were, in fact, provable?

Josh's thoughts suddenly changed directions. *Maggie, Maggie. What am I going to do about you?* Leaning back in his chair with his hands locked be-hind his head, he put his feet up on his desk. He felt all torn up over Maggie, and he truthfully didn't know what to do about it. Maybe when the Gardner case was solved and they were no longer working together, he could stop thinking about her.

But, hell, there'd be another case, he thought dis-gustedly. Even so, he might be able to avoid Maggie most of the time, but how could he avoid what was going on inside his own body? He wanted her. There, he had finally admitted it. He wanted to make love to Maggie Sutter, and not just a quick slam, bam, thank-you-ma'am kind of love. He wanted to hold her, to stroke her beautiful long hair, to look into her eyes while he...while he...

Josh dropped his feet to the floor and told himself to get a grip on reality. Good God, she was ten years younger than he was and Tim's kid sister, to boot. Besides, she sure didn't act as though she would welcome a seriously adult pass from him.

Wishing that he'd refused her dinner invitation— he could have come up with some excuse—he pulled on his heavy coat. But there was consolation in knowing about the other guests. Probably wouldn't be many because Maggie's apartment wouldn't accommodate a crowd, but there was safety in even small numbers. Two or three other guests would be enough to make him keep his hands to himself. It might even turn out to be a pleasant evening.

"Yeah, right," he muttered on his way out.

The next day, Maggie worked intently on those photo enhancements until noon. She had printed out five of the best ones and put them in the case file, although she still wasn't satisfied with their quality.

Benton hadn't shown his face all morning, and

she was glad because her stomach had been doing somersaults as it was. She rushed away a few minutes after twelve, made several stops to purchase the things she needed for dinner tonight, and finally got home at one-thirty. After working in the kitchen for two hours—now all she had to do to feed Benton was turn on the oven for about fifteen minutes— Maggie hurried to the bathroom to start on herself. She had cleaned the apartment last night, and everything shone like a looking glass. This morning she had put fresh linen on the bed. Everything was ready for the evening ahead except for herself and a few final touches to the apartment. She had hours to get ready, and she planned to use every minute of them. She began with a foot soak and a pedicure. No part of her was going to remain untouched. She was going to be as perfectly groomed as any woman could be.

And she was going to learn tonight why Josh kept looking at her with hot, desire-filled eyes and never did anything about it.

Her virginity scared the hell out of her. What if he did something about it tonight and then came unglued because she had never been with another man?

"Oh God," Maggie whispered. If they should happen to end up in bed together, was there anything she could do to prevent his understanding her pristine state? What scared her most was that she'd heard all her life that the first time for some women was horribly painful. If she were in that category, Josh would know in an instant that he was the first.

Maybe she could pretend everything was wonderful, and really, why did she keep thinking it was even going to happen?

Because you're going to make it happen, that's why! It's why you cleaned until midnight last night, and the reason there's fresh linen on your bed, and why dinner is ready and just needs a few minutes in the oven, and why white wine is chilling in the refrigerator, and two bottles of red are uncorked and breathing on the kitchen counter.

It's the reason that it's going to take you at least three hours to get yourself ready for the evening. When you open your door to let Josh in, his eyes just might pop right out of his head, because he's going to see a Maggie Sutter that he's never seen before.

Maggie was working on her pedicure when the telephone rang. Walking on her heels so her toes wouldn't touch the carpet, she picked up the receiver. "Hello?"

"Hi, Mag. How're you doing, kid?"

"Tim! Oh my gosh, it's so good to hear your voice. How are you?"

"Couldn't be better. But you didn't answer my question. How are *you* doing?"

"I'm great. Working hard and loving my job."

"And?"

"And what?"

"I ask how you're doing and all you can talk about is your job? Baby sister, what about Mr. Perfect? Haven't you met him yet?"

"Are you trying to get me married off?" Maggie teased, though her heart had begun thumping over Tim's reference to the perfect man for her.

"Of course I am. That's what big brothers are for. Seriously, you must be seeing someone. Tell me about him."

"Sorry, but my dates have been only casual events for years and years. How's Laurie and the boys?"

"The boys are healthy, happy whirling dervishes, and Laurie is pregnant."

"Pregnant! Oh, Tim, I'm so happy for both of you. You're hoping for a girl this time, aren't you?"

"Laurie is. We'll know if it's a boy or a girl in about another month. I'll let you know, okay?"

"You bet it's okay."

"So, what's going on with your job. Working on a big case?"

"Actually, yes. It's a homicide, and…and…" Maggie knew the only way to say this was to dive in headfirst. "I'm working with Josh Benton on the case."

"Josh! Hell's bells, is he still on the force? Say hello for me, all right?"

"Why not call him and say hello for yourself?"

"Maybe I should do that. Do you have his number?"

"Sure do. Hold on." Maggie was back with Josh's business card in seconds. She read off the numbers, assuming that Tim was writing them down. "It's too bad you two lost touch," she said. "If memory serves, you were pretty tight."

"To some degree. Oh, we had some good times, that's for sure, but Josh came by to see Ma as much as he did to see me."

Maggie was floored. "I don't remember him spending time with Mom."

"Well, he did. His own mother died when he was in his teens, you know, and he took a big liking for Ma. She thought the world of him, too. Used to cook his favorite dishes when she knew he'd be there for supper. You don't remember any of that?"

"No," Maggie said quietly. "Obviously my mind was elsewhere when that was going on." *Yes, it sure was. It was dreaming about Josh Benton noticing that you were all grown up and dying to be kissed by him.*

"Next time I see him I'll tell him to expect a call from you," she said before ending the call.

Maggie found herself even more unnerved about Josh coming over tonight than she'd been before Tim's phone call.

Maybe her upset stomach was because she'd lied to her brother about never having met Mr. Perfect. After all, she'd met him ten years ago, when he'd dropped by the house to see her mother!

Chapter 5

"Nat, I've gotten myself into the most ridiculous mess. Before I explain, let me ask how you and your new guy are getting along."

Natalie sighed dreamily in Maggie's ear. "He's wonderful…absolutely wonderful. I think I'm in love."

"I'm glad. Are you seeing him tonight?"

"He should be here any minute. Why, Maggie?"

Maggie gave her friend an abbreviated explanation of her dilemma. "I invited Detective Josh Benton to have dinner here tonight. He thinks there are going to be other guests. There aren't. Or there weren't going to be. I can't do it. He's going to end up thinking I'm a total moron. Could you possibly bring your boyfriend and act as though I invited both of you yesterday?''

''Oh gosh, Maggie, we have tickets for that big fund-raiser concert everyone's been talking about. Dozens of music and movie stars have donated their time and talents, and Tom paid a fortune for the tickets. I can't disappoint him. I mean, *how* could I disappoint him?''

Maggie had heard about the big affair for weeks now. It was great that Natalie was getting to go to it. ''You can't,'' Maggie said, adding, ''I can't believe I got myself into this.''

''Wait a sec. What time is your detective supposed to show up?''

''I told him seven.''

''Well, the concert starts at nine. Tom and I could come by, talk about the concert and how excited we are about attending it, eat a bite if you want us to and leave. Actually we could already be there when Detective Benton arrives. I can walk out my door the minute Tom gets here, and he's such a sweetie that I'm sure he wouldn't mind going to your place first. Would that help you out?''

Relief flooded Maggie's system. ''Immensely. Nat, I owe you, big-time. Come over the second Tom gets there.''

''This Benton guy must be important to you.''

''I don't know if he's important or simply a challenge. We…we have a history. I'll tell you about it the next time we get together, after tonight. Anyhow, I nearly made a huge mistake. Thanks for the rescue, Nat. I won't forget it.''

"See you in a few.''

"Right.'' Maggie hung up then checked the time. She had about an hour until Josh got there, if he was on time. Thank God Nat and her friend Tom would precede his arrival.

Maggie, Natalie and Tom were sitting in the living room, talking, laughing and sipping wine when the front door buzzer went off in her kitchen. After the third refill Maggie no longer had to pretend to be having a good time but now her stomach did a flip-flop. Josh had arrived.

Maggie excused herself and went to the kitchen intercom. "Who's down there ringing my bell?'' she asked brightly.

The lilt in her voice startled Josh, but then it pleased him. Obviously the party was already in process and Maggie was enjoying it. Great. She was usually far too serious.

"It's the big bad wolf,'' he growled playfully. "Let me in or I'll huff and I'll puff and I'll blow your house in.''

"*Which* big bad wolf? There's more than one in this neighborhood.''

"This one happens to be your boss, my dear,''

Josh said in his best imitation of a villain in a melodrama.

"You just said the magic words, my dear," Maggie drawled back at him. She laughed and pressed the button that would unlock the front door.

She checked the table that was set for four, turned on the oven and then returned to the living room. "He'll be right up," she announced.

"Maggie, we can only stay long enough to meet him," Natalie said with a concerned expression. "I didn't know it when we talked on the phone, but Tom promised to pick up several of his friends on the way to the concert. They'll all be waiting, and...well..."

Tom spoke up. "I'm really sorry we can't stay for dinner, Maggie. We'll do it some other time, I promise."

Maggie's stomach sank, but she forced a smile. "I understand. I'm glad you were able to come by at all, considering your plans for the evening."

They were getting into their coats when the doorbell rang. Maggie let Josh in, introduced the trio, then said good-night to Natalie and Tom. Natalie hugged her and whispered in her ear, "He's gorgeous. We'll talk tomorrow."

Maggie closed the door and leaned her back against it while she looked at Josh. His overcoat was wonderful. *He* was wonderful. Wonderful looking, at least. No telling what he would say or do when the truth came out.

Josh stood there in his overcoat and wondered what in heck was going on. As far as he could tell, there wasn't anyone else in the apartment. Was he late? Had everyone already eaten and gone? Maggie *had* said seven, hadn't she?

"Did they leave early or am I late?" he asked. He couldn't stop his eyes from wandering over Maggie, down, up, down, up. She looked ravishingly beautiful in a blue skirt and blouse that were very close in color to her eyes. Her hair was exactly the way he'd been wanting to see it, loose, bouncy and framing her face. Her skirt was short, with the hem about two inches above her knees, and her legs in hosiery were stunning. This was a Maggie he'd never seen before, and he liked the view immensely.

She pushed away from the door. "Let me take your coat. Natalie and Tom had previous plans. They left early. You're not late."

"And the other guests?" Josh handed her his overcoat.

Maggie hung it in the tiny foyer closet. "There aren't any."

"Your other friends were all busy?"

"So it appears." Maggie stepped into the living room. "Come and sit down. Would you like some wine? We've been drinking this bottle of Cabernet

Sauvignon, but I also have some white wine in the refrigerator.''

''The Cabernet is fine.'' He noticed the one un-used wineglass upturned on a napkin, which told him that Maggie had expected only three guests. Four wineglasses, including her own, were all there were. Obviously her spur-of-the-moment dinner party hadn't panned out.

But he didn't mind being the only guest, he didn't mind it a bit. In fact, as he sat on Maggie's sofa and sipped her wine, he began feeling cozy and con-tented. Sort of like he was sinking into a big, soft, warm pillow. Not that he'd actually ever done that, not literally, but the sensation was delicious, all the same. Here he was, alone with a beautiful, sexy woman, drinking wine and hearing soft music along with the wail of the wind beyond the walls of the building. Could heaven be more pleasurable? he wondered with a smile at Maggie.

That smile said a thousand things—Lord, he was a stunner!—and discombobulated Maggie. Nervous again, she stammered, ''Uh, dinner is warming in the oven as we speak. We'll be able to eat in about ten minutes.''

''Whatever you say. *Anything* you say.''

He was much too sweet and affable tonight, not at all the man she'd been working with these past few days. Even his face was different. Still outra-geously handsome but without the granite his gray eyes usually portrayed. In fact, there was softness in his eyes that she certainly hadn't seen before. Not even the morning he'd almost kissed her.

He's on the prowl, you ninny! You could have him in your bed tonight with one small hint from you that he'd be welcome! Wasn't that what you wanted to happen? The reason for this farce of a dinner party? After all, do you want to die a virgin?

No! But I don't know what to do.

Just...just smile and feed him! He's a man, isn't he, and haven't you heard for most of your life that men basically want two things from women, sex and nurturing? He's not stupid. Be nice and he'll catch on, and when he does, watch out!

Maggie nearly choked on her swallow of wine over that wild and woolly progression of thoughts. Her head was spinning more than it should be. She'd consumed too much wine on an empty stomach. It was time to eat.

She got up. "I'm going to put the finishing touches on dinner. You sit back and relax. I'll let you know when it's ready." She started for the kitchen, never dreaming that he would do what he did next.

"I'll help. I'm not the kind of guest who lets the hostess do all the work," he said smoothly. Josh was no more than one step behind her when they entered the tiny kitchen. "Oh, you have the table all ready. What else needs to be done?"

"Nothing. I mean, nothing big or…you know…important." This was not going well, although she honestly didn't know how to improve the status quo. Her stomach was in knots and her head was spinning, but the peculiar sensation down very low in her body was by far the most disconcerting symptom of whatever malady had attacked her at the very same moment that Josh had stepped inside her apartment. It was, of course, his fault.

"Sit down," she said, deliberately sounding curt. She went to the refrigerator and brought out the bowl of salad she had prepared earlier. She removed the plastic wrap from the bowl before setting it on the table. Then she dared to look directly at her guest. "You're not going to sit?"

"I will when you do. Besides, there are four place settings. Where would you *like* me to sit?"

"Oh. Sorry." Such a small oversight should not have been an embarrassment, but Maggie felt her face flame. Instantly she became defensive. She wasn't perfect, especially in this sort of situation. She should have removed two of the place settings from the table before doing anything else in the kitchen. "If you're still looking for something to do," she said a bit sharply, "you can gather two of the place settings and put them on the counter."

"Glad to do it." Josh could tell she was terribly uneasy. Almost clumsy, in fact, when at work she walked and moved with the utmost grace. He moved the extra settings to the counter then turned to look at her. She was just about to open the oven door when he asked quietly, "What's wrong, Maggie? Do I make you uncomfortable?"

She straightened, stared wide-eyed at him and then humiliated herself beyond belief by getting tears in her eyes. "I…I'm so…stupid," she whispered, and grabbed a paper towel from the roll near the sink and dabbed at her wet eyes.

Josh took one big step and clasped her upper arms. "Why would you say something like that? Why would you even think it?"

"*You* make me think it." Her voice was thick from emotional unshed tears.

Josh studied the moist depths of her eyes. They were standing no more than six inches apart. His hands on her arms were like a live-wire connection, and he felt the desire for her that had been badgering him off and on since the night of the murder taking control of his system, including his ability to deny how much he wanted her.

"If I've been doing that, then I'm sorry," he said huskily.

"I…I don't think you mean to do it," she whispered. "It's me, and…"

"And what?"

Maggie slid her eyes away from his. "I'm sure you didn't know it, but I…I had an awful crush on you when…when you and Tim were friends."

"And that makes working together now tough for you?" Josh laid his hand on her cheek. "Look at me." She brought her eyes back. "First of all, I knew all about that crush. I also knew it wouldn't last and that teenage kids seem to love torturing themselves with crushes..."

"That's not true! It lasted...forever!"

They stared into each other's eyes. Josh dampened his lips with his tongue. "You're not saying those old feelings are still making your life miserable, are you?"

Again she angled her gaze away. "Something is," she said in a shaky little voice.

Josh was astounded. "Maggie, I'm ten years older than you!"

"And that's important because?" she asked with heavy sarcasm.

"I could almost be your father!"

"Oh, for crying out loud. Don't overdo the drama, Benton. Who ever heard of a ten-year-old father?" She wriggled free of his grasp and went to the oven. "Sit on the far side of the table. We're going to eat." She took the hot dishes from the oven and placed them on the table.

Then she brought out a bottle of chilled white wine from the refrigerator and set it and a corkscrew near Josh's plate. "Do the honors, if you don't mind," she said and brushed away one more errant tear.

Josh didn't know what to do. Maggie couldn't seem to stop crying, dinner was on the table, and he felt like pond scum, although he didn't know why he should. So what if she'd had a girlish crush on him ten years ago? It was a common enough occurrence and shouldn't be bothering either one of them at this late date.

But it was. It was the reason Maggie couldn't keep her eyes dry, and maybe had a lot to do with why he wanted to haul her off to the bedroom instead of sitting down to eat the fine meal she had prepared.

Just to do something with his hands, he opened the wine and poured some into the stemmed glasses by each plate. Then they sat and Maggie said, "Help yourself. The chicken is baked and I'm sure you'll remember that vegetable casserole."

Josh looked at it. "You're right. Your mother used to fix that."

"It's her recipe. You know, Tim called today and he said something that sort of surprised me. He said that you used to come by the house to see Mom, as well as him. Is that true?"

"Probably. I like your mother. How is she?"

"Dead."

"My God, Maggie, you didn't have to say it like that!"

"Fine, I'll try to say it in such a way that it won't affront your tender sensibilities. She passed away at age fifty after one hell of a battle with cancer. Is that better?''

"It's terrible. I never knew."

"Well, after Tim moved to California, Mom got a better job in Detroit, so we moved, too. It never occurred to me that you would come by after Tim left, so you probably never knew. Unless Mom talked to you."

"No, she didn't. I went by your old place about a month after Tim had gone, and someone else was living there. Now that I think about it, I'm pretty sure I thought you and Lottie had also moved to California."

"But you never really tried to find us."

"Through the department, you mean? No, I never did. Did you ever try to contact me so I would know where you were?"

"Did you ever talk to Tim again after he left?"

Josh realized that they had both raised their voices. He put down his fork and sat back. "Why are we at each other's throats?"

"I can't speak for you, but I'm sore because we...none of us...meant enough to you for you to keep in touch."

"Nor did your family keep in touch with me, Maggie. And everyone knew where I was."

"Which makes the Sutters the villains and you Mr. Innocent."

"I didn't say that, but maybe it's partly true."

Josh shook his head. "No, it isn't. None of us kept in touch and with only a small effort we could have." After eating a few more bites he said, "This is good, Maggie. You want to know something? You don't look anything like a cop tonight."

"And you do?"

Josh grinned. "Don't I? What do I look like to you?"

"If you think I'm going to say something dorky, like a movie star, think again."

"A movie star!" Josh roared out a laugh. "That's the funniest thing I've heard in a long time."

Maggie smiled weakly. "Hilarious. Actually you look like a banker in that striped shirt. Or a stockbroker. Maybe an attorney...a well-dressed attorney."

"Ah, so it's this shirt that eradicates my cop image. I'll have to remember that. Want to hear what destroys your cop facade? It's the way your hair looks tonight, and that pretty blue outfit, and your legs and feet in high heels, and..." Abruptly Josh fell silent. What she'd said about her crush lasting forever had finally sunk in. Should he believe that she had feelings for him now that had endured through ten years of separation?

His pulse quickened. So what if he was older? Thirty-six wasn't ancient, by any means, and she was twenty-six now, no longer a teenager and certainly no novice to male-female relationships.

Maggie became aware of the changing expression in his eyes as he regarded her. She'd had just enough wine to be bolder than usual.

"What're you thinking?" she asked.

"You don't look like a cop tonight, but now you're sounding like one. What are you suspicious of, Maggie?"

His soft voice touched like a whisper of silk. "I'm wondering just how far you would let your imagination carry you."

"How far does your imagination take you?"

"Unlike yours, not far at all. But then it's hard to even try to imagine things that one has never experienced." Maggie froze. She'd said too much! "Uh, how about some dessert? Ice cream and chocolate sauce?"

"No dessert. Your dinner was great. I'll have some of that coffee, though."

Maggie rose. "I'll bring it to the living room. Please let me do a few things in here...I won't be a minute...then I'll join you."

Josh got up. She was suddenly nervous as a cat. Because of what she'd said about not being able to imagine things she hadn't experienced? What was that supposed to mean?

But he really had no wish to keep her strung out, so he nodded and walked from the kitchen. "The bathroom?" he called.

"Down the hall. On the right," Maggie called

back. She put her forehead against the refrigerator and wished the floor would open up and swallow her. She'd given away enough information tonight for a half-wit to figure her out, and Josh Benton was no half-wit. Was it because her tongue and privacy inhibitions had loosened from the wine she'd drunk, or would she have found a way to make a fool of herself without ingesting a drop of alcohol?

Maggie forced herself to put away the leftover food, then quickly cleared the table by putting the dishes in the sink. She would deal with them later, after she got rid of Josh. It was strange how her priorities had changed. She'd wanted him in her home badly enough to lie about it, and now she could hardly wait for the moment when he would say "Thanks for dinner and good night," or something to that effect.

She filled two cups with coffee, put them on saucers on a small tray and went into the living room. Josh was again using the sofa, and when he saw the tray he shoved things aside on the coffee table to make room for it. Maggie set it down and stood to go to a chair, but he caught her by the arm.

"Sit here, by me," he said quietly.

Her heart nearly burst through her chest wall. "I...I think I, uh, might have given you the wrong, uh, impression during our dinner conversation," she stammered.

"You gave me the impression you wanted me to

have. Sit down, Maggie. I won't lie and tell you I
don't want you, because I do, and I'm sure I don't
have to spell out in what context. But no woman's
ever been in danger of having her principles compromised by me. One word is all I ever need to hear,
one little word. It's *no,* Maggie. Say it once and
everything stops. Do you follow me?''

''You have assumed far too much from some of
the silly things I said because I was half-tipsy
throughout dinner.''

Josh frowned. ''That sounded like a no right out
of the starting gate. Was it?''

Maggie gulped. Yes or no? This was the moment
of truth. The awful truth, actually. *She didn't want
Josh to know she was still a virgin!*

''It was a no,'' she said in a shaky whisper.

Josh slowly rose. ''Would you like me to leave?
Never mind, you don't have to answer that. I'll
make that decision myself and tell you it's time for
me to go.'' He went to the closet for his overcoat
and looked at her while putting it on. ''Something
odd is going on with you, Maggie. Maybe I'm part
of it. I sort of feel as though I am.'' He stopped to
think a moment, then asked with a frown, ''Did I
lead you on ten years ago? Make you think something could happen for us?''

''No, you didn't.''

''That's a relief. I enjoyed all of the Sutters' company, but I never thought of you back then as any-

thing but a cute kid. Decent men don't fool around with teenagers.''

''You don't have to rub it in. I know the score now. According to what you told me the other day, men don't fool around with women who want more than a roll in the hay from them, either.''

Josh's eyes widened. ''Are all of my sins written in concrete so that you will never forget them?''

''Why would I give a damn about your sins? I have enough of my own to worry about.''

Josh went to the door and turned to look at her. ''You know, that's where I think you're pulling my leg. You don't have any sin in your past, do you? Oh, maybe a romantic love affair or two, but no real sin.''

Maggie's breath almost stopped in her throat for good. As she'd already known, he was no half-wit. He was very close to figuring out her every secret. He would have hit the bull's-eye exactly if a twenty-six-year-old virgin wasn't beyond his realm of realistic thinking.

''You're right,'' she said after catching her breath. ''There's no real sin in *my* past. I left that for you to handle, Detective. Here, let me unlock the door for you.'' Maggie moved next to him and began unbolting the locks. She felt his eyes on her profile and flushed hotly. Expecting a pass any second, she finished quickly and stepped back. ''Good night.''

Josh touched his forehead in a semblance of a

salute. "Dinner was delicious, and I have to say one thing before I go that you're probably not going to like. You, Maggie Sutter, are a flaming coward. Good night."

He vanished through the door, closing it behind him. Maggie wilted into a weak-kneed heap while struggling to lock the dead bolts.

Then she fell onto the sofa and cried her eyes out. She hated Josh Benton.

But the real truth, she realized with another spate of tears, was that she didn't hate him at all. She loved him. Madly, passionately, eternally. With all her heart and soul. She always had, from the first time they met when she'd been a starry-eyed teenager and he'd been her big brother's friend until this very moment. It would go on, she knew. It would never disappear and let her lead a normal life. She was destined to die alone and miserable.

But her apparently indestructible feelings explained one thing very clearly. It was no wonder she'd never slept with another man—none had ever come close to measuring up to Josh.

Chapter 6

Josh slept restlessly that night. Along with images of Maggie haunting his dreams, he couldn't clear his mind of Franklin Gardner's premature demise. Something told him they were getting closer to the truth in the case, but there were still some perplexing pieces missing from the puzzle.

By morning Josh was feeling testy and out of sorts. It was a gray, cloudy day, which didn't lift his spirits any. Grumbling about the lousy weather, he put on a pot of coffee to brew and then opened the door of his apartment to retrieve his copy of the Sunday newspaper from the hallway.

There, on the front page, was an inflammatory headline: Politicians Demand An Arrest In Gardner Murder.

Josh sank onto a chair at his kitchen table and read the article, which harped mostly on one theme: The police department was being pressured by everyone in the city with a modicum of power to find and arrest the murderer of Franklin Gardner. Various persons were quoted and had expressed shock over the heinous crime and perhaps some laxity in what should have been a speedy arrest. "After all," one public figure stated, "it was a simple burglary until poor Franklin tried to protect his possessions. I understand that one of the missing treasures from his home is a priceless and very identifiable jade Buddha, carved in the sixteenth century. Now, how is the killer going to pawn something like that?"

"Moron," Josh muttered. Anything could be sold. Besides, the items that had gone missing that night, according to the housekeeper, were not "priceless." Valuable, maybe, but not priceless. Josh never had believed the burglary theory, not when Franklin's killer *could* have taken things that might truly be categorized as priceless.

But Josh knew that anyone wanting to put their image before the public jumped on any bandwagon that happened to pass through their territory. An article like this one often got results, though. Josh might hate the pressure the media had the power to apply, but he couldn't deny its effectiveness. Everyone involved with this case would feel bullied and unappreciated today, him included, but they would work just a little bit harder to find the killer and bring him to trial.

After drinking the entire pot of coffee and going through the Sunday paper, Josh shuffled back to his bedroom, threw the blankets over his bed, which was how he made it every morning, then continued on to the bathroom for a shower.

Even that didn't bring up his mood, but he knew something that would. He got dressed in comfortable old jeans and an ancient Chicago Cubs sweatshirt. He was in his outside jacket and ready to leave when his house phone rang.

He almost left without answering, but that was only because of his bad mood. He went to the nearest extension phone and said a gruff "Benton."

"The decision to release Franklin Gardner's body for burial was just made. Mrs. Gardner has planned the funeral for Tuesday morning. I expect you'll be attending the service?"

"Yes, sir," Josh said to his commander, even while thinking about how quickly that newspaper article had jacked everyone up. "Detective Sutter and I will both be there. Do you know the exact time and place?"

"Eleven o'clock at the Pines Cemetery. The church service before that is private. Family only. But the graveside service will be open to Franklin's many friends."

"Mrs. Gardner's words, I take it?"

"Precisely. I've some other calls to make. Have a good day."

"You, too, sir." Josh put down the phone, then wondered if he should call Maggie now or delay telling her about the funeral until he saw her at work tomorrow.

The mere thought of talking to her on the phone caused what felt like a low-voltage electrical shock to leap through his body. It left him feeling a bit numb but it didn't surprise him. His whole damn system was out of sync because of Maggie Sutter.

She was becoming a larger-than-life person to him, making him rethink attitudes and standards that had seemed pretty much settled years ago. God, he was even beginning to think that getting married and having kids wasn't such a bad way to go.

Cursing out loud, he grabbed his athletic bag and left the apartment. He drove to the gym that most of the cops used, changed into shorts and running shoes, then hit the indoor track.

Two hours later he had run at least five miles, worked out with weights, showered away the perspiration and donned his bathing trunks to finish his workout in the huge indoor swimming pool. He was at the door to the pool area with a towel around his neck when his heart actually skipped a beat. Just getting out of the water, climbing one of the far ladders, was Maggie.

She was wearing a plain black one-piece suit, she was dripping wet and she was, without a doubt, the prettiest sight he'd ever seen.

He knew when to admit defeat. *You're a gone goose, Benton. Be a man and admit it.*

Entering the echoing pool room he walked straight to Maggie. She was drying off with a big soft-looking towel, and when she saw him her eyes got very big.

"Hello," he said with a smile.

"Uh, hi," she said, unable to conceal her surprise.

"Do you come here often? I don't remember seeing you here before."

A spurt of her normal gumption prompted a wry retort. "Since you didn't even recognize me until the night of Gardner's homicide, why would you have noticed me here, at the gym?"

"Maybe because you're *very* noticeable." Before she could hit him with another zinger he said, "There's something I need to tell you about the Gardner case. How much longer are you planning to be here?"

"Not long." She had used six different exercise machines and finished her regimen with about twenty laps in the pool. "After a shower, I'm out of here."

"I was going to swim a few laps, but I don't have to. I've been working out for over two hours already. That's enough for today. So, how about meeting me in the lobby in about what? Ten minutes? Fifteen?''

"Fifteen. I need to dry my hair."

"Great. See you in fifteen."

They went in different directions, Maggie to the women's locker room, Josh to the men's. She hurried through a shower and then drying her hair, wondering all the while if he really had something to tell her about the case or was using some feeble tidbit as an excuse to lord it over her one more time.

She groaned, because she wasn't thinking clearly. Josh had his faults, but insisting on being king of the hill wasn't one of them. Besides, why on earth would he want to spend time with her today for anything remotely personal when he'd had ample opportunity only last night to haul her willing if incredibly ignorant butt to bed?

He has absolutely no wish to haul any part of you to bed! Good Lord, you're the one with the completely insane imagination, not him!

And you told him everything last night...all the secrets hidden in your foolish brain for so many years.

It was true, Maggie realized with a sinking sensation. She hadn't revealed her secret passion for him in one long uninterrupted confession, but anyone with half a brain could connect the dots. Not only did Josh Benton possess a full and complete brain, he was an exceptional detective. The only thing that would prevent his grasping the content of her alcohol-induced blathering last night was a lack of interest. He just might not give a damn.

Also, exactly how mature was it for a woman to confess to the object of her affection that she had worshipped him from afar for ten damn years?

Groaning because she was behaving so out of character these days, Maggie unplugged her hair dryer and put it in her bag. She hadn't brushed the natural curl out of her hair as she did on workdays, and her head was a mass of dark red curls. Yesterday, because of her dinner party—Maggie pursed her lips over that phrase—she had taken the time to actually give herself a hairdo, leaving some curl in strategic places, brushing it straight in others. Today she had taken no such pains.

Nor would she put on makeup, she thought spitefully. Why should she care if her face was practically colorless? Josh probably wouldn't even notice.

And then she remembered what he'd said by the pool. *Maybe because you're* very *noticeable*.

Did she have this thing all wrong? Was she reading Josh wrong? Where was her intuition, her instinct, her normal good sense?

Grabbing a small zippered case from her carryall bag, she went to a mirror and applied a touch of blusher to her cheeks and put on a bit of lipstick.

She was ready. "Go forth and face the enemy," she said under her breath, wishing she knew for certain if Josh was a friend or merely her current working partner. Truthfully, she wished for more than that. If only she could read his mind just once and learn how he really felt about her.

"Yeah, like that's going to happen," she muttered.

A few moments later Josh saw her coming toward him. The large lobby contained a snack bar and some small tables, one of which he had held for their usage. He got to his feet and smiled. Maggie arrived and set her bag on the floor next to his.

He motioned to the other chair. "Have a seat. How about something to eat? And drink?"

"Thanks, but I'm not crazy about the snacks in this place."

"Too healthy?" Josh asked with a twinkle in his eyes.

"Something like that, I suppose, though I prefer to call them tasteless. I'll have one of those tropical fruit drinks, though. They're pretty good."

"Maybe we should leave this health-nut place and hit my favorite cheeseburger hangout," Josh said with a little laugh.

He was surprising Maggie, she realized, teasing her, maybe even doing some flirting. Talking like a man did to a woman he liked. A thrill she couldn't control rippled through her system, and her pulse began fluttering as she wondered if maybe she had somehow attained the power to read his mind after all.

"You know something?" she said pertly. "I would love to have a cheeseburger. Let's go."

Josh chuckled. "A woman after my own heart. By the way, I love what you did to your hair."

Maggie cocked her eyebrow and spoke drolly. "It's what I *didn't* do to it. It would be a mop like this every day if I didn't brush out the curl while I dried it."

Josh reached across the table and stuck his finger into a curl. "It's incredible," he said softly. "Believe me, it doesn't look like any mop I've ever seen."

Okay, she hadn't expected this! Not in a public place, at any rate. She backed away from his hand. "If we're leaving, let's get moving."

"Sure, why not?"

They stood, picked up their bags and left the building.

Maggie drove her own car and followed Josh in his.

Josh was thinking with something other than his brain. In truth, his blood was running hot and fast. He would tell Maggie about the Gardner funeral service, of course, but that would use up about three minutes and what else could he talk about to hold her interest? He could always ramble on about the case, of course. He could mention Desmond

Reicher…ask if she'd read Colin's report on the man…talk about the shadow that possible underworld ties had cast on the whole affair…things like that.

"Damn," he said, wishing he'd hung around her apartment a while longer last night, even though in his estimation they hadn't gotten along all that well. But maybe the feelings she had admitted to having for him years ago still meant something today.

Wait a damn minute! What was that remark she'd made about her crush lasting forever?

Josh's pulse rate quickened as he went over their conversation again, or tried to. It had occurred in starts and stops, he remembered that clearly, which made it nearly impossible to recall it word for word. But the gist of it all made a crazy kind of sense. *Maggie felt the same about him now as she had ten years ago!*

"You are imagining things," he told himself flatly, refusing to believe that a woman with her looks, intelligence and magnetism would carry a torch for a guy who'd never done anything but kid around with her and treat her as the teenager she'd been back then.

Driving behind him, Maggie's thoughts were practically in the same ballpark. She'd said far too much last night. Nervous again because of Josh's rare display of affection and watching the back of his vehicle, Maggie kept thinking of his philosophy toward women in general. After that hair compliment—or forked-tongue flattery—she probably should worry that Benton had decided she was worthy of one of those brief affairs he had professed to prefer. Or else he had put it all together and that was the reason he was being flirty and cute today. She had made herself easy prey, giving him the impression that she would go wherever he led her.

She truly felt like bawling. Yes, she'd run off at the mouth, but not just to lure Josh into a cheap affair.

Or had that been her motive all along?

Maggie gasped. Of course that had been her motive! Why else had she contrived a dinner party with Josh as the only guest? *For God's sake, stop lying to yourself! You want to make love with him so much that you would do just about anything to get him into bed. You're just afraid of how he'll take his being the first!*

It was the painful truth, and she wished ardently that she had slept with some guy, *any* guy, just so she wouldn't be in this ludicrous place now.

Maggie gave her head a small shake. Josh had made a quick right turn and she didn't want to lose him. He had invited her to ride with him just before leaving the gym, but she had thought it best if she took her own car. How silly could she get? She was so damn cowardly with Josh it was a wonder he didn't kick her off his team at the Bureau.

Maggie's lips thinned in further self-reproach. Wasn't it time she acted her age in Josh's presence? In every other area of her life she was independent as hell and afraid of nothing. The mere thought of how she behaved around Josh sickened her. Her adolescent ploy to get him to her apartment last night was bad enough, but then she'd chickened out and called Natalie. *Then* she'd drunk too much wine and made a fool of herself.

There'll be no more of that, she thought grimly, squaring her shoulders. From this moment on she was off silly games and pretense. If she felt like saying something, she would say it.

Josh pulled his vehicle to the curb and parked, and Maggie followed suit. She was getting out when she saw Josh walking toward her.

"It's Sunday," he said with a look of chagrin on his face. "I don't know what's wrong with me, but Sammy's Hamburger Haven is never open on Sunday. That's why we had no trouble with curb parking. I should have remembered, but I guess I was thinking of other things."

"Oh…well, no problem. We can do it some other time." She got settled behind the wheel of her car again. "Do you want to talk right here about the case? You said you had something to tell me."

"Yeah, guess so, though I don't mind admitting I was all set for one of Sammy's cheeseburgers and I'm feeling disappointed as hell. I'll get in, okay?

It's too cold to stand out here.'' He shut Maggie's door and walked around the back of her car to reach the passenger door.

She realized that she hadn't agreed to him getting in her car, but so what if he did? With lunch together out of the picture they were back to a business-only basis.

That was fine, too, she thought with a sigh, although she couldn't help being at least as disappointed over the missed cheeseburger as Josh had said he was. But her sense of loss was more focused on what might have been said and done while they ate. Who knew where a simple lunch together might have gone?

Damn, was she back to grasping at straws?

Josh got in and pulled the door closed. ''This cold goes straight to a man's bones,'' he said with a slight shiver.

''I'll start the car.'' Maggie turned the ignition key and the heater came on immediately.

''Thanks,'' Josh said and proceeded to tell her about the funeral service on Tuesday.

''I think we should be there, too. I'd like to see the Gardner family for myself, for one thing. They seem to be an odd lot, if you read between the lines of Waters's and Wilson's reports about them.''

''You may be right,'' Josh murmured. He turned his head to look directly at Maggie. ''Can we talk about us now?''

She blanched. "Us?"

"Yes, us, as in you and me. I told you the latest information on the case, but I don't want to just drive off now in one direction and watch you driving off in another." He saw the color return to her face and knew he'd really given her a jolt. "I've changed a lot this week," he said quietly. "I've changed because of you."

She swallowed and realized how dry her mouth had become. Remembering her vow to be herself with him, she said, albeit hoarsely, "I...I've changed, too."

"Because of me?"

"Yes." She turned in the seat to face him. "It's always been about you." She watched the changing expressions on his face and within the depths of his incredible gray eyes. "Whenever we've been together I tried to act as though it didn't matter, but it does matter."

Their gazes locked and nothing short of an atomic blast could have broken their admiration of each other.

"I want to make love to you," Josh said thickly.

"I want to make love to you," she whispered, and had to forcibly stop herself from saying too much. It would be better for him to find out her last and final secret for himself.

"Your place...or mine?" Josh asked.

"Which is the closest? I don't know where you live."

"Yours."

"Then we'll go there."

"Maggie…" He leaned forward, cupped the back of her head and touched his lips to hers, once, twice, a third time. And then he *really* kissed her, letting go of every inhibition and overwhelming them both.

She felt his tongue, the movement of his lips on hers. She inhaled his scent and realized how much bigger than her he was. The desire racking her body caused her to tremble, and she actually wondered if women ever fainted from this kind of passion.

He raised his head and looked into her eyes. "Drive safely," he said, and heard in his own voice how deeply affected he was.

"You, too."

"Follow me again." He got out hurriedly and strode to his own vehicle.

"I'll follow you anywhere," Maggie said as a tear spilled from her eye and coursed down her cheek.

Once they got to her apartment building, she couldn't remember actually driving home. Her mind had gotten stuck on that kiss and what they were going to do in her bed. She'd felt feverish one minute and chilled the next. Anxiety had eaten at her one minute and more happiness than she'd known existed had warmed her soul the next. She was eager and she was frightened. But most of all she was swirling in a sea of the kind of excitement she'd only been able to imagine before today.

Finally they were both parked and in her apartment. They tore off their heavy jackets and dropped them on the floor just inside, right near the door, and then they fell into each other's arms and began kissing hungrily.

Josh picked her up and mumbled two words. "Your bedroom."

"Next to the bath."

"I know."

He set her on her feet next to her bed and began undressing her. It was lovely and startling and arousing for Maggie, all at the same time. No man had ever undressed her before, and looking at Josh's face between hot, passionate kisses and the almost magical way he made her clothing disappear, she saw a reflection of her own feelings. This was as exciting for him as it was for her! How could that be? He certainly wasn't a novice to…

No, she wasn't going to think about his previous lovers. She adored him, and she loved every striking feature of his handsome face. She suddenly felt the need to see the rest of him, all of him, and she shoved the bottom of his sweatshirt up and pressed her lips to the hot skin of his bare chest.

He helped by grabbing the back of the shirt and yanking it over his head. Naked to the waist, he concentrated again on getting Maggie out of *her* clothes.

"Maggie, do you even know how beautiful you are?" he asked in a ragged shard of a voice.

She was pushing down his jeans and fitted boxers, and she didn't care how beautiful she was, she only cared how beautiful *he* was. The sight of his hard belly and manhood weakened her knees. She stepped backward, to the bed, and quickly threw back the covers. Then, with him watching intently, she took off her bra and panties and lay down.

He was on her in the very next second, covering her body with his, covering her lips with his, and managing to whisper again and again, "Maggie...Maggie...Maggie."

Nearly overcome by the pleasure of having his body on top of hers, with his arousal nestled in the perfect spot between her legs, Maggie ran her hands up and down his back and kissed every part of him she could reach with her lips. "Josh...oh, Josh," she whispered. "My beautiful man, my love."

Josh brought himself down so he could kiss her breasts. When he lavished attention to her nipples, he heard her moan softly and felt her twine her fingers into his hair. From the movement of her hips and the way she was rubbing herself against his erection, he was certain she was as hot as he was for the real thing.

He moved up again, took her mouth in a long,

feverish kiss and slid into her. Or tried to. Startled, he raised his head and looked at her. "Maggie..."

"Don't say one word. If you stop now I will never forgive you."

"But..." She turned her head on the pillow, but he still saw the tears. "Don't cry, sweetheart," he said in a hoarse, emotional voice. "You should be proud. You're giving me the only gift a woman can give once in her life." He kissed her cheek. "I'll be gentle, little love," he whispered.

And he was. He caressed her back to writhing passion, and when he finally entered her she was so breathless and needy that she barely noticed any discomfort. Fully inside of her, he began an easy rhythm. In seconds she was riding the same crest of passion that he was on. It built, not hurriedly but steadily, and the first spasms of completion were so amazingly pleasurable that she dug her fingertips into his back and began moaning. The sounds coming from her would not be held back; she heard herself and realized that the mere thought of control at this point was laughable.

She wasn't laughing, though. She was soaring far above the mundane world that had been her life for twenty-six years. She was in love, and being loved, and nothing else that had ever happened to her could compare. When Josh moved faster and breathed harder, she went with him. And incredibly delicious minutes later, when he yelled her name, she was only strong enough to whisper his. He had taken her to the stars, and she was in no hurry to come back down to earth. She clasped him tightly and vowed that she would never let go of him. It seemed to be a completely reasonable oath in her dazed and bedazzled brain.

But it was over, and she was floating. The sensation of dreamy satisfaction she felt was certainly a close second on the pleasure-list, with the actual act of lovemaking being the first.

"I never knew," she said softly.

Josh moved his weight from her to the bed and lay up against her. "Tell me why you never knew, Maggie," he said softly while stroking her damp hair back from her face.

She looked into his eyes. "I guess I waited for you. I love you. I've always loved you. It wasn't a kid's crush, after all. It was the real thing, and maybe I knew that."

He was overcome with emotion and tears filled his eyes. "I love you, Maggie."

She snuggled closer and pressed her lips to his before whispering, "I've never been happier."

Josh and Maggie went—in the same car—to the Pines Cemetery on Tuesday morning. They talked about the case, but they also kept smiling at each other. They had spent last night together, and while they hadn't yet discussed marriage, they each knew they were heading in that direction.

"At least there's a little sunshine today," Maggie said as they exited the vehicle.

"Very little," Josh said with a quick glance at the weak sun hanging in the sky.

"Spring has to be just around the corner. I, for one, can hardly wait."

"I, for two, feel exactly the same." Josh took her arm as they approached the group standing around the open grave. He stopped about twenty feet away. "This is close enough," he said under his breath. "Look at each face. Who do you recognize?"

Maggie named some of the bigwigs in the Chicago government that were present.

"The woman seated is Cecelia Gardner, Franklin's mother," Josh said. "Lyle, her eldest son, is sitting on her right. Stephen, Franklin's son, is sitting on her left."

"Oh, there's Colin and Darien."

They were on the other side of the small crowd, doing exactly what Josh and Maggie were doing, checking out the attendees.

"And there's Desmond Reicher," Josh murmured. "The man standing right behind Mrs. Gardner. Do you see him?"

"Yes."

"I wonder if any of those men is left-handed," Maggie murmured.

"Because?"

"Even though I still can't make out a clear design of the killer's ring from Franklin's facial bruises through photo enhancement, I'm certain that the person who delivered the brutal blows is left-handed. I did a report detailing the proof of that opinion but I need to verify one piece of it before I put it in the file for Detectives Waters and Wilson to follow up on."

Josh looked at her. "You're amazing."

"So are you, my darling, in bed and out."

"Are you asking for trouble, my sweet?"

"Umm, could be."

"Then let's go and find some." With a wicked smile he tucked her hand around his arm and walked her back to his vehicle.

Epilogue

The news that night did a special on the Gardner family, with emphasis on their good deeds in the Chicago area.

Snuggled together on the sofa, Josh and Maggie watched the report. They both snapped to attention when the special segment was followed by a statement from the anchor.

"Desmond Reicher, COO of the Gardner Corporation, was taken into police custody today and charged with the murder of Franklin Gardner."

Josh and Maggie looked at each other, each of them conveying shock. "Is Reicher left-handed?" Maggie asked in a hushed, startled voice.

"I think we had better find out, don't you?" Josh

got up and went over to the phone. In a moment he had identified himself and asked, "Which facility is holding Desmond Reicher?" After another moment he said, "Thanks," and broke the connection to place a second call. "This is important, Sergeant. You've got Desmond Reicher in a holding cell. Is he left- or right-handed?"

Josh turned to look at Maggie. "He doesn't know," he told her. "But he's checking."

She sat without moving, tense as a coiled spring, waiting to find out. Finally Josh said, "Thanks, Sergeant," and put down the phone. "Reicher's right-handed," he said quietly.

"They've arrested the wrong man!"

"Yes, they have, but I would bet anything that Colin and Darien are already on top of it."

Maggie relaxed some. "You're right. But if it's as simple as which hand the killer used to pummel Gardner, wouldn't Reicher have been released by now?"

"There are complications in the case still to be ironed out, Maggie."

Maggie sighed and put her head back. Josh resumed his place on the sofa next to her and took her hand. She smiled at him.

"There's something I'd like to tell you," he said.

"Feel free."

"I led you to believe I never even got close to a

genuine commitment with anyone and that's not true.''

Maggie sat up straighter. ''You don't have to…I mean, you're entitled…''

''You're dying to know all about my life during the past ten years, so don't get phony on me now, sweetheart.''

''All right, fine. Go ahead and bare your soul.''

''Well, my soul is hardly overburdened with deep, dark secrets, so my little story isn't apt to leave me naked and bleeding.''

''Aw, heck. And there I thought I'd finally see the real Josh Benton.''

''You've *always* seen the real me, Maggie. You just didn't know what went on behind the scenes ten years ago. And why would you have? Adult men don't tell kids about the women they're dating.''

''Oh, you were dating…someone,'' she said, speaking almost wistfully.

''Your mother knew I was getting pretty serious about…would you like to know her name?''

''Do you still see her?''

''Nope. Haven't seen her in years. The last I heard of her was that she had gotten married and moved to Savannah, Georgia.''

''Then, no, I don't want to know her name. But you told Mom about her. How come?''

''Probably because your mother sort of became my mother for a while. Guess I missed my own mom, and Lottie was always willing to talk to me. Anyhow, I was on the verge of popping the question when the woman of my dreams started sleeping around. My friends all knew it before I did. Tim was the only one with the guts to finally tell me about it. I was wounded, I can't say I wasn't, and it took a long time before I healed enough to even take a woman to a movie.''

"I knew there was more to your negative attitude about relationships than bad statistics, darling,'' Maggie said softly. "I'm sorry you were hurt but I'm glad it happened.''

He chuckled. "Want to know something? So am I.'' He kissed her until they were both breathless, then whispered, "I've been thinking of a honeymoon in a nice warm place, maybe Hawaii or the Bahamas. What do *you* think?''

"A honeymoon?'' Maggie leaped up from her spot on the sofa and straddled his lap. She wrapped her arms around his neck. "Yes...yes...yes!''

"Looks like we're going to get married,'' Josh said with a big grin.

All Maggie could manage was another "Yes!''

*   *   *   *   *

BEHIND THE BADGE

Justine Davis

Dear Reader,

When I was first asked to participate in this project, a book covering a single crime from the perspectives of forensics, detectives and lawyers, each by different authors, I thought it was a great idea. It sounded like something I'd really like to read, which is the best sign for something you're going to write!

My second thought was "Gee, I wonder which part they want me to do?" I'm joking, of course. With my background, I knew I'd be doing the cops. But I was excited about this new twist; my story would not only have to mesh carefully with the others, but when it was done, I'd get a chance in fiction to do what I rarely got to do in real life. I'd be able to follow a case closely even after it left my little section of the law-enforcement world and was investigated, documented and handed to the prosecutors, a chance to be there every step of the way to the verdict.

It turned out, however, to be much like reality; I knew my part of the process in great detail, but the rest only in a general way. I'll have to wait until the book is in my hands to find out exactly how the rest happens. So I'll be reading just as you will. After getting to know Joan and Jackie and our tireless editor on this, Ann Leslie Tuttle, I think we're all in for a treat!

I enjoyed writing "Behind the Badge," and I hope you'll enjoy reading it and the rest of *Body of Evidence*.

Justine Davis

Chapter 1

"Franklin Gardner? Of *the* Gardners? As in Gardner Corporation?"

Colin Waters hated days that started like this.

"Yep, those Gardners. That's why the commander put out the call to Detective Benton personally at one this morning."

"Are they sure the body's Gardner himself?"

"Benton says so. And he asked for you specifically. You're to meet with him at the station before you go to the scene."

At the dispatcher's answer Colin sighed into his cell phone. He'd already been on his way, hoping to get in early to try and catch up on some things, but if this was true, he could kiss that opportunity goodbye. And if forensic detective Josh Benton said it was Gardner, it was true; the man didn't make mistakes.

"Great," Colin muttered. Just what he needed, a dead mover and shaker.

He ended the call and began to maneuver his worse-for-wear city vehicle back into traffic. No sooner had he gotten to the number one lane than his cell rang again. This time it was the district commander, Eliot Portman.

"You're on the way?" he asked without preamble.

"Yes."

"Good. I'm counting on you to keep the lid on as long as you can. I don't want the press getting wind of this before we're ready."

Assuming the vultures aren't already circling, Colin said to himself. The media seemed able to scent society murder like sharks scented blood in the water.

"Wilson's going to meet you there."

Colin frowned. "Wilson?"

"The new hire. And your new partner."

Well, that's the capper on my day, Colin thought. Not only did he have a case involving one of the most socially prominent families in the state, let alone Chicago, but now he had the new pet dumped in his lap.

He hadn't joined in the general grumbling about

Wilson sliding into a coveted detective slot, even though there were cops on the street who'd been trying for years to get the assignment, while she had only a couple of years on a department a small fraction of the size of Chicago PD. The fact that Wilson had computer skills sadly lacking in the division had kept him from jumping on that bandwagon, but that didn't mean he thought it was a good idea.

So now he had not only a rookie detective but practically a rookie cop on his hands, on a high-profile murder case. A very high-profile murder case.

"Problem, Waters?" Portman asked, making Colin realize he'd been silent a little too long.

"Just dodging some traffic," he improvised. "I'll keep you posted."

"This is a big one, so you do that."

As if I don't know that, Colin muttered to himself. "Yes, sir," he said aloud.

It was going to be a very long day.

"You look," Colin said frankly, "like hell, buddy."

"I feel worse," Josh Benton said, his voice sounding grim as he ran a hand over his black hair.

Benton was only six years older than Colin, but there was an eon of weary experience in his eyes. Wondering if someday the eyes he saw in the mirror

would look like that, he handed Benton his own cup
of black coffee.

"You need it more than I do."

"Can't argue that," Benton agreed and took it.
"It's been a long night."

"Want to sit down and bring me up to speed?"

"No." At Colin's startled blink, Benton grimaced. "If I sit down, I may never get up." He
eyed Colin. "But you might as well sit. It may be
the last rest you get for a while."

"Yeah, I get that feeling. Where are we at?"

"The maid, Miriam Hobart, found him at about
one this morning. She's pretty upset, she's worked
for the Gardners for more than ten years."

"Signs of a struggle?"

"Yes. He fought, all right. There's some oddly
shaped bruising to the face, severe blow to the back
of the head that we're guessing is from a fall against
a table. That one could have been fatal, if you ask
me. Stab wounds, small but deep, any of which
could also have been fatal."

"Knife?"

"More like an ice pick. And there was a collection of picks at the scene."

Odd thing to collect, Colin thought, but said only,
"Forced entry?"

"No. Some valuable stuff missing, but a lot, including a chunk of cash, weren't taken."

Colin frowned, but said nothing. He knew Benton

would have the same questions he did. They both had enough experience to know what those facts could signify.

"Where do you want us to start?"

"Us?"

Colin stifled a sigh. "Yeah. The boss informed me I have a new partner. We're supposed to meet up at the scene."

Benson studied him for a moment. "The propeller head?"

Colin rolled his eyes at the slang for computer geeks. "How'd you guess?"

"She's the only one unassigned, and you're the only one partner-free," Benton said with a shrug.

"And I was kind of liking it that way."

"At least she's not hard to look at."

Not a great recommendation for a cop, Colin thought, but he left it at that. And Benton apparently agreed because he went right back to business.

"We'll have photos as soon as they're dry, and the preliminary crime scene reports. There's a son, Stephen, age twenty-three. Lives at the Gardner estate. Mother is Cecelia, widowed. If you even glance at the society pages of the paper, you'll know her on sight."

"If you watch five minutes of the evening news, you'll know her on sight," Colin said wryly. "Who else?"

"Family, only an older brother, Lyle."

"Who's been notified?"

Benton grimaced. "The mother. In person, by two captains, sent by the commander himself."

Colin grimaced in turn; as a reminder of the horsepower of the victim, it was potent, but it was also a loss to the investigation. On a murder case, a detective always tried to be the one to deliver the grim news, not out of any ghoulish enjoyment, but to see the reactions of the family, who frequently weren't all that sorry to see the dearly departed depart.

"If she was surprised, they said it didn't show. Shock, maybe."

Since Benton didn't elaborate, Colin assumed no one had reported any other reaction that triggered more suspicion than usually fell upon the family of a murder victim; Benton was among the best at his job, despite that world-weary look in his eyes, and he wouldn't leave out anything crucial.

"Canvas of the building?" Colin asked.

"We had patrol start it, but you'll need to follow up."

Colin nodded. "Anything else?"

Benton nodded. "There are security cameras in the lobby and in the hallways. The super, a guy named Carter, said the recording equipment is in the basement. We put in a call to the security company, they should be getting there about now. They're sending a Mr. Bergen."

"We'll get on that right away," Colin said; a videotape of the elevators and hallways could wind this case up in a hurry. But he knew better than to hope for such a tidy package; this was murder, and murder was almost always messy. Very messy.

Darien had to park so far from the address she'd been given on the Gold Coast that she should have changed to her running shoes. But she hadn't wanted to delay, not when the district commander himself had given her this assignment.

After a dash to the right address, she paused for a few seconds to gather herself before she went inside. She knew she should be feeling appropriately solemn—someone's loved one was dead in the worst imaginable way—but some small part of her couldn't help being excited at working on her first murder case. She'd have to be careful that it didn't show; she knew that much, that inappropriate rookie enthusiasm could brand her forever.

She also couldn't dwell on the fact that the sexiest guy in the division would be her partner.

The March sun didn't provide much warmth, but it turned the stone of the upper stories of the building a golden cream that nicely set off the amber tint of the windows. Thirty stories or better, she thought, and she was headed for the top. Of course. If the victim was the kind of high-roller the commander had said, it would only figure he'd live in the penthouse.

Telling herself that she hadn't gotten this far to give in to doubts and qualms now, she straightened her spine and stepped inside. Still, the lobby caught her off guard with its expanse of gleaming marble. Springfield might be the state capital, but it had a population of about one twenty-fifth of Chicago and for a moment she again felt like the small-town girl lost in the big city.

No, she thought. *That man lying dead upstairs is lost. And it's my job to help find out who did this to him.*

Steady now, she strode across the marble floor to the bank of elevators, trying to thaw her fingers as she went. A uniformed officer stood outside one of them, and she quickly found out it was the private elevator to the penthouse. She showed her ID and after the officer examined it as if he doubted it was real, she stepped inside the car. It, too, was elegantly appointed with gilt and marble, and she told herself to expect more of the same when she reached the penthouse. Considering the size of the building, she could guess how big the place must be.

The elevator doors opened directly into the foyer of the penthouse. She ran into a uniform the moment she stepped out, and had to produce her badge once more to get him to allow her in. Even then the man looked at her skeptically, and she wondered if that would ever stop.

"Look, I'm supposed to meet with Detective Waters. We're partners. On this case," she added as an afterthought, since she had no idea if the assignment would last beyond this case.

Something flickered in the man's eyes, and she thought the corners of his mouth twitched. But all he said was "He's in the kitchen."

She tried not to speculate about the officer's thoughts as she stepped past him. Now all she had to do was figure out where the kitchen was in this place. As she walked, she forced herself not to gape at the opulence evident in every square foot of the place, from huge Oriental carpets to a pair of matched sofas that had to be big enough to seat twelve people each, from sculptures on lighted pedestals to paintings on the walls that looked as if they should be in museums.

She walked until she heard voices. Stopping, she realized they were coming from two different directions, straight ahead and off to her left. She listened for a moment, then heard the low, rich baritone of Detective Colin Waters. Even after her short time assigned to this job she couldn't mistake it. She turned left.

"—need the videotapes for the elevators for that time period."

"I'll get them right to you, Detective." This promise was followed by the sound of footsteps, and she decided it was all right for her to go in.

"You do that," Waters was saying. "I appreciate it."

She was sure she imagined the slight break in his words as she stepped into a kitchen that looked more suited to a five-star restaurant than a home, because he didn't even glance in her direction. The other man, a shorter, stockier man with a goatee, didn't just glance, he stopped in his tracks and stared at her.

"About time, *Detective* Wilson," Waters drawled pointedly, and Darien fought not to let color stain her cheeks. He knew how long it took to get here from probably anywhere in the city, so why was he—

"Detective?"

The other man almost squeaked it, and Darien stifled a sigh. And then stopped as the thought occurred to her that the statement might have been aimed at the other man as much as at her, letting him know who she was before he said anything embarrassing. She studied the tall, powerfully built man assessingly, wondering if there was indeed such tact and consideration hidden behind an exterior that had seemed, to her at least, decidedly gruff until now.

By the time she decided she had no way of knowing and that it wouldn't make any difference anyway, the other man had escaped out another door—

way. She also decided against making any comment about his unfair dig about her arrival time. If she was right, she'd look silly, and if he really was criticizing, he didn't deserve a response.

Start as you mean to go on, her father had always said, and she meant to start this partnership on the right foot.

"What have we got?" she asked briskly.

There was the slightest of pauses before he answered, and she was very aware of his steady gaze. With those unusual golden-brown eyes, it was hard not to be. There was the slightest bit of emphasis on the first word when he finally spoke.

"*We* have a homicide case that could turn into the nightmare to end all nightmares."

"Victim's a big shot, I gather," she said, as neutrally as she could.

"And then some. They're more recognizable in this town than the mayor. And they've got friends in higher places than that."

"I thought I heard eggshells crunching," she said.

To her surprise, Waters grinned. "And very expensive eggs we're walking on at that."

She felt absurdly pleased. And decided to make it clear right away that she understood her position. "What do you want me to do?"

He gave her a look she couldn't quite interpret. "You're waiting for me to tell you what needs to be done, Wilson?"

She wasn't sure what she was supposed to say to that, so she went with the truth. "I know what needs to be done. I know what my area of expertise is, so I would assume I'm supposed to tackle his computer. But I also know I'm the rookie here, so I was asking what part of it you want me to do."

After a brief moment, he nodded as if she'd gotten the answer to some difficult test question correct. "Benton and Sutter have the evidence situation under control, and we should have their preliminary written reports by the end of the day. We'll take the computer with us as evidence; it's a laptop—at least it's the only one I could find—so we don't need to wait for transport, as long as one of us has it in our possession from the time we leave here until it's booked in, for chain of evidence."

"Did Benton or Sutter draw any early conclusions?"

"Limited. This is the highest-profile kind of case, so those eggshells are pretty thin. So far all we know for sure is Franklin Gardner's dead, he didn't do it himself, and there's no sign of forced entry."

"Anything missing?"

"A few valuable items. But whoever it was left cash and other easily portable—and fence-able—things behind."

Darien frowned. "Interrupted burg, maybe?"

"Maybe."

"By the victim?"

"It's possible," he said. "There are signs of a struggle in the study where he was found. I'll show you in a minute."

"But that still doesn't explain the lack of forced entry."

"Nope."

"Nobody heard anything?"

"The live-in maid, who found him, was the only one here. But the study is soundproofed, according to her, so he could work undisturbed."

"You've talked to her?"

"Not yet. She's first on the list, but she's pretty distraught."

"He have any enemies?" Her mouth curved wryly. "As if anybody could reach such an exalted position in life without making at least a few along the way."

"Safe bet," Waters agreed. "But we don't have names yet."

"So…we start asking questions?"

"Indeed we do."

Chapter 2

"I understand it was a shocking experience for you, Mrs. Hobart," Waters said.

"It was terrible!" The woman shuddered. She looked tired as she sat on her employer's elegant sofa, and Darien supposed she'd been up most of the night. The notes she had said the woman was fifty-three, but right now she looked at least a decade older.

"So I'm sure you want to help us find who did this to Mr. Gardner," Waters said, his voice gentle.

"I already told the other detectives, I don't know anything. I heard a noise, then I found him on the floor in the study."

"You didn't see anything at all?"

A suddenly wary look crossed her face. "No. I told you, a noise woke me."

"What kind of noise?"

"Just a noise," she insisted. "I walked to the hall, I saw a light on. I found Mr. Gardner. I called 9-1-1. That's all."

She sounded almost defensive, Darien thought. And on her thought she saw Waters incline his head a fraction, as if the woman's tone had also caught his interest.

"I see. Then I guess we won't need much more of your time," Waters said. The woman relaxed visibly. "We'll just need the names of everyone who was here yesterday and last night. And anyone else who came regularly."

Immediately the woman stiffened up again. And Darien saw Waters notice it.

"I'm afraid I couldn't do that. It would betray my employment contract."

"Your contract?" Waters said, looking puzzled.

"A confidentiality clause?" Darien asked, the first time she'd spoken since the interview had begun.

The woman looked at her. "Exactly. I've not broken that trust for ten years, and I'm not about to start now."

Darien hesitated, then asked softly, "But the person you promised confidentiality to is dead. Doesn't that void your responsibility, especially if it will help find who killed him?''

Mrs. Hobart looked thoughtful, gave a half nod, opened her mouth to speak. And then abruptly stopped.

''Mrs. Hobart?'' Waters said.

''I work for the Gardner family,'' she said. And crossed her arms in front of her as if that answered all.

''And I work for the city of Chicago,'' Waters said, his voice suddenly flinty. ''It's my job to find out what really happened here last night. And I will, Mrs. Hobart. By whatever means necessary.''

The woman drew back slightly, as if she felt intimidated. *I would,* Darien thought.

She'd never seen Colin Waters in investigative mode before, but she knew his reputation, and she quickly decided to stay quiet so she could watch and learn.

''I'm sure the Gardner family wouldn't appreciate it becoming public knowledge that one of their employees had to be forced to cooperate with the investigation of the homicide of one of their own.''

His tone had gone icy, and it worked. The woman visibly quailed, and Darien saw her swallow nervously. But she still maintained her silence. So did Waters, until Darien wondered if he was waiting for her to step in.

''Perhaps we should call Mrs. Gardner,'' Darien

said. "I'm sure she would tell you she wants you to cooperate."

Waters shot her a look that told her without doubt that he thought she'd just made a big mistake. But she'd begun now, and he didn't stop her, so she had no choice but to go on.

"I mean, she's already told our commander she wants all the stops pulled out in this investigation."

"She has?" the woman asked, looking doubtful. "Well..."

Waters's expression changed, although Darien wasn't sure what the sideways look he gave her then meant.

When the woman still hesitated, Waters put in, "We'll check the security tapes, of course, but you'd save us a lot of time."

The woman's eyes widened. "Oh. The cameras."

She'd forgotten about them, Darien thought. *And now that she's remembered, she's not happy. Interesting.*

Waters gave her a moment longer to consider before he said, "And after all, we only need to know the names of any frequent visitors Mr. Gardner had, and of course any he had last night."

With a tiny sigh, she surrendered. "Many people came to see him often. Business people, and friends."

"Family?"

"Of course," she said, giving Waters a withering

look. "Mrs. Gardner comes frequently, and Mr. Lyle."

If Waters noticed the absence of Stephen, the dead man's son—and heir—on the visitor list, he didn't show it. But Darien was certain it had registered.

"Who came the most often outside of family?"

She frowned. "I suppose Mr. Bartley. And Mr. Reicher."

The victim's administrative assistant and the chief operating officer of the Gardner Corporation respectively, Darien thought, recalling the organizational chart she'd seen in the file Waters had given her to scan when they'd arrived.

"Who was here yesterday?"

"Mr. Lyle, early in the day, for just a few minutes. No one else that I know of."

"And last night?"

"I said I don't know if anyone came to visit him last night. He went out for dinner, didn't get home until ten, like I told those other detectives. He told me to go on to bed, he wouldn't be needing me."

"Was that unusual?" Darien asked.

"No. Mr. Gardner liked his privacy."

Waters studied her for a moment. "Especially if he was going to have female company?"

Darien realized he'd voiced the thought she'd just had, and she wondered what had been in the woman's voice to make them both think of this.

"I don't intrude into such things."

"It must have been hard to keep track anyway," Darien said empathetically. "He was a very handsome and wealthy man."

"Yes." For a moment genuine pain showed in the woman's face. "But it was more than that. He had something special. Charisma, they call it."

"Did Mr. Gardner's lady friends tend to be happy with him?" Waters asked.

"Not that it's anyone's business, but he always treated them well."

"But never married any of them," Darien observed.

"He had to be careful. A man in his position could never be sure if they were genuine or after his money. It's always been that way."

Poor little rich boy, Darien thought, but said nothing.

"Did he anger anyone in that process?"

"A woman he was seeing, you mean? Enough to…murder him?"

Oddly, her voice sounded merely thoughtful, not startled or shocked at the question. And it was only seconds before she was shaking her head.

"No. I can't imagine any woman he'd been seeing doing such a thing."

"You knew them, then?"

"I met most of them."

"Liked them?"

"It wasn't my place to like or dislike them."

That was the end of the woman's cooperation. Darien couldn't decide if she was showing loyalty to her long-time employer, or if she had something to hide. Judging by the way Waters was looking at her, he was wondering the same thing.

"Now what?" Darien asked as Waters dismissed the woman.

"What do you think?"

Darien knew he was testing her. She wasn't a fool, she knew some people thought she'd sailed into this position over the heads of others who had more right to it than she had. She'd thought about refusing it for that reason, but Tony had talked her out of it, pointing out they might decide she didn't want the job badly enough and she'd never get another chance. Her ex-husband was good for that, twisting the point of view to make you see the other side. It was one of the things she loved about him although it didn't outweigh the reasons she couldn't live with him.

But now she had to focus on what was happening here. Patrol officers had thankfully already done a canvas of the immediate neighbors, with minimal results, not surprising given the separation between the penthouse and the rest of the building.

"We need to interview the family, but while we're still here and he's primed...the super?" she asked.

"Benton already talked to him this morning when they got the call. Think we need to bother him again?"

She weighed that one for a moment, then went with her gut. "We're going to be who he sees from now on, he might as well get used to our faces."

Waters grinned suddenly. It lit up those amber eyes, and Darien felt as if the sun had come out on this blustery March day. "His place is on the ground floor. Let's go," he said.

On the way down in the elevator, Waters leaned against the wall and looked around at the expensive marble and carved wood. He gave a slight shake of his head as he mused aloud. "Looks, power, wealth, charisma. He had it all, didn't he?"

"For all the good it did him," Darien said.

"There is that," Waters agreed, and Darien knew he was thinking, as she was, that all the wealth in the world couldn't help the man who now lay on a slab in the morgue.

She was doing okay, Colin thought. Wilson had picked right up on the cue he'd given her when the building superintendent's wife had launched into a tirade about the arrogance of Franklin Gardner, not letting the super himself get a word in edgewise.

"Is he in trouble with the police? Good," the woman had snapped. "Some kind of financial fraud, I'll bet. That's what it always is with his kind."

It was then Colin had tried to signal Darien Wilson with a flick of his eyes. She caught it and smoothly took the woman's arm, using body language and tone of voice to invite the woman for a nice, long venting session.

"It seems that way, doesn't it? Perhaps you can help with the investigation, I'm sure an observant citizen like yourself must have noticed some things."

The woman smiled, clearly pleased as she was led away. "Oh, I have all right, I could tell you…"

Relieved to have her removed, Colin turned back to Carter. The man gave him a look that was both sheepish and wary. "I didn't tell her he'd been killed. The detective last night, he said I shouldn't talk about it to anyone. Since she can't keep anything secret, I figured that included her."

"You made the right choice."

"I'll remember that when she chews me out for keeping such big news from her."

As jarring as it was to have a murder reduced to such cold terms, Colin knew it was true; the death of a Gardner was just that, big news.

"I'll need a list of all the tenants from you."

The man grimaced. "They're not going to like that. They pay a lot of money to live here, and they expect their privacy."

"So did Franklin Gardner," Colin pointed out.

"Yeah. Yeah, you're right. But, do I need to see like a search warrant or something?"

Rescue me from sidewalk lawyers, Colin thought. "I can get you a subpoena for the records, if you want," he said easily, pulling a notepad out of his jacket pocket. "I'll just need to verify all your identifying information for the court records, in case they need you to testify about the delay."

It worked, as he had guessed it would. The only thing the average citizen disliked more than getting involved was having to appear in court to explain why.

"We've already talked to many of them," Colin said. "It won't come as any surprise to them when we go to follow up."

"I'll get the list," Carter grumbled. He turned and disappeared through a doorway that led to a bedroom he apparently used as an office.

The apartment itself, although smaller, was as elegant as the others Colin had seen in this building. But there the resemblance stopped; Carter might be the super of one of the fanciest buildings on the Gold Coast, but obviously they didn't pay him enough to match the other residents in decor.

Or maybe his tastes are just more like mine, Colin thought ruefully; his own furnishings ran to whatever was comfortable and things he could put his feet up on. After four years of marriage to a woman who kept the living room for company only, he'd sworn he'd never have a room he couldn't live in.

He continued his cursory inspection, looking for anything that jumped out at him, anything out of tune. Nothing looked out of the ordinary. There were afghans tossed over every chair and the couch, and someone living here was obviously the source, judging by the large basket full of yarn festooned with scissors and what he guessed were knitting needles. There were some amateurish oil paintings on the walls, of floral arrangements and bowls of lopsided fruit, and he wondered if they were by the same hand. The upholstery was floral, much like the things his mother had preferred, which probably explained why he felt more at home here; he might not like all the fussy details but he'd grown up with the stuff, unlike the marble and leather of the late Franklin Gardner's abode.

Carter came back with the list of tenants. "Must have been tough," Colin said, pretending to scan the list while in fact he was watching Carter with his excellent peripheral vision, "to have your wife dislike your star tenant so much."

"She's that way about anybody with that kind of money, not that we're doing all that bad. I mean, we live in this building, after all. Anyway, I just try…tried to keep her out of his way."

"Hmm," Colin said, wondering just how deep Mrs. Carter's dislike of the penthouse tenant had gone. It seemed unlikely a woman could take him. Gardner had been a strong, healthy, athletically built man, but the element of surprise could turn any situation on its head.

"Who were the regular visitors to the penthouse that you knew about?"

Carter thought for a moment. "Ladies, of course. He had lots of those. And he held a lot of business meetings and dinners up there. He and Mr. Reicher."

Hmm. Second time that name had popped up. "What was he like? Mr. Reicher."

"Oh, he's much worse than Mr. Gardner. Mr. Reicher wasn't very pleasant at all. Very cold, my wife says."

Colin asked a few more routine questions, gave the man his card and told him to call if he thought of anything that might be useful.

"What's your take on the wife?" he asked his new partner as they left the apartment.

"Bored out of her mind, so she minds everyone else's business," she answered.

"Social climber? Aspires to the Gardner level?"

She thought about that one. "I don't think so. She doesn't really like them enough to want to be one. It's not envy, she seems to view them more as an affliction."

"To be eliminated?"

She stared at him. "You're thinking of her as a suspect?"

He shrugged. "Just curious about her attitude. And thinking those knitting needles in there could leave a wound a lot like an ice pick."

Quickly she glanced back over her shoulder as if she could still see into the apartment they'd just left. When she looked back at him there was acknowledgment in her eyes, he supposed for seeing something she'd missed.

"I don't think so," she said after a moment of thought. "She's more of a complainer than a doer, I think."

Colin listened, then nodded. "All right."

He saw an odd expression flit quickly across her face, as if she were surprised he had accepted her assessment so easily. But he'd arrived at the same conclusion after his short interaction with the woman, so in fact she was simply confirming what he already thought.

"What's next? A door-to-door?" she asked, indicating the tenant list he now held with a nod of her head.

"Chances are you'll get mainly staff this time of day," he said. "Family should probably come first."

"Okay."

She didn't sound particularly nervous about going up against a family the stature of the Gardners. Colin didn't know if that meant she was sure of herself, or too naive to realize what she was about to get into.

"You drove from home?" he asked. She nodded. "Let's take my city car, then. I'll bring you back here when we're ready to head to the barn. Or on my way home." He didn't mention that would likely be well after normal quitting time; he guessed they'd be putting in a lot of long hours on this one.

"All right. Shall we pick up his computer now?"

"Might as well. I've got an evidence lock box in the trunk. We'll secure it there."

The lock boxes were an innovation added after one too many cases had been lost due to a fast-tongued defense lawyer convincing a jury that somebody could have broken into a police unit trunk, tampered with evidence, and then locked it back up and leave no sign, nor be seen by any witnesses. They never explained why that "somebody" simply hadn't stolen the evidence altogether, but logic didn't seem to apply much to such things.

He doubted logic would apply much to this case, either.

"Now this is more like it," Darien said.

"Think you could live like that, Wilson?" Waters asked, gesturing toward the huge house in the distance as they drove up the sweeping, half-circle driveway.

She glanced at her new partner. "I didn't mean the house. I just meant the space."

The grounds of the Gardner estate were, indeed,

spacious. She was a little surprised at how comforting it felt to be able to see more than a tiny patch of sky between towering buildings.

"What's the point, besides to impress people that you can afford it?" he asked

"Peace. Quiet. Privacy. Room to breathe. Air to breathe. Trees. Grass to walk on, lay down in on a sunny day. A garden. A dog." She looked around once more and grinned. "Or a horse."

She thought she saw the corners of his mouth quirk. But he only said, and grudgingly, "Okay, I'll give you that. But who needs *this* much room and privacy?"

"Hey, I grew up near farm country. This is nothing but the back pasture. Besides, what if you want to go out and get the paper in your pajamas?"

"I don't."

"You don't ever want to just sneak outside—"

"I don't wear pajamas."

The image that shot into her mind was overpowering. Trying to recover, she muttered, "T.M.I."

He slowed the car as they neared the house. "What?"

"Too much information," she translated with a wry grimace.

"Computer talk?"

"Started out that way," she said, not quite sure if he was ribbing her or if he really didn't know the acronym that had come into general usage.

He braked the car to a stop, then leaned forward to look at the majestic stone steps that led up to the covered portico. "Suppose they'll want us to use the servants' entrance?"

"Would you?" she asked, curious.

He shot her a sideways look. "Not a chance. Murder doesn't take a back seat to anyone."

"Amen," she said softly. And for a long moment their gazes locked. The sense of being caught and held by a pair of amber-gold eyes was unlike anything she'd felt before. She wondered if it had the same effect on a suspect. She guessed it did; it would certainly account in part for his stellar arrest rate.

He turned his attention back to driving. He inched the car up until it was not exactly in front of the front doors, but no farther. He put it in park and shut the motor off; out of the way was apparently as far as he would accede to wealth and position.

"I'll bet you forgot to call ahead for an appointment, too," she said.

His head snapped around, and this time the grin broke loose. "Darned if I didn't."

"Oh, well," she said with a dramatic sigh.

Still with the grin, he said, "Let's go."

When they walked up the grand steps, Darien felt a sense of camaraderie for the first time since she'd been on this job.

Chapter 3

They followed the butler—an honest-to-God butler in full regalia who had quizzed them at the door before finally allowing them entrance to the Gardner domain—into what the man had called the drawing room.

"What is a drawing room, anyway?" his partner whispered, and Colin had to stifle a chuckle. "Beats me." He took a quick look around the room. It seemed just as rich, but somehow different from the apartment. The art was of the same caliber, the fittings and furnishings just as elegant, but still it wasn't the same. And he couldn't put his finger on the difference.

"This feels like old money. More class, less flash," she murmured.

That was it, he thought. This room felt like it had been here for generations of wealth. Wilson had immediately assessed and summed up the difference, and he felt yet another stab of respect.

Colin had been expecting a grande dame sort of entrance, and Cecelia Gardner didn't disappoint him. She might be nearly eighty years old, but she still swept into the room as if she expected crowds, water, or whatever she confronted to part for her. As they likely did, in most cases, Colin thought. There was something about the woman, her haughty demeanor, her cool, assessing gaze, the elegant and obviously expensive designer suit, or the formal upsweep of silver hair, that told you this was a woman used to being in control, used to getting her own way. A strong woman, who looked much younger than she was.

But she is still a mother who has just lost a son, Colin reminded himself.

"I'm sorry to come here under such painful circumstances for you, Mrs. Gardner," he said when she came to a halt in front of them.

"I already spoke at length to the other detectives. So what I'd like to know," she said, her voice crisp, "is why you are here, instead of out looking for the murderer of my son."

Colin had heard that countless times before. It didn't matter if the victim had been rich or poor, they always wanted to know why the police didn't instantly, magically know who the killer was.

"Out of respect, ma'am," he said smoothly. "I knew you would want to personally meet Detective Wilson and myself—I'm Detective Waters—since we'll be handling the criminal investigation."

"I see."

That had slowed her down a bit, he thought with no little satisfaction. But as he expected, she recovered quickly; he imagined it took a great deal to rattle the poised, proud Cecelia Gardner.

"As I told Mayor Jones, I expect quick results. Anything less is unacceptable. I want the person who did this found immediately."

"As do we, Mrs. Gardner. So the sooner we can get the formalities out of the way, the sooner we can get back on the real case."

"Formalities?"

"Speaking to the family members." As she stiffened, he added, "It's routine, but it has to be done."

"Ridiculous, you're wasting precious time."

"No, Mrs. Gardner." It was the first time his partner had spoken, but her voice was pleasant and even. "We're making sure no one can later get the killer off because we didn't go by the book now."

Her words seemed to appease Mrs. Gardner. "Very well. Ask your questions," the older woman said as she ushered them over to the couch and sat down.

"At the risk of sounding like a cliché, where were you last night?" Colin asked, smiling to indicate he knew how ridiculous the idea that she might be involved really was.

"I was at the Windy City fund-raiser," she replied impatiently. "In front of several hundred friends, I might add."

"Until what time?"

"Nearly eleven. I arrived home just before midnight. Any of the staff can tell you."

"And you didn't go out again?"

"Of course not," she said impatiently. "I'm nearly eighty years old, young man. I don't stay out until all hours."

"Most people I know who are your age wouldn't even make it until eleven," Wilson said, sounding genuinely admiring. Mrs. Gardner looked at her consideringly, then nodded as if in acceptance of the compliment. As if it were her due.

"Was any of the rest of the family there?" Colin asked.

"No."

She didn't, Colin noticed, offer any explanations of where her other son and her grandson had been. She might cooperate in answering their questions, but she wasn't going to volunteer anything.

"Is there anyone who might have had reason to want your son dead, Mrs. Gardner?"

The older woman sniffed audibly. "Reason?

Some people don't need a reason. The fact that he was a Gardner engendered envy and malice in some. Anyone in our position is a target of sorts these days."

It was the oddest combination of arrogance and stark reality, and Colin couldn't argue with a word of it. Just being a Gardner was enough to attract the wrong kind of attention from the wrong kind of people. And a malice killing would explain why so much of value had been left behind; if revenge or hatred was the motive, theft would have been secondary.

"Then is there someone who comes to mind? Someone who stands out? Anyone he argued with, or had a business disagreement with?"

"Franklin didn't argue."

"Ever?" Colin didn't know anyone who *never* argued.

Cecelia Gardner waved her hand dismissively. "Never seriously. If you'd known him, you'd know that no one would argue with Franklin."

Because they wouldn't dare? Colin wondered. What he'd read about the man indicated he'd been a powerhouse, a high-profile international businessman who was at home around the world. The kind of man few others could stand up to.

The kind who could, with the right touch of arrogance and contempt, drive someone to murder?

"What about his son?"

"Stephen?" Cecelia Gardner became instantly tense, and her demeanor changed to a protective fierceness he had to admire. "My grandson is not to be subjected to your interrogation. He is distraught, of course. And he would be of no help. He spends most of his time at school, or here studying. He's working on his graduate degree."

Interesting, Colin thought, that she was so forthcoming with all that after we had to pry the rest out of her.

"We'll need to talk with him anyway, I'm afraid," he said.

The icy look nearly became a glare. "I'll see when we're available."

"Just Stephen," Colin said firmly.

"Alone? I don't think so. His parents are both dead now, so I will stand for them."

"No, Mrs. Gardner." The woman blinked, and Colin wondered just how long it had been since anyone had said no to her. "He's an adult now. We will speak to him alone, here, or at the station, he can choose."

Cecelia Gardner drew herself up and gave him a stare that was nothing less than insulting. "How dare you?"

"He dares," Wilson said, unexpectedly speaking for the first time since her comment about the killer getting off, "because your son has been brutally killed, and no one has the right to secrets in a murder investigation. I would think you would want it that way."

For a moment Mrs. Gardner shifted her stare to the younger woman. Colin stayed silent, watching, but he cheered inwardly when Darien Wilson stared down the imperious woman without faltering. She might just be tougher than she looked.

Amazingly, the older woman gave in first. "You're quite right. I'm protective of my grandson. I always have been. Too much, Franklin used to say."

And just why would a kid's father say that? Colin wondered.

"I will have Stephen call you as soon as he arrives home."

"Thank you, Mrs. Gardner." His voice was as polite as it had been cool before.

They left shortly thereafter, the only useful bit of information they'd gotten being that Lyle, who also lived in the estate house, was at the Gardner Corporation offices in the business district.

"Impressions?" he asked his partner when they were back in the car.

"One main one, with two possible interpretations." She hesitated, but he nodded at her to continue. "I didn't see a single trace of any grief, pain or loss. She was more worried about us talking to her grandson than the death of her own son, which in itself makes me wonder about the grandson."

"I agree," Colin said. "What does your impression tell you?"

"That either she truly doesn't care, which makes her a very sick sort of mother. Or she's grieving as any mother would, and just hiding it extremely well, which makes me wonder what else she's hiding."

"Indeed," Colin agreed. *Maybe she does have the instincts for this, after all,* he added silently. "And the brother is doing business as usual at the office? Great family love there, wouldn't you say?"

"Nobody can tell anyone else how to grieve, but so far I'm not impressed with the Gardner approach."

"Nor am I."

"So we go see if the brother is shedding any tears?"

"That we do."

Lyle Gardner was not, in fact, shedding any tears. It didn't surprise Darien to find he was, as Waters had said, doing "business as usual." The secretary who greeted them outside his office was showing more emotion than either Mrs. Gardner had or Lyle Gardner was now.

"Maybe the rich are just different," Darien whispered as she opened the door to the inner sanctum of Gardner Corporation.

"At least this place isn't gilt and marble," Waters retorted under his breath, making her smile. She was much more at ease with him now, much less nervous at having been assigned to him as a partner. She quickly quashed her smile when the secretary turned back to them. She gestured toward the door and indicated they could go in.

It was true, the glass-and-steel structure that housed the Gardner Corporation clearly demonstrated success, but it was sleek, businesslike and modern rather than ornate and classic. And the office they walked into now had the same feel, that this was a place where efficient—and profitable—business was done.

The man behind the desk had the same black hair and blue eyes as his dead brother, but there the resemblance ended. Where Franklin had been trim, tan and athletic, Lyle looked as if he spent a bit too much time behind that huge expanse of cherry wood. They knew he handled the family trust fund and oversaw all their general business interests, while Franklin had handled the oil refinery and their international dealings.

"What have you found out?" he asked as he rose and strode around the desk.

They really do expect a miracle, Darien thought. Because they're the Gardners?

"We're in the information-gathering stage," Waters said easily. "We just need to clear up a few things with you."

"Me?"

Why on earth doesn't the family expect to answer at least a few questions? she wondered. *Don't they watch the news, and know how often in a murder the killer is family?*

"Where were you last night, Mr. Gardner?"

"Me?" he repeated, his tone incredulous.

"Yes," Waters said patiently. "Routine questions, sir. Eliminate the obvious so we can find the hidden."

Gardner looked as if he were torn between ordering them out or venting his anger at being suspected at all.

"I was at home," he said finally, stiffly. "As I told the other detectives."

If that made any difference to Waters, it didn't show. Again, Darien held back; she didn't think he'd welcome her intruding until he trusted her. He hadn't shut her up yet, so she assumed she hadn't done anything that irritated him, but still she kept quiet; learning, she told herself, was her primary goal right now.

"You were at home?" Waters asked. "Doing?"

"Watching television."

"Until when?"

"A little after midnight."

"So you spoke to your mother when she arrived home?"

He seemed to hesitate, but it was so quick Darien couldn't be sure. "No. I was already in bed, and I didn't want to bother her. I knew she'd be in a hurry to get to sleep.''

"Who knew you were home?"

He frowned. "No one. I was alone."

"Staff?"

"No. I mean, they knew I was home, but I'd dismissed them before I went up to bed."

Convenient, Darien thought.

"So you have no alibi."

"I don't need an alibi," Gardner said, rather vehemently.

Waters kept pushing. "You didn't leave the house?"

Gardner drew himself up and looked down his nose at Waters, abruptly every inch the haughty Gardner. "I don't care for your implications, Detective. No, I did not leave the house. And to answer the question underlying all your other questions, no, I did not kill my own brother!"

"Any idea who did?" Waters asked, with a cool she admired in the face of Gardner's anger.

"None."

"No one who was angry at him, maybe someone who got the short end of a business deal, something like that?"

"The Gardners don't deal like that, Detective."

Waters didn't even react. "The oil business is a delicate thing these days, any problems there?"

"None." Gardner's voice was becoming icy.

Waters retracted the point of his pen with a click of the top, and looked at Gardner straight on. "So, nobody had any reason to kill your brother."

"None that I'm aware of."

So why's he dead? Darien muttered to herself.

"Who stood to benefit from his death?" Waters asked.

Lyle Gardner ran out of patience. "You're on the wrong track, Detective, and you're wasting valuable time. Yours and mine. Weren't things taken from the apartment? Doesn't that make it clear this was a robbery, and poor Franklin interrupted it?"

"Perhaps." Waters tapped the pen against his notepad. "What about your nephew, Mr. Gardner?"

"Stephen? What about him?"

"He'll be quite a wealthy young man now, won't he?"

"He already is," Gardner snapped. "He's a Gardner."

"But now he'll have his own money, won't he?"

"He's never lacked for whatever money he needed."

"But now it's his," Waters persisted. Darien wasn't sure what he was up to, but guessed it had been triggered by Mrs. Gardner's fierce protectiveness of her grandson.

"He's doing graduate work, getting ready to take his place with the corporation. The family takes care of his expenses. He doesn't need more money now, doesn't want the worry of it.''

''I don't know any twenty-three-year-olds who don't think they need more money. Of their own.''

''Look, they may have fought about the money he was going to inherit, but Stephen had nothing to do with this!''

Waters froze. And the moment the words were out, Lyle flushed.

Well, well, Darien thought.

''I wonder,'' Colin mused aloud.

''What?''

''How long it would take to get to Franklin's apartment from that fancy college his kid goes to.''

As they walked toward the elevators, his partner glanced at her watch, as if to see if they had time to make the run themselves. ''Maybe we should find out firsthand,'' she said. ''Before grandma has a chance to talk to him about what to say.''

''Good idea,'' Colin said. ''But first I want to track down those security tapes. The guy should have contacted me by now.''

''So we go back to the apartment building?''

He nodded again. But as they continued down the hall, the name on an office door slowed him. ''Hold on a sec,'' he said, and made a turn in that direction. He opened the first door, to find a blond, tan young man behind a desk.

"Can I help you?" the man asked quickly.

"We'd like to see Mr. Reicher."

"And you are?"

"Detectives Wilson and Waters."

"Oh!" The young man leapt up. "I'm sure he'll want to see you. He's very upset about Mr. Gardner. Just a moment."

He opened the door behind him, and disappeared inside. Less than a minute later he emerged again, and gestured them into the inner office. Again, the room was exquisitely and expensively decorated, but they had little time to notice the decor.

"What took you so long?" the man standing behind the large desk snapped.

Well, hello to you, too, Colin thought. He studied the tall man in the very expensive-looking suit. His assessment stalled at the man's gray eyes; he'd seen warmer eyes on a python. Score one for Mrs. Carter, he thought. Cold was definitely the word. The chief operating officer of the Gardner Corporation was clearly a man used to being the boss. *And pity the underlings,* Colin added to himself.

"We're working our way down the possible suspect list," Colin said bluntly.

"Suspect list!" The eruption came just as he'd expected.

"Of course," Wilson put in with an icy cool that would have done Cecelia Gardner proud. "You're merely another name on it. We've eliminated several, we're hoping to eliminate you.''

Reicher looked torn, as if uncertain whether to react to her placating words, or the disdain with which she spoke them. Silently Colin congratulated his new partner; he doubted Reicher often was at such a loss.

''As Detective Wilson said, we're here to eliminate you from the list. So if you can just tell us where you were last night?''

''I was right here. Working late, as I often do.''

''Can anyone verify that?''

He turned on Wilson as she spoke. ''My word isn't good enough for you, Ms...*Detective?*''

To his own surprise, Colin took offense for her. But he said nothing, knowing she had to learn how to handle such things herself. Which, with her next words, she did quite effectively.

''Absolutely good enough for me, Mr. Reicher.'' Her tone was sweet now. ''I wouldn't presume to doubt you without evidence. It's just not good enough for the D.A., a judge and a jury.''

Reicher seemed to accept her new approach, but Colin had the strangest feeling he should have taken it as a sign to be even more careful.

''John, my assistant, can verify I was here. I'm afraid I kept him quite late on a project I've been trying to wind up.''

She continued her questioning. ''As COO, you'd

be aware of any business enemies Mr. Gardner might have?''

''Enemy enough to commit murder? I would be, if he had any. You're wasting time if that's your angle.''

''No deals that fell through, or hostile take-overs?''

''No. I told you you're wasting your time. You should be looking for a dope-crazed burglar. Now if you'll excuse me, I have work to do. Franklin's death has caused a bit of chaos.''

Colin said nothing until they were back in the elevator and the doors had closed behind them.

''A dope-crazed burglar,'' he repeated.

''Oh, please,'' Wilson groaned.

''You don't buy it?''

''I don't buy that any doper would leave all that portable wealth behind. He'd take everything he could stuff in his pockets and then start filling the pillowcases.''

Okay, she does have it, he thought.

''What do you think of misters Gardner and Reicher?''

''One's an arrogant bully and the other's a cold, pompous snake. You pick which is which.''

Interesting that she'd thought snake just as he had. ''With those eyes? No question, Reicher's the rep-tile.''

They headed to the car for the trip back to the

penthouse building to check on the videotapes. When they arrived, he parked in the loading zone in front, slapped an identifying placard on the dash, and they headed for the door.

"Where's the equipment?" she asked.

"The basement."

She nodded, and they took the stairs down.

The basement was as utilitarian as the rest of the building was elegant. Cool and a bit dim, it took up barely a third of the building's footprint. The rest, he guessed, was given over to the parking garage that housed what was likely a fleet of vehicles as elite as their owners.

They stepped into a wide hallway. Off to the left were two doors labeled Maintenance and Utilities. To the right was a single, unmarked door. Without a word, they both turned that direction. As they got closer Colin saw light coming from under the door. He tried the knob, but it was, as he expected, locked. He rapped twice on the metal door.

For a moment there was only silence, but finally the sound of footsteps came from the other side of the door. After another moment, it opened. The man who handled the security cameras stood there, and Colin didn't like the expression on his face.

"Something wrong, Mr. Bergen?"

"I…it's impossible. It's never happened before. I don't know how… The equipment was fine when I got here, but…"

Something way down in Colin's gut knotted. "But…?"

"The tape for last night…"

The man swallowed tightly, his eyes flicking nervously from Colin to Wilson.

"What about it?" Colin asked, his voice very quiet because he already knew the answer.

Bergen swallowed again.

"It's gone."

Chapter 4

"Now what do you suppose the odds are of that particular tape, and that tape only, going missing?" Waters mused aloud as they made their way into the station. Their quick run to the younger Gardner's private college had netted them only the fact that it didn't take long if you drove fast; the youngest Gardner had been off campus.

Darien shifted Gardner's laptop, the evidence they were here to book, to her other arm. "About the same as the Cubs winning the World Series," she muttered, without thought starting up the stairs for the detective office, even carrying the extra few pounds of the computer.

"Or less. If that's possible," Waters added with a quirk of his mouth as he started up with her.

"So, does that narrow us down to residents and their families? Those who knew about the cameras and where the recording equipment was?" Darien asked.

"And everyone from the security company. And anyone any of them might have told."

"Or anybody who went looking, I suppose," she said. "It wouldn't be tough to figure out it would be in the basement. And we knew instantly the unlabeled door had to be it."

"Exactly."

They reached the Detective Bureau door, and Waters leaned around her to open the door. She'd long ago given up making an issue out of such things—she'd found too often they were a test of sorts—but when she stepped through she turned and held the door for him as he followed. He accepted the gesture without comment, and she wasn't sure if she'd passed this test. If indeed it had been a test.

"Hey, if it isn't the two-W detective team of Waters and the lovely Miss Darien. What have you two been up to in the stairway? Don't you know it's easier in an elevator?"

"Oh, joy," Darien muttered. Then she flashed a quick look at Waters, hoping the mustached Detective Palmer, a man she'd only recently met but still could only describe as rude, crude and obnoxious, wasn't his best buddy.

"Well, now, if it isn't every woman's dream come true," Waters drawled.

"Hey, hey, you know they love me," Palmer said, in jovial tones, proving to Darien what she'd already thought, that the man was too stupid to even know when he was being insulted. "You're not the only chick magnet around here."

Oh, puhleeze, Darien thought. "Excuse me," she said. "I must be a matching pole."

Palmer looked blank, but she caught Waters's quick, appreciative grin just before she tried side-stepping around the sleaze to head for her desk.

"I'd take it easy, honey," Palmer said, his voice taking on a nasty undertone. He gave the computer she carried a look of disdain. "There's a lot of people not very happy that you got this spot over guys who deserved it more. A lot of people asking why. And how."

She stopped in her tracks. She knew exactly what he was implying, that she had slept her way here. She turned, and gave the man a level gaze.

"Are you trying, in your Neanderthal way, to make a point?" she asked sweetly. "If so, you're going to have to spell it out. I'm just a silly little ol' woman, after all."

"Keeping in mind there's a witness," Waters said softly, surprising her.

Palmer frowned. But even he seemed to realize if

he came right out and said what he was thinking it could boomerang on him.

"Yeah, right. Well, I don't have to say a thing. We all know." He slid Waters a sideways look, as if uncertain if he should include him in his generalization.

"Don't you have some missing persons to look for?" Colin asked, knowing there had been several reports recently.

"Yeah, yeah," Palmer muttered. Apparently deciding he was better off abandoning this particular ship, he turned and walked away, leaving them in the deserted hallway.

Darien felt a queasiness in her stomach that she fought not to show. She flicked a glance at Waters, who was watching her, his expression unreadable.

"So that's what everybody thinks?"

"That's what Palmer thinks," Waters said. "I'd say you'd have to ask to find out what everybody else thinks."

"No, thanks. I don't care." She took two steps, then stopped. She looked back at him. "No, maybe I do. If it's what you think."

He studied her for a long, silent moment. "I may not be sure why you're here, but no, I don't think you slept your way into this job."

"Why?"

He seemed surprised at the question. "Almost ten

years of being a cop teaches you to read people. If you're paying attention.''

''Oh.'' Then, as she realized she probably should, she said, ''Thank you.''

''Don't bother.'' As if it were an afterthought he added, ''Why did it matter what I thought?''

''Because it would be very hard for me to work with someone who thought I sold myself and my soul for the job,'' she said bluntly.

This time she'd only gone those same two steps when he called her.

''Wilson?''

She turned to look over her shoulder at him.

''You handled him just right.''

A slow smile curved her mouth. ''Thanks.''

Those simple words warmed her much more than they should have. And she thought that she could come to like Colin Waters, even if he was the resident division hunk.

They walked past Joshua Benton's cubicle and Waters joked that he was likely locked up in the lab with Maggie Sutter, working miracles. She laughed in agreement; she'd seen the lab, but what went on there was as incredible to her as her expertise with computers was to techno-phobes.

An hour later, she realized she'd been mistaken. Not about feeling she could like Colin Waters, but about the height of his hunk status. Now, in close quarters with him—she'd been given a desk in the same cubicle in the open office area—she was aware of just how much attention he got from most of the females in the entire building. They were always stopping by on some pretext or other, hand delivering a phone message, a copy of a report, anything, all of which could have been sent through normal delivery channels. She felt a faint distaste growing as the parade continued. And the fact that Waters apparently saw nothing unusual about it told her how often it happened.

She wasn't spared herself; the close and not very subtle inspection she got from the women told her that word of her assignment as his partner had spread rapidly. She couldn't fault their taste—Colin was a very attractive man—but their methods made her feel a little bit ashamed to be female just now. Even if she had been interested, which of course she wasn't, she would never try those kinds of maneuvers.

They'd agreed to divide up the reports on their initial interviews, and she'd been secretly relieved not to have simply been told to do it all, being the female, the rookie, and thus the most likely secretarial material available.

Once they were done, almost simultaneously, they filed the reports and headed back out to the parking lot. She'd retrieved her car when they'd returned to the apartment to find out about the missing tape. They had just reached it when her cell phone rang.

"Hi, babe, it's me."

"Hi, Tony. What's up?"

"Getting ready to leave for the Yucatán, so I wanted to check in."

"Check out, you mean," she teased.

"That, too," he said cheerfully. "Everything okay, fuzz lady?"

"Just busy. Have a good trip. Send me a post-card."

"Don't I always?"

"Unless you forget," she said.

"Love ya," Tony said.

"Love you, too. Be careful."

"Always."

She disconnected, then slid the phone back into her coat pocket. And became aware that Waters hadn't walked on to his own car but was still here watching her.

"Boyfriend?"

It wasn't any of his business, really, but she found herself answering him anyway, just to see what he'd say. "No. Ex-husband."

That got you, she thought, hiding a smile at his startled look.

"Ex?" he asked after a moment. "Didn't sound ex to me."

"How do you talk to yours?" She knew from office gossip that he'd been married and divorced.

"I don't," he said flatly.

"That's too bad."

She thought she'd kept her voice fairly even, but he turned on her anyway. "You think all divorces should be...what's that stupid word, amicable?"

She shrugged. "I just know mine was. Tony and I are still good friends."

"Friends," he muttered, still in that sour tone.

"We were friends before we got married, and should have stayed just friends. We were too young to understand what marriage was really all about."

"Don't tell me you were high-school sweethearts."

"No. I was twenty, he was twenty-one, but we were still too young. It worked at first, but after about three years he got to thinking about how he hadn't played enough."

"So he cheated on you?"

"Tony? Good grief no. He would never do that. I didn't mean that kind of playing. I meant literal play. Ski, bike, climb, you name it."

"And you didn't?"

"I enjoyed fun as much as anyone, but I also wanted to have kids. That was the break point for him. And it's just as well. He wasn't mature enough to raise a child, and he knew it. I respect him for that."

"So, Wilson, you married a playaholic?"

She ignored his sharp sarcasm, but she did wonder what kind of nerve she'd hit. "Tony is who he is. Above all he's honest. And that saved us both a lot of pain. I'm glad he's my friend. Besides, my parents like him and he's good to them, and I wouldn't want to ruin that.''

"Honest," Waters muttered.

He lapsed into silence, which left Darien wondering why on earth that had come pouring out of her. It was true she wasn't uncomfortable talking about Tony and her marriage, but she didn't usually tell near strangers all that.

It was too late now to worry about, so she turned her thoughts to something else, something that had just struck her when he'd made that comment about Tony being a playaholic. He'd called her Wilson. Unlike Palmer.

…Waters and the lovely Miss Darien.

She'd noticed that most cops called each other by their last names unless they were personal friends. But they called women by their first names. She hadn't thought much about it until Palmer had made that rude, suggestive comment. And suddenly she was seeing it as something more, some subtle symptom of a man's world that had yet to completely accept the intrusion of females.

But Colin Waters called her by her last name, just as he did most others. That comforted her somehow.

Great, Colin thought as he rubbed at his eyes. *So your new partner, besides being gorgeous enough to stop most men in their tracks, was on the kiddie track. Was friendly with her ex-husband. Kept her parents happy. The proverbial, perfect girl next door. Exactly the kind of woman I always avoid.*

He wasn't sure why this realization bothered him. She was only his partner, after all.

It was odd that he was actually thinking of her that way already, as his partner. She hadn't said all that much, either in interviews or in between, but what she had said had been right-on. She'd surprised him, more than once. As she'd been surprising him today; she'd set herself up this morning with a diet soda, then dug into Gardner's laptop computer and had been hacking away ever since. She showed no sign of being aware of time passing, merely kept at it, with the occasional mutter to the computer screen that he'd noticed before in those who had carnal knowledge of the things.

He'd thought the words "carnal knowledge" as a joke about computer geeks, but somehow when applied to Darien Wilson, they managed to make him feel damned uncomfortable. He shifted in his chair and made himself go back to filing the last of their reports, and going through what had been added by the forensics team thus far.

"Sutter says the bruises on his face were likely made by a heavy ring of some kind."

She paused then, looking up at last. "That helps."

"If he's still wearing it," Colin said glumly.

She went back to her work. More and more time passed. There were moments of silence, followed by a series of quick keystrokes. More muttering, then more silence, more keystrokes. She was so intent that she didn't even glance up as he went to the copy machine and then returned.

For a moment he stood looking over her shoulder. Instead of the usual software interfaces he was familiar with, there were strings of odd-looking characters on the screen. They made no sense at all to him, but she seemed to find them easily understandable. But then, while he was fairly computer literate, his comfort zone ended outside his regularly used software.

"Come on, come on," she murmured, then let out a tightly compressed breath when the screen flashed and went blank. She leaned back in her chair and rubbed the back of her neck.

"Problem?"

"Not sure. He's got some odd chunks on his hard drive that could be hidden files. I just have to find my way into them."

"Hidden files?"

"They could be junk, but we won't know until I can get in there."

He leaned against the edge of his desk and gestured at the computer. "How'd you get so into all this?"

"I started out doing research for school online.

Then a Web site. The more I got into that, the more I wanted to know.''

"And the jump from there to police work?"

She swiveled the chair around to look at him straight on. "My mom got taken in by an online scam. During that case, I saw a whole lot of innocent people who got taken by thieves who used this medium I loved for their crimes. I wanted to stop that kind of thing. It's going to be the crime scene of the future. It's already here.''

God, she really was the girl next door, out to avenge her mom. "It's not all nice, clean computer crime, you know.''

She gave him a wry look. "Believe it or not, I knew that. And if I hadn't, this assignment would have taught me in a big hurry.''

"Sorry,'' Colin muttered.

"Look, I know I was hired for this—'' she gestured at the open laptop "—because the department is recruiting computer people, but I didn't come into this blind. I thought long and hard before I applied. And longer and harder before I took the job because I knew there were going to be people who felt like Palmer does.''

"Palmer is just a jerk.''

She studied him, long enough to make him wonder what she was thinking. "Thanks, but you know there are others who think the same thing.''

"They may question your being given the job, but

if you prove you can do it, eventually that's all that will matter.''

"Promise?'' she asked, her mouth quirking up at one corner.

"Yeah," he said, hoping he wasn't being too optimistic.

She studied him again for a long moment before saying, ''So, now that I've told you my life story, tell me yours.''

He blinked, startled. ''Mine?''

"Why don't you talk to your ex?''

"Why would I?'' He was aware he sounded a bit defensive.

"That bad?''

When he realized he'd tensed up, he made a conscious effort to relax his muscles. She had, after all, told him about her ex. So he told her, although the words came out stiffly.

"She couldn't take these kinds of hours, so she found somebody who came home on time. Unfortunately, we were still married at the time.''

"Ouch. No wonder you jumped to that conclusion about Tony.''

"Yeah. Well.'' He grimaced. ''And she *was* my high-school sweetheart.''

"That must have been rough.''

He shrugged, back in control now. ''It wasn't her fault. I'm just not cut out for the whole wife and kids thing. Married to my job, Anita used to say.''

"I can see being married to a cop would be difficult. But I believe an affair is the fault of the person involved. If you want out, get out, but you don't cheat."

Yes, he thought, surprising himself. He'd spent so much time listening to Anita telling him it was all his fault that he'd almost forgotten that what Wilson had just voiced had been his original reaction to his wife's infidelity.

When he didn't speak, she lowered her gaze. "Sorry about the soapbox bit."

Then she turned back to the computer. He thought he saw a faint tinge of color in her cheeks, but he couldn't be sure. She stared at the screen for a minute, then hit a few keys.

"Come on," she muttered. "I know you're in there."

He let it go, and sat down to make some calls to residents of the building they so far hadn't been able to contact. He did a little net surfing of his own for mentions of Franklin Gardner or the Gardner Corporation in the business and financial sections of the area newspapers, looking for potential enemies on that front. Hours later, when he'd hit the wall, she was still at it, and showing no sign of letting up. The office was deserted, the rest of the division having gone home long ago. He crossed out the last name on his list, tossed down his pen, and groaned audibly as he stretched.

She looked up. Glanced at the watch he'd noticed before; nothing fancy or glittery for this woman, just a simple, utilitarian metal band. She wore only small, gold earrings as well, no rings or necklaces.

"No wonder my stomach's growling," she said. Then she stood up and stretched much as he had. Except on her, the sinuous movement was downright sexy.

She grinned at him, and for a breath-stopping moment he wondered if she'd read his mind. But she only said, "Let's go out. Feed me."

He recoiled, as much from his own unexpected response to her as to her words. "I don't think that would be wise. The commander frowns on fraternization."

She stared at him. "Excuse me?"

"I don't mix business with pleasure," he said bluntly.

She crossed her arms in front of her and gave him a level look. "Which part did you figure was going to be the pleasure?"

He blinked, startled. "What?"

"I gather you're used to women falling at your feet, but it was a simple request for a food break, Waters. Not a declaration of undying passion."

He supposed he'd been more embarrassed in his life, but just now he couldn't recall when.

"Uh…yeah. Sure. Let's go."

He noticed that she carefully shut down the computer and resecured it in the evidence locker before picking up her coat and purse. Then she started across the empty office toward the door. And she did it without once looking at him.

Nice work, Waters, he told himself.

And didn't dare think about what thoughts had leapt to life in his mind at the words *undying passion.*

Well, she'd really put her foot in it that time, Darien thought as she fastened her seat belt. She'd meant only to keep things businesslike, to make clear to him she wasn't like the other women at the department who seemed to be chasing him at every turn, and she'd ended up insulting him.

She didn't understand. She didn't usually say such stupid things. The fact that he was the most attractive man she'd spent time with in far too long shouldn't make any difference.

Well, not much anyway.

She was grateful that, when he finally spoke, he seemed to have put the awkward scene behind him.

"Where do you want to go? Luciano's maybe? Or Sullivan's?" he asked, naming a couple of popular restaurants on the Magnificent Mile.

"To tell you the truth, I'm dying for a Gold Coast Dog."

He laughed. She let out a silent sigh of relief; he

wasn't mad. "That's one I haven't indulged in for at least a week."

She widened her eyes. "You've gone a whole week? You poor man, we must remedy that immediately!"

"I appreciate that."

"Drive on, James," she said, so relieved that he wasn't angry—or at least wasn't showing it—that she was able to carry off the breezy tone.

He chuckled, and in moments they were heading toward Hubbard and the nearest Gold Coast Dog franchise.

When they had eaten enough of their hot dogs laden with onions, tomatoes and hot peppers to quiet growling stomachs, he took a long draw on his soda—caffeinated, he said, in anticipation of another long night—and leaned back.

"You think there's really something there on that computer hard drive?"

"Just some space that I can't account for. There's data there, in some form. It may be nothing, old files that weren't erased or overwritten, but..." She shrugged, not wanting to try and explain the suspicion that had so little basis in hard fact.

"But what?"

"It's just a feeling. I know that's not much to go on."

To her surprise, he nodded. "Sometimes it's all you have."

She was used to the computer world, which had little room for things as ethereal as gut feelings. "No cracks about intuition versus hard data?"

"I never underestimate intuition because I don't think it's intuition at all."

That caught her attention. "You don't?"

"No. I think it's more a finely honed perceptive ability that leads to valid deductions, but it goes through the middle steps so fast it seems like wild jumps."

She'd never thought of it that way, but the explanation made sense to her. "You mean it's like that sense you get just looking at some person, that they're up to something?"

"Exactly. Maybe it's only that they have a heavy coat on when it's seventy degrees out, or that they're carrying an umbrella when it hasn't rained in days. Something you don't really consciously think about, but it registers and you...wonder." He took another sip of soda, then gestured at her with the paper cup. "Like your unaccounted for space."

His assessment was so logical that it relieved her own uneasiness about the instincts that occasionally prodded her and that she couldn't explain to her hard data-minded colleagues.

They finished and drove back to the station. Without discussion, Darien realized; she'd always intended to return to continue working on the computer, but she'd never said so. She decided she was pleased that he had made the assumption. It meant that he was taking her dedication to the work seriously, despite the others who seemed to think she was playing at this.

Hours later, her back aching from being hunched over the laptop's small keyboard, she could have told them all how wrong they were. There was nothing about this that was anything like playing.

Chapter 5

Colin was exhausted. While his new partner had
been hacking away at the victim's computer, he'd
done the rest without even taking a break on Saturday or Sunday. He'd fielded calls coming in, including one from District Attorney Evan Stone, who
was well aware this case would be headed his way
as soon as they made an arrest. He made interview
calls following up on the initial canvas until
9:00 p.m. every day, knowing that after that he took
the chance of really irritating the citizens he was
asking for help. He'd taken repeated calls from both
the district commander and the deputy superintendent of the Investigative Services Bureau. He assured them all possible progress was being made,

and that he would personally contact them when there was anything to report.

After that he finished the reports from those calls and interviews, then reread the case reports Sutter and Benton had filed. He mentally crossed the maid off his suspect list when he'd learned she had had a gentleman caller herself the evening before the murder; no wonder she'd been a bit edgy.

He mentioned it to Wilson. She nodded, but didn't look away from her screen. He tossed down his pen, closed the computer file, and sat for a moment rubbing at gritty eyes. Just another in the string of long nights.

He glanced over at his partner. He didn't know how she did it, sat and stared for so long at a computer screen day after day. His eyes started to scream back at him after a few hours. But she was just as intent as she had been when she'd started, clearly with no thought of quitting. She had the drive, he had to admit that. And she'd made some good observations. Maybe this wouldn't be as bad as he'd feared.

At that moment she leaned back at last, arching her back in a slow, graceful move. She shoved one hand through her hair. He'd never thought of short hair as particularly sexy before, but he just might change his mind. The blond cap fell back in a tousle that looked as if she'd just run her fingers through it after getting out of bed.

Shock jolted through him as his body clenched. For a moment he refused to believe what he was feeling, but the rush of heat that followed, pooling low and deep inside him, made it impossible to deny.

Are you nuts? he asked himself. *Isn't it bad enough she's the epitome of everything you've proven you can't handle, a woman made for a marriage that would last a lifetime, with kids gathered round? Add the fact that she's a colleague, and your partner to boot, and you're not playing with fire, you're tossing around napalm.*

"Gotcha!"

He nearly jumped, wondering how on earth she'd guessed his reckless thoughts. It took him a moment to realize her exclamation was directed at the laptop she was working on. He stood up.

"Go—" He cleared his throat and tried again. "Got what?"

She looked up at him, satisfaction warming her blue eyes. "The files. I found the files. They were buried a bit, but they're there, right where I thought."

"Can you get them open?"

"I think so. I've got this program that's designed to do just that." She looked up at him again. "I'm going to have to do it on this machine, or risk corrupting the files trying to copy them. Is that going to be a problem, evidence wise?"

"Worth it, if it works. We'll just have to log every step. Go for it."

She nodded, then turned and pulled a jewel case out of her purse and removed a CD-ROM. She inserted the disk into the laptop's drive.

"Hang on," she said.

He waited while she opened a software program with what looked to him like a very rudimentary interface. He decided not to ask what it was or where she'd gotten it. After a moment she typed a series of commands, then leaned back and waited, her eyes fastened on the screen. Several minutes passed, during which she assured him the wait was not unusual.

Then the computer let out a high beep, the screen flashed and changed, and row after row of jumbled characters raced across and down the screen.

She let out a low, hissed breath.

"What is it?"

She sat back and rubbed at her face in obvious weariness. Then she looked at him.

"It's all in code."

He blinked. "What?"

"They're all there, the files I mean, but they're encoded."

"Hot damn," he breathed. "That means there's something there really worth hiding."

Realization dawned on her face, and he knew she had been so intent on solving the new problem that she hadn't thought of the ramifications of the results she'd already gotten.

"Hot damn," she echoed. And grinned.

Darien was exhausted. Exhausted, but still determined. They'd brought her into this job because of her computer skills, so she was darn well going to prove that they'd made a good choice. So she kept at it. She'd taken a three-hour nap last night in one of the few offices with a couch in it, but at 5:00 a.m. she'd been up and at it again. She'd been antsy to get back to working on Franklin's computer. She knew it was in part because that was safe, familiar ground where she knew what she was doing, unlike this seemingly endless legwork.

She didn't look up until her partner wandered in about a half an hour later.

He'd obviously been to the locker room and taken a shower; his hair was wet and slicked back. It emphasized the even, chiseled features of his face, strong masculine jaw and cheekbones she hadn't really noticed before. A drop of water from his hair trickled down the side of his face, then traced a path along his neck.

"—having any luck?"

She jerked her gaze away from the unexpectedly fascinating travels of that droplet.

"What? Oh, no, not yet." She looked at the message that had flashed on her screen, tapped a couple of keys, then looked back at him. "What do you suppose he was hiding?"

He leaned a hip against his desk, and she noticed then he'd put on a pair of jeans. *And judging by how snug they fit, it must have taken him ten minutes just to get into them, especially if his skin was still damp,* she thought.

At the images that raced through her mind she felt a blush that began somewhere around her navel. And again she missed the first part of what he said.

"—anything. Could be just secret business files, maybe something on a takeover."

"Maybe he cooked some books," Darien said, still working to recover a poise shattered by her own too-vivid and suddenly overactive imagination.

"Or if we're real lucky, it could be even worse, something criminal."

"You mean something bad enough that it could have gotten him killed?"

"It's a possibility," he said.

"All the more reason to get this broken fast," she said, and turned her gaze back to the screen.

"Coffee?"

She looked up again, surprised. "Yes, please."

"How do you take it?"

"One each cream and sugar."

He nodded and exited the cubicle, leaving her still a little bemused that he'd even offered. When he returned a few minutes later, a luscious aroma made her look up.

"The guy was just bringing them in, they were still warm, and I couldn't resist."

He set a small plate down in front of her, and put a matching one on his own desk. She looked down at the obviously freshly baked cinnamon roll, and nearly grinned as her stomach growled in Pavlovian response.

"I can see why," she said with heart- or stomach-felt sincerity. "Thanks."

She tore a piece off the edge, and found it tasted as divine as it smelled. She looked up to thank him again, and found him licking icing from his fingers in a way that made her think again of those rebellious shower thoughts she'd had earlier. Immediately she tried to distract herself by peeling off another layer of the roll and popping it into her mouth.

So, the hunk has a sweet tooth, she thought.

"It's a weakness," he said rather sheepishly, and for an instant she feared she'd spoken aloud. "Baked stuff. Can't help myself."

She found that rather endearing. "Did your mother bake a lot?"

"No. She was all thumbs in the kitchen. But my stepmother, now she can whip these up with her eyes shut. Cakes, cookies, you name it. She always joked she had to run five miles a day to keep from weighing a ton just from sampling."

Darien grinned. "Sounds like my kind of woman."

"She's great. I was ten when my mom died, so when my dad brought her home a couple of years later, she stepped into a pretty difficult situation. She did a great job, though. Even if I didn't really appreciate it until much later."

That he appreciated it now said a great deal about him, Darien thought. "You're close, still?"

"Yeah. My dad was killed in an accident three years ago, but we've stayed close. She's the mother I lost, and a friend, too."

She gave him the warmest smile she could, and he shrugged as if embarrassed and turned his attention back to his own treat. In short order, she finished her own.

"I'd better get back to this. Use the sugar rush," she said wryly, knowing the crash when the sugar burned off could be ugly.

She hadn't spent a lot of time trying to break coded files, but she knew the basic approaches and she had the software to run them. She had tried them all, so far with no results. So now she was starting on combinations, knowing she was shotgunning, hoping a few pellets would hit.

"I wish I knew how you thought," she murmured.

"Gardner?"

She nodded without looking up. "Then maybe I

could figure out what he would have done to protect these files.''

"Well, you know he both hid them and encoded them,'' Waters said.

"Yes. That right there tells us something, I guess. But I would think the complexity of the code itself would depend on the importance of the information.''

"That makes sense,'' her partner agreed. "If this is a list of his girlfriends, it would likely have less protection than, say, if he was dealing drugs or something like that, and those were his contacts.''

She glanced at him. "If there really is a connection between these files and his death, then we know this is dynamite. Of some sort.''

"That's a big if,'' Waters cautioned her.

"I know. So I'm just going to break this sucker so we can either act, or move on.''

"Anything I can do?''

She smiled at him. "You just did it,'' she said, indicating the crumbs that were all that remained of the cinnamon roll. "That'll keep me going for a couple of hours, at least.''

And it did, Colin thought later, watching her with amazement. She might be everything he stayed away from in a woman, she might have the kind of looks that had Neanderthals like Palmer guessing she'd slept her way here, but Colin had to admit now that she not only had good instincts, but she had the dogged determination the job required.

Looking up, he saw that the brass was filtering in. He knew it was only a matter of time before they came calling; on a high-profile case like this, no one had any peace until it was resolved. And every day that passed only increased the pressure.

"Brace yourself," he told his partner. "The powers that be are starting to arrive."

She glanced up, frowning. "Rats," she muttered. "I need a little more time, quiet time. I'm almost there, I know it. I can feel it."

"I'll try to keep them off you," he said.

"That would help," she said, "if you don't mind."

He shrugged. "I can't do what you're doing, so I might as well do what I can."

"Thanks," she said, her voice carrying a little more gratefulness than he would have expected for the simple offer he'd made.

He looked up and saw the commander headed toward them. Colin stepped out of the cubicle and went to head him off.

"What progress?" Portman asked, dispensing with any amenities.

Quickly Colin outlined the interviews they'd conducted, both in person and on the phone, and his own business search.

"Suspects?"

"We've got a lot of possibles," Colin admitted. "Just as you'd expect with somebody as rich as Gardner. A couple that stand out, but nothing I want to hang the name on yet."

Portman scowled. "You know I'm fending off the media over this. They're getting impatient. I need something to give them."

"Surely the usual 'We're investigating all avenues' will hold them for a while longer, won't it?"

"Not much, not when it's a Gardner who's dead." He turned as if to go, and Colin sighed inwardly in relief; he didn't want to mention the computer files, not until they had something solid. But then Portman turned back. "How's your new partner working out?"

Colin was glad now he hadn't complained at the time. "Fine. She's got good instincts, I think, and she's working as hard and long as anyone."

Portman nodded shortly, then turned and headed back to his office. Colin went back to the cubicle where Wilson was still working.

"That should hold him for a while, but—"

She didn't look at him but threw up a hand to hush him. Startled, he shut up. He noticed then she was leaning forward, eyes glued to the screen, and he wasn't quite sure she was breathing. He took his cue and kept quiet, and less than a minute later he heard her hiss under her breath a triumphant, "Yes!"

He stood up and took a step toward her. "Yes?"

"Got him!"

He stepped around to look at the screen, and saw the rows and rows of gibberish morph into lines of readable text. He let out a low whistle. "You go, girl," he said.

She looked up at him and smiled. And he thought suddenly that was the kind of smile that started—or ended—wars. And that she was the kind of woman men fought them for. Or alongside. That scared him, and he backed away to a safer distance, retreating to the edge of his desk again. The moment he realized what he'd done, he swore silently at himself. *You are* not *going to do this!* he ordered himself.

She turned back to the screen and began to read. After a moment her smile faded, then a crease appeared in her forehead.

Uh-oh, he thought. "It didn't work after all?"

"No, no, it did," she said without looking up. "It's just that…this makes no sense. Unless Franklin Gardner was going to some kind of dating service or something."

Colin snorted inelegantly. "Not likely. Guys with his looks and money have to beat them off with sticks."

"But he's got lists of women here, broken down by month, with physical descriptions, and odd little notations like 'jock' or 'schoolgirl.'"

He frowned. "Do they all have notes like that?"

She read further, and nodded. "Here's one that says 'girl next door.' Oh, and here's a nice one, 'brunette and trashy.' But the strange thing is, the physical descriptions are really vague."

Colin went very still. "Vague how?"

"Like…well, maybe *general* is a better word. Like this one. 'Blonde, five-two to five-six, voluptuous, hidden assets, innocent look.'"

Colin stood up, slowly this time, in contrast to his racing thoughts.

"And this one," she went on, her voice rising slightly, "this one's *sick!* Listen to this! 'Redhead, pigtails, freckles, no more than five feet, immature body, must look no more than twelve.' What is this?"

"It sounds," Colin said grimly, "like a shopping list."

Even with the questionable help of Palmer it took them another hour to track down the reports—but only moments to match up the physical descriptions on four of the missing females to the list Darien had decoded on the computer. Palmer finally seemed to wake to the possibilities, and dug out three more reports that had been filed as open but not active. Those matched up with three more of the entries in Gardner's file.

Even more damning were the dates; it was Colin who first realized that in only one case was there more than five days between the date of Gardner's entry and the date of the missing persons report. And that one case was a sixteen-year-old who had already been gone several days, but hadn't been missed due to her propensity for disappearing for days at a time anyway.

"Are all these girls runaways?" Darien asked Palmer, for the moment setting aside her dislike of the man.

"Yes," Palmer said, apparently also focusing on business for now.

Colin gestured at the files. "They only got reported because somebody noticed they weren't showing up at their usual hangouts anymore. Only one was reported by the family."

"Not many care what happens to these kids," Darien said. "I guess these are the lucky ones, to have friends with enough nerve to call the police."

"Hey, there's also the fact that these kids are runaways and don't want to attract any attention," Palmer said defensively.

"Palmer's right," Colin said. "And there are probably a dozen who never got reported for each one of these."

And some that someone tried to report, Darien thought, but got shined on because it was just another runaway among hundreds, if not thousands. But she knew she'd gain nothing by speaking the thought. At least, not in front of Palmer.

But when he had to go back to his own cubicle to take a phone call, Waters opened the subject himself, saying thoughtfully, "I wonder how many on Gardner's list might be among those unreported missings?"

"You mean the girls who were shrugged off as just another street statistic?"

He didn't pretend not to understand, which gave him points in her mind. "We're not perfect. But there are only so many of us, and so many hours in a day. Things get kissed off."

"Like girls who are addicts or thieves, or have taken to selling themselves on the street out of desperation, so their disappearance isn't worth the effort?"

He looked at her silently for a long moment, and she wondered if she'd gone too far. Then he spoke softly. "I had a cousin who ran away and disappeared into the wilds of Los Angeles. I didn't expect L.A.P.D. to find her. Even then I knew L.A. was too big, and she was just one girl among thousands."

She was surprised at the personal story, but couldn't help asking, "What happened to her?"

"She turned up dead six months later." He grimaced. "Ironically, not drugs, or killed by a john, or anything like that. She got hit by a car. Stupid, huh?"

"I'm sorry." Not knowing what else to say, she turned back to the matter at hand. "So, what do you think this means?'' she asked. ''Why would Franklin Gardner have a list of women who match the descriptions of missing runaways?''

Colin gave her a surprised look that gradually changed to one of sympathetic understanding. ''Guess you wouldn't hear much about this kind of thing out in the country.''

''What kind of thing?'' she asked, trying not to sound defensive at being called, in the gentlest way, a country bumpkin of sorts. ''And why did you say it looks like a shopping list?''

''Because it looks like Gardner was taking orders for particular types of girls, and then filling them.''

She felt a bit slow. ''Orders?''

''Probably from some overseas client with a picky customer base. Some men are very particular about what they want.''

Darien's eyes widened, and suddenly she did feel very much a country bumpkin. ''You mean…some sort of white slavery thing?''

''Some call it that, yes. We're guessing these girls were kidnapped, very specifically, and sent off to be used as prostitutes somewhere where nobody asks questions.''

''My God,'' Darien breathed, stunned. She'd heard of such things, of course, but they had always seemed the stuff of lurid documentaries, nothing she would ever encounter firsthand.

''What I don't understand,'' Waters said, ''is why

somebody like Franklin Gardner would be involved in something like that. With his family name, and they already have more money than they could possibly spend in a lifetime.''

''Some people aren't content to treat their own women as property,'' Darien said, rather fiercely now that she knew what they were dealing with. ''They look at all women that way.''

He gave a half shrug, half shudder, as if he were trying to shed a distasteful idea. ''Hard to believe he'd risk it.''

''Or his partner in crime,'' she said.

Her own partner went very still. ''His partner?''

''Yes. Didn't you see who the files were copied to?''

''No.''

''Here, it's in here,'' she said, pointing to the lines still in gibberish—or what had looked like it to him— at the top of the list. In the middle of a long string of characters he saw *D.Reicher@gardnercorp.com.*

''He's in this, too? Damn, I knew he had snake eyes.''

''All I can say positively,'' she warned, ''is that he got sent copies of the list, and—''

She stopped suddenly as another thought struck her.

''What?'' Waters asked.

''I was just thinking. If they were both involved

in this enterprise, maybe there was a falling-out among criminals?''

"One that occurred at Gardner's penthouse, and ended up with Gardner dead? Yeah, that thought has occurred to me.'' His grim expression lightened suddenly, and he gave her a crooked smile. "You might just have nailed our killer, partner.''

The words warmed her beyond rationality. "Thank you…'' She hesitated, then risked it. "Colin.''

"You're welcome, Darien.'' He said it so easily, yet it was pointed enough to acknowledge the change.

Now we're partners, she thought with satisfaction. Just the tiniest bit of anxiety tinged that satisfaction as she acknowledged that Colin Waters was a very unsettling associate. He would be for any woman, she told herself, not just her.

And managed to ignore the fact that how it would affect other women didn't matter because she was the woman being unsettled.

While waiting for the search warrant they'd requested, they had attended the funeral. Mrs. Gardner had apparently made enough noise to enough important people that the autopsy had been rushed to a finish and the body of her son released. There had been a side benefit, to them anyway, in that the autopsy report had been completed faster than they could have gotten it no matter how hard they'd pushed. Ironic, she thought.

But they'd learned that the injury to the back of the head had indeed been the fatal blow, with the stab wounds inflicted postmortem. And who knew what Benton and Sutter would turn up when they analyzed the autopsy that might open up new avenues to pursue, she added silently as she stifled a yawn.

Waters had indicated with nothing more than a nod and a whisper, Detectives Benton and Sutter, present at the funeral for the same reason they were: to see who showed up on the chance their killer was among them. Given the size of the funeral, and the upper crust of society who were present, it only added to the nightmare size of the investigation. The three remaining Gardners of course were there, wearing very expensive black and suitably grim expressions. However, so were the mayor and several other high-powered notables, and Darien wasn't sure they'd learned a thing. Other than that she still hated funerals.

By the time they returned, the search warrant was ready. They got it for Reicher's home, since they doubted he would be foolish enough to store information like that on his office network. It had taken so long because they'd been fighting to make it as broad as possible in case they stumbled across anything else incriminating besides the matching computer files they were hoping to find. They'd encountered the resistance they'd expected, but not nearly as much as Gardner's maid had given them, and Colin wondered rather cynically if it was because Reicher was a less-than-kind employer.

His residence was a condominium both larger and flashier than Gardner's penthouse, with stark, modern furnishings and lots of exotic lighting. The servant who answered the door had taken one look at the warrant and welcomed them with ill-concealed glee. Colin doubted Reicher would find out about this from that quarter.

"This place is as cold as his eyes," Darien had said, and Colin couldn't argue with her.

They'd found two computers, one laptop and one desktop, and confiscated them both to be inspected in depth at the station. And now that she knew how they'd been hidden, Darien was able to find and decode the files in relatively short order once they got them there.

"Got it," she said, and Colin saw the same change from garbled text to a match for the files they'd pulled from Gardner's computer.

"Looks like we'll need to go chat with Mr. Reicher again."

Colin stood up, but before he could reach for his coat Darien said, "Wait a second. There's more here."

"More? More on the list?"

"No. Another file. Hang on...."

He waited, knowing she'd tell him when she could.

"There. Dates and times and some sort of abbreviations."

He leaned in to look over her shoulder. He studied the new list she'd uncovered for a moment, but it didn't mean anything to him. A couple of the abbreviations seemed familiar, but he couldn't place them. After a few fruitless minutes, he walked to a cubicle across the aisle and up one.

"Palmer? Can you come here and take a look at something?"

The man lumbered over. If he noticed Darien pulled back so there was no way they could even brush, he didn't say anything.

He looked at the new list. "I don't know. Doesn't mean anything to me. Unless there were events scheduled at each place on those days. I could check, if you want."

Colin stared at the detective and asked carefully, "Each place? What places?"

Palmer gestured at the third column in the list. "Those. You know, Safe Haven, Laurel House, Lakeshore."

"Of course!" Colin exclaimed. "That's why those abbreviations seemed familiar."

"What are they?" Darien asked.

"They're halfway houses and shelters for run-aways."

It didn't take her long to figure it out. Colin saw her eyes widen as it hit her. "That's where they...went shopping?"

"Let's just say when we correlate this list with the other list and the missing persons reports, and check with those agencies, I won't be surprised if there's yet another series of connections," Colin said.

"Gardner was on the board of the charity that funded three of these," Palmer contributed, and Colin knew they had yet another nail in Reicher's coffin.

Within an hour of concerted effort, they knew he was right. Everything matched. Phone calls to the shelters and halfway houses verified the last facet of his guess.

"I think we've got it," Colin said. "Thanks to Darien," he added. The words were for her, but he was looking at Palmer, who had the grace to look abashed.

"So Gardner did the shopping, off this list, at these halfway houses and shelters, sent the list to Reicher, who arranged the kidnappings?" Darien asked.

"Probably helped deliver them to the buyer," Colin said.

"And I'm supposed to be sorry he's dead?" she asked.

Colin and Palmer gave her a startled look. "Ah," Colin said. "Under that beautiful exterior beats a justice-craving heart."

Darien stared at him, so intently he felt nonplussed.

"You going to go get him?" Palmer asked.

Colin shook off the odd sensation Darien's steady gaze had given him.

"That we are," he said.

Chapter 6

"**T**his is an outrage!"

"You're right about that," Darien said, her voice cold. "Did you figure you could get away with it because nobody cared about those kids?"

She'd been stunned when, after discussing interrogation strategy, Colin had told her to go ahead and start the questioning. She'd asked why, and he'd told her she was just angry enough to face Reicher down.

"I'll step in when the time's right," he said.

So, quashing the nerves that were making her stomach jump, she had begun.

"I don't know what you're talking about," Reicher snapped now. "I've taken all the insults I'm going to take. I demand to see my lawyer."

"Your request has been noted. You'll get your call as soon as a line is free."

She saw him glance at the phone on the interview room desk. All the buttons were indeed lit or flashing. They'd made sure of that.

"In the meantime," she said, "you might want to figure out how you're going to explain this."

She tossed the printout of the list on the table in front of him. He glanced at it, and she had the extreme satisfaction of seeing him pale visibly beneath his carefully maintained tan. His gaze flicked up to her face, and she saw a trace of apprehension in those cold, crocodile eyes.

"Where did you get that?"

Not what is it, she noted, satisfaction flowing through her again.

"Right off your hard drive, unedited and uncut."

"How dare you?" he sputtered.

"Oh, with a warrant, Desmond." She used his first time intentionally, almost insultingly. "Rest assured, the legal system is already fully engaged."

"You can't prove a thing. My attorneys will make a hash out of your warrant. And then I'll slap this department with the biggest lawsuit it's ever seen. Anybody could have put that on my computer."

"Interesting. Your staff told us you were paranoid about it, that no one was allowed to touch that computer, or even clean the room it was in unless you were physically present."

Reicher muttered something under his breath, and Darien doubted any of that staff would be employed by Reicher much longer. But she also guessed none of them would be particularly upset about that fact.

"Was it really worth it? You can't need the money, so was it for kicks? The thrill? Or just the pure joy of putting a few more women in their place?"

"Someone should put you in yours," he snapped.

She lifted a brow at him, and he flushed, as if realizing he'd betrayed something he should have kept hidden.

"My place," she said softly, leaning over the table to invade his space, "is to make sure you go to jail, where no one will care how rich you are, for a very, very long time."

"That will never happen," Reicher said. "You'll never prove I had anything to do with those women disappearing."

"Who cares?" Colin asked, speaking for the first time.

"What?" Reicher said, clearly startled.

"That's just our reason to hold you until we gather up the last bit of evidence for the big one."

Reicher frowned. "The big one…what?"

"We know when and how you did it, but what we don't know is why. Did he want out, maybe, cutting off the flow of easy cash? Did he develop a conscience, threaten to go clean, maybe confess?"

Reicher looked puzzled, and Darien thought it seemed real. ''What are you talking about?'' the man asked, in an entirely different tone than he'd used when he'd said similar words before.

''Nice try, Desmond,'' Colin said, using his name familiarly just as Darien had; the man was used to more respect than this, and with his ego, not getting it could only add to his anger, which might make him make a fatal mistake. ''If I didn't have all this evidence, I might even believe you didn't do it.''

''Whatever evidence you think you have, my lawyers will tear to pieces. I had nothing to do with those women.''

''And it won't matter, when you go on trial for murder,'' Colin said flatly.

''Murder?'' Reicher's eyes widened. ''Wait a minute...you think *I* killed Franklin?''

He looked so astonished Darien found herself thinking, *I almost believe him.*

''Are you crazy? Why would I do that?''

''I think I gave you some possible reasons,'' Darien said.

He gave her an irritated glance, but then looked back at Colin. ''I'd be crazy to kill Franklin. He was the goose that laid the golden egg.''

''That goose, if you recall, wound up as dead as your partner. So did he want out? Did he want to put an end to your little scheme? Is that why you killed him?''

"I didn't kill him. This is insane."

"Insanity is overrated as a defense," Darien said, letting her disdain show in her voice, knowing it would needle him, coming from her. "And by the way, your alibi didn't hold up. Your assistant could only swear you were at your office until ten. Not late enough to save you, Desmond."

Reicher looked at her as if he wished he could send her the way of the women he'd already sold into hell.

"Look, we know you and he were in on this slavery ring," Colin said. "You're going to go down for that. Which makes you the most likely suspect for the murder, too, unless you can give us a very good reason to go looking elsewhere."

"The very good reason is I'm not a fool, Detective," Reicher snapped at Colin. "I did not kill Franklin Gardner. And whatever else you think you've got, you will *never* be able to prove I did because it's not true."

"What's bugging you?" Colin asked, judging by the crease between her brows that Darien wasn't happy about something. "You did great with him."

"Thank you," she said, with that smile that he'd finally had to admit knocked him for a loop every time. It was so warm, so gentle, so...personal, that it was hard not to read too much into it.

"You earned it," he said. "So what's putting that furrow in your forehead?"

She shook her head. "It's nothing."

"Well, something's bugging me," he said, and she looked at him quizzically. His mouth quirked wryly at one corner. "After all this, my gut isn't cooperating."

"What do you mean?"

He let out a compressed breath. "I believe him."

Her forehead immediately cleared. "You do?"

"I know, I know, it's crazy, but slime that he is, I don't think he killed Gardner."

"Neither do I."

He blinked. "You don't?"

"I believe him, too."

"He had to have known killing Gardner would cause more trouble than it was worth."

She nodded. "The only way I could reconcile it was if he killed him in an out-of-control rage, and…"

When she hesitated, he finished it for her. "And Desmond Reicher has never been that far out of control in his entire lifetime."

"Exactly. He's too cold, calculating. He would never act without figuring what it might cost him first."

"Same conclusion I came to." Colin sighed audibly. "I just don't know where that leaves us."

"At square one?" she suggested wearily.

"Well, not quite," Colin reminded her gently. "We did just put a forced prostitution ring out of business."

"Yes, we did. No way now Reicher could pick a new partner and start again, or try to carry on alone."

"And when they trace the other end of the chain, we might just save some of those girls."

She brightened at that. "I hadn't thought of that. Now that would be worth it all and then some."

"I thought you'd like that."

"I do. But now what? And what if we're wrong about him not killing Gardner?"

He shrugged. "He'll still get turned over to the feds for the forced prostitution charges. That will hold him for a long time. More than long enough for us to keep turning over rocks and looking for anybody else that might crawl out."

She yawned suddenly, then embarrassedly apologized. "Sorry. Guess it's catching up with me."

"We've been pushing pretty hard for days now, and it's—" he glanced at his watch and was surprised himself "—it's nearly eight. Let's knock off, get some dinner and some sleep."

"Food? Real food?"

"Honest. Then we'll start fresh in the morning."

"Early," she said.

"Of course."

He grinned at her, and got himself that smile

again. He could get used to that, he thought. And
before he could recoil from the danger of that
thought, she was on her feet. She grabbed her coat
and, seemingly without embarrassment, his hand,
tugging.

"Let's go," she said. "I don't care where, as long
as it's food I didn't cook on dishes I don't have to
wash."

"Yes, ma'am," he said, trying to ignore the heat
that shot through him at even her casual touch.

This could be a long night, he thought. In more
ways than one.

She shouldn't have had that second glass of wine,
Darien decided too late. She didn't drink often,
didn't like the feeling of being out of control, but
tonight she'd been having trouble winding down and
thought it might help. She needed sleep, after too
long with too little, but her mind wouldn't slow
down. She knew too many cops went down that road
too far to get back, so she was in little danger of
following, but still, she could understand how it happened when you felt like this.

Right now, she felt full of good food and a bit
buzzed. And it was not a bad feeling. But then, neither was sitting across the table from Colin Waters.
She'd liked his looks before she'd ever spoken to
him, but now that she'd spent hours and days on
end with him, she liked him as a person as well. She

liked the way he handled himself, the way he'd let
her deal with Palmer, the way he'd subtly warned
the man when things got out of line. She liked that
he gave her a chance to prove herself before he
passed judgment, and that he didn't belittle her instincts, even though they weren't honed with as
much experience as he had.

And most of all, she liked the way she felt when
he looked at her with approval in those amber-gold
eyes.

"Thank you," she said suddenly.

"For what?" he asked, clearly surprised by the
out-of-the-blue gratitude.

"For not making this harder than it had to be for
me. I knew there was going to be a certain amount
of resentment to deal with. I'm grateful to you for
not being part of that."

"Even if I had been," he said, "I'd be over it by
now. You do your job, you give it full effort, and
you know when to back off and learn. That's all I
ask from a new partner."

This reminded her of something she'd been wanting to know. "Your former partner retired?"

He nodded. "Sam had thirty years on. He taught
me most of what I know." He grinned. "Sometimes, he just let me learn the hard way. He called
it tough love."

"Sounds like quite a character."

"He was one of the best. Before he left, I tried

to thank him for all he'd done. He said the best thanks I could give him would be to pass it on. That way he'd feel he didn't do those thirty years just for a paycheck.''

"I'll have to look him up and thank him some day.''

"He'd appreciate that.''

A few minutes passed as the check came, Colin insisted on paying, saying she could pick up next time. The idea that there would be a next time, and conceivably a next and a next, both thrilled and frightened her. She could so easily get into trouble with this man, and trouble was just what she didn't need now, on a new job that was already hazardous enough, in too many ways to count.

And then he looked up, caught her staring at him, no doubt with everything she was thinking showing plainly on her face.

"This way lies trouble,'' he said softly. "For both of us.''

She didn't, couldn't, pretend to misunderstand. "I know.''

"Are we going anyway?''

"Do you want to?''

"I'm not sure.'' He shook his head. "I hate being a cliché.''

She knew he meant the cliché of cop partners falling for each other. She'd had the same thought herself more than once since they'd started working together.

"So do I."

Later, when they were outside walking to the car, Darien still wasn't sure of anything except that this was asking for trouble. Yet when he entrapped her with his arms against the car, even though she could easily have escaped, she didn't make a move.

"Maybe," he said, his voice low and husky, "we should dip a toe in the water and see just how hot it is."

"I suppose," she said rather breathlessly, "we should find out what we're resisting. Maybe it won't be so hard after all."

"Yeah, right," he muttered, and lowered his mouth to hers.

Darien knew in the first three seconds that fighting this was going to be next to, if not beyond, impossible. His mouth was rich with the taste of wine and the chocolate they'd had for dessert, and with something indefinable that was pure Colin. Her nerves came to life with startling speed, as if they'd been waiting for this moment, this man. Anything she'd known before paled next to this.

She heard him make a sound, deep in his throat. He seemed to hesitate, and she thought he was going to pull back. Her response was immediate, without thought; she flicked her tongue over his lips in an effort to keep him there.

It worked. The sound he was making became a groan, and his arms came around her, pulling her hard to him. He probed her mouth with his tongue, taking the hint she'd offered. Fire leapt through her, and all thought of danger, all the reasons they shouldn't do this, were seared to ash.

By the time he finally did pull back, Darien was shaking. And it didn't comfort her much to realize he was breathing fast and hard as he stared down at her, his eyes as hot as the flames that had scorched her.

"That answers that," he said roughly.

"It certainly does," she whispered.

They were both in trouble now. For a long, tense moment they simply looked at each other, and somehow Darien knew he was thinking the same thing she was: what had they unleashed?

When his cell phone rang, he didn't even react until the second ring. Then, with an effort that was obvious, he pulled it out and pushed the talk button.

"Waters." He listened for what seemed like a long time. Then, finally, he said, "No, I'm not surprised. We'd already reached that conclusion. But now we have proof. Thanks."

He informed the caller that they would start anew tomorrow, and then hung up.

"That was the sergeant from the facility where Reicher's being held," he said. "Benton called him.

Sutter's determined our killer had to be left-handed.''

Her brows shot up. "And Reicher is right-handed.''

He nodded. "So we've got the satisfaction of knowing we were right. And the job of starting all over to find our killer.''

"Joy," she muttered.

"And," he added softly, "the extra job of figuring out what to do about this personal fire we've started.''

"That, too.''

Chapter 7

"When in doubt, start with the family," Darien said. "Isn't that what they always say?"

Colin nodded. "That's what the statistics say."

"Well, all I can say is the matriarch should be the last one we talk to, or we'll be dead in the water before we start."

"I had that same feeling," he said, stifling a yawn that reminded him too clearly of a restless night spent remembering that heated kiss they'd shared. "I'm thinking we hit the son again first, since he's the one dodging us."

...they may have fought about the money he was going to inherit, but Stephen had nothing to do with this!

Lyle's vehement defense of his nephew had been echoing in his head, and he wondered if perhaps the man had reason to think the young man needed it.

A single phone call not only set the course of their day, but gave them a piece of information that made them both react with interest; Stephen Gardner had dropped out of school.

This trip to the Gardner estate was considerably different than the last one. For one, they were now looking for a suspect in the family circle. Secondly, they had the memory of that kiss between them.

And this time, there would be no insulating her grandson from reality for Cecelia Gardner.

"Get any sleep last night?" Colin asked.

"Not much," she admitted.

"Me either. What are we going to do about it?"

"Get over it?" she suggested, but without much conviction.

"I wish," he said dryly. He wasn't particularly stung by her words, mainly because they were uttered with such acknowledgment of the impossibility of what she'd said.

But doing anything else seemed impossible, too.

"It would never work," he said.

"Probably not," she agreed, surprising him; he'd expected her to disagree. "But," she went on, "I'm curious why you think that."

"Because you want everything I'm no good at.

You're cut out for marriage, kids, the white picket fence, the whole bit.''

When she answered, her words came slowly, as if she'd chosen them very carefully. ''You don't know what I want, proven by the fact that I don't like white picket fences. But that aside, why do you say you're not cut out for the rest?''

''My marriage proved that.''

''Hmm. My marriage failed, too, but all it proved was that we were too young. But you assume yours proved that you were unfit for all time? A little premature, wouldn't you say?''

He'd never thought of it quite that way before. ''Maybe,'' he muttered.

''At least you didn't decide that because you couldn't trust one woman, you can't trust any,'' she said.

''It was my—'' He stopped in the middle of the old refrain, that his fractured marriage was his fault.

I believe an affair is the fault of the person involved. If you want out, get out, but you don't cheat.

Her words came back to him, and now that he knew her a little better, he knew she meant them. That's the code she would live by, an honesty he'd thought didn't exist. If there was a problem in the relationship, the guy wouldn't get blindsided, because Darien Wilson would come out and say so. He knew that with a bone-deep certainty that surprised him, given the short time he'd known her.

She was quiet the rest of the drive, giving him time to think. He appreciated that she didn't feel the need to fill each silent moment with chatter. Then again, he was nervous about what he was thinking, so maybe he shouldn't be so glad she was allowing him time to do it.

When they arrived at the Gardner estate, the only thing they revealed was that they had an update for the family. It was enough to get the butler—or whoever answered the intercom—to open the massive driveway gate for them. And then they got lucky; Darien spotted Stephen Gardner outside the large garage beside the house, apparently directing a chauffeur or servant in how to correctly wax what appeared to be a brand-new European luxury coupe.

"New toy?" Colin wondered aloud.

"Not wasting any time spending daddy's money, is he?" Darien said.

"So it would seem," Colin agreed as he halted the city vehicle, which looked derelict in comparison, a few feet from the garage activity.

He looked little like his father, with thick, medium-brown hair and brown eyes. And had none of Franklin Gardner's reported charisma; Stephen Gardner seemed a bit sulky, almost sullen. And, Colin guessed, more than a little anger was hidden away under that surface.

If I had a son, he wouldn't end up like this, Colin muttered to himself. And nearly stopped breathing when he realized what he'd thought. And that the child who popped into his head had blond hair.

"Colin?" Darien said, sounding a bit odd, although she never looked away from the younger Gardner.

"What?"

"He's left-handed."

Colin leaned forward, in time to see Stephen Gardner writing something on a small piece of yellow paper with his left hand.

"Well, well," he murmured. "Shall we?"

They got out and headed toward the two men and the fancy coupe.

"Nice car." Darien caught the young man's attention with the comment. And kept it with her looks, Colin thought wryly as he watched the young man smile at her. When they'd spoken to him briefly a few days ago, his responses had been short and unhelpful, no doubt as instructed by his grandmother. This was an entirely different young man.

"Yeah, isn't it?" he said enthusiastically. "I've been wanting it for ages, it's the latest—" He broke off, belatedly recognizing them. "Hey, you're the cops. The detectives."

"Yeah, we are," Colin acknowledged, noticing the unobtrusive man with the car wax quietly departing the scene.

"You have news? Did you catch who killed the old man?"

So much for the respectful "my father" he'd used before, Colin noted. *Over the shock? Or just more certain he's going to get away with it?*

"We're getting very close," Darien said. "That's why we're here."

"Oh? So was it a burglar like Uncle Lyle says, or did somebody finally get ticked off enough to just do him?"

"Think that's likely, do you, Stephen?" Colin asked.

The young man scowled. "Look, I told you before, the old man and I didn't get along. I told you if it hadn't been for him, my mother would still be alive."

"I looked into that, Stephen, after we spoke," Darien said. "The official report says accidental overdose."

The young man's mouth twisted scornfully. "Of course it does. What would you expect it to say? My father was *Franklin Gardner*. But he drove her to it. He could drive anyone to it. She wouldn't even have had those pills around if she hadn't needed them to get through every day of living with him."

Colin thought about asking why she hadn't just divorced him, but he could guess at the reasons and it wasn't really relevant anyway.

"Did you hate him, Stephen?"

"I'm not going to lie about it. He was a control

freak who had to have everything his way. Nothing was good enough for him. Nothing.''

"Even you?''

"Especially me,'' the young man said bitterly. "Did I hate him? Yes. Enough to kill him? No. I didn't want him to think he was that important to me, that he could get to me like he did my mother.''

There was bitterness in the younger Gardner's words, but also the ring of stark truth.

Apparently Darien felt the same way because she said, "Do you have any idea who might have done it, then?''

Something flickered in the young man's eyes, and Colin's instincts came to alert.

"No,'' Stephen said.

"If you have even a guess, we'd like to hear it,'' Colin said.

"You're the cops, it's your job to figure it out.''

"That,'' Darien said softly, "sounds like something your father would have said.''

Good shot, Colin thought as he watched the young man wince.

"My father was always throwing his weight around,'' Stephen acknowledged. "But he was bigger on family loyalty.''

Colin's already alerted instincts spiked higher. But before he could continue, an imperious voice rang out, interrupting the proceedings thoroughly.

"I told you you were not to speak to my grandson without myself or his uncle present!"

They turned to see Cecelia bearing down on them. The chauffeur, he guessed, must have sounded the alarm. Cecelia was followed by Lyle, who looked rather anxious. Colin wondered if that was his normal mien when in the presence of his overbearing mother, or if he was nervous about something else.

"And, ma'am, I told you he is an adult, and we're not required to allow a relative present while questioning him."

"Questioning him?" Lyle asked sharply. "You make it sound like he's a suspect when we know you've arrested Desmond!"

"I think we've come to an understanding," Darien said, glancing at Stephen and giving him a smile that made the young man redden.

I know how you feel, kid, Colin thought ruefully. *She does the same thing to me.*

Oddly, although Cecelia backed off a bit, Lyle didn't seem to relax. Or maybe it was just his normal demeanor; as Darien had said after their original contact with him, he was a bit full of being a Gardner. But they shooed Stephen away, and turned on Colin and Darien.

"If you don't have anything worthwhile to report to us," Lyle demanded, gesturing rather wildly, "why are you here and not out hunting the person who killed my brother?"

Because we're here hunting the person who killed your brother, Colin thought, eyeing the man. Something was bothering him about Lyle, and he couldn't quite put his finger on what it was.

"Because we have some additional questions to ask." He turned to Darien, letting his gaze flick from her to Mrs. Gardner and back. She picked up on his cue quickly, and more efficiently than he would have thought possible she had ushered the redoubtable woman away, leaving him with the surviving Gardner brother.

Now he just had to decide where to start, and how far to go.

Darien studied the woman sitting beside her, wondering if she was imagining that she looked older, less intimidating than before. She certainly hadn't expected it to be so easy to separate her and get her alone.

"I'm sorry this is so difficult," she said, going on instinct. "It must seem like this process takes forever to you."

"At least you finally have the killer in custody now," the woman said, but her critical tone seemed more automatic than truly snappish. As had the order for coffee; Darien doubted, had the woman been herself, that she would be serving one of the cops she held responsible for all the delay.

"We thought we did, but it turns out the evidence proved us wrong and we had to begin again."

Mrs. Gardner actually looked startled. "Wrong?"

"Yes. He's still being held on…other charges, but it appears he's not guilty of murdering your son."

"Then who is it?"

"We don't know yet. I'm sorry."

"It's my son who's dead," she snapped. "First I have to fight to get them to release his body for burial, and now you're telling me the man you arrested is innocent and you don't have any idea who killed him?"

"I didn't say we had *no* idea. Just nothing I can talk about yet."

Mrs. Gardner subsided, but not happily. Darien looked at the elderly woman, who looked not stylishly slender just now, but thin and frail. And no matter how she tried she couldn't picture her killing not just her own son, but anyone.

Except perhaps by slicing them to death with that tongue of hers, she added silently.

"We understand your need to protect your family," Darien said. "Especially when you've already lost a son. But doesn't that son deserve your total honesty, if it will help find his killer?"

For a long moment Cecelia Gardner looked at her, a steady, assessing gaze that made Darien want to draw back. But she held her place, met the woman's gaze, and refused to avert her eyes. Finally, as if defeated, Mrs. Gardner broke first and looked away.

She's hiding something, Darien realized with a little jolt. *She knows something, and she's hiding it.*

Her mind began to race. Could she have found out about her son's little sideline? Was she afraid we'll also find out, or already know? Or did she know something about her son's murder that she wasn't telling? She still couldn't believe the woman could have done it herself, but neither could she doubt that Cecelia Gardner knew something she wasn't telling.

By the time she was back in the car with Colin, she wasn't any closer to figuring it out. So when he asked her what she'd gotten, all she could say was, "She's hiding something. She knows something, or is afraid we'll find out something she doesn't want us to."

"Protecting someone?"

She considered that. "Possibly." And then, after a moment, she added, "And I can't think of all that many people she'd take the risk for."

"Neither can I."

"So if we follow this to the logical end…"

"We've narrowed our suspect pool considerably," Colin said, finishing the thought for her. "Especially after Stephen's comment about his father being big on family loyalty." The two prime suspects were obviously what was left of Cecelia Gardner's family. And that made the morass they were treading through even messier.

"And if our suspect is someone important enough for Cecelia Gardner to protect…"

Colin again finished her unspoken thought. "It's somebody we're going to have to be very careful with."

"So now what?"

"Back to the station, I guess. I need to find something, and I may need your help."

"All right. What is it?"

"A photograph. Probably a society page type of thing."

"And it's at the station?"

"No. I'm not even sure it exists, but if it does I figured you could help me find it online."

"If you need an online search, let's go to my place. I've got a cable connection, and it'll be a lot faster."

"All right. Where to?"

She gave him the address of her apartment, and he nodded.

Darien barely noticed the quiet as they drove; she'd found silence with Colin soothing rather than unsettling. Besides, she was sure he was thinking as hard as she was about what they'd learned today. And about what they'd guessed at. What she didn't know was if he was worrying as much as she was whether those guesses were right. What if she was wrong about Mrs. Gardner, or about Stephen? What kind of instincts did she have, after all?

She suppressed a shiver, and told herself she hadn't done anything based on her guesses, so it didn't matter. But it still made her edgy, and she wondered if Colin had ever felt like this.

And wondered if she now had the right to ask.

Darien's apartment was small, but Colin immediately felt comfortable in it. It was decorated in bright, warm, cheerful colors that were pleasant after the cold outside. The living room was narrow, containing only a sofa, a chair, coffee table and an entertainment center, but they were arranged cozily and looked comfortable. It felt like a home, unlike his own spartan digs. Or maybe it was just that she made him feel as if he was coming home. The thought stopped his breath, and he was glad when she spoke.

"Coffee? Or something stronger?"

"Coffee," he said, then added, "with the option for the other later."

She walked to the small kitchen that was tucked into one corner and divided from the rest of the room by a small island. She filled a coffeemaker that sat on the counter and started it. Then she walked to an alcove that housed a desk and computer that looked much more impressive than the ones at the station, and pushed a button to boot up. It took a moment as things whirred and beeped, and data flashed across the screen. When it was done, she leaned over and made a couple of mouse clicks. She opened a browser, then glanced back at the coffee-maker, which was already dripping the dark brew into the pot.

"I'll get it," Colin said. "Cups?"

"Mugs in the cupboard just above. Milk in the fridge, sugar in the green canister."

He nodded, and she pulled up her desk chair and sat down. "All right," she asked, "what am I looking for?"

He told her, and while it didn't make sense to her—they'd just left the real thing, after all—she started the search.

He came over and set a steaming cup beside her. She glanced at it, and saw it was exactly the shade she liked.

"Thanks."

"You're welcome." He watched for a moment as she clicked on various search results, then let out a low whistle. "Whew. You weren't kidding about it being faster."

"I'm spoiled," she said. "At the station it seems to take forever."

"I can see why, if this is what you're used to. I've never seen—" He stopped suddenly. "There. That one, with the woman in red. Can you go back to it?" She clicked once and the image reappeared.

He studied it for a moment, then shook his head. "No. Sorry."

"Keep going?"

"Yes, please."

The steady process began again, and he sipped at his coffee as he watched. Occasionally he stopped her on a shot, but always seemed to decide it wasn't what he wanted.

"Dare I ask exactly what it is you're looking for?"

"Something with a clear, closer shot of the left hand."

She blinked. And in that moment guessed his intent.

With a series of clicks that went so fast he could barely keep up she went back to a photograph he'd rejected a few moments ago. She clicked on it, a menu popped up, and she seemed to pull it right out of the article—a report on the annual Gardner Corporation Christmas Gala—and it appeared in another window.

She began to work with what appeared to be some kind of photo software, and within a few minutes, she hit one last button and a new window began to fill with an enlarged, sharpened image.

When it was done, he was standing there staring at a piece of evidence that could make the case. It wasn't razor sharp, and it lacked detail, but it was enough to make it clear his idea was possible.

"Can you print that?" His voice was a little tight.

"Sure."

She hit two more buttons, and he heard the whir of a printer starting up. Then she turned to him.

"How did you know?"

"Something's been bothering me every time we saw him." He gestured at the subject in the photo. "And today, I finally figured it out. I think it was because we were out in the sun, so it was more obvious. A tan line, where a ring used to be."

She turned to look at the picture still up on her monitor, and made the jump instantly. "The ring that explains those facial bruises. And he's left-handed."

"Yes."

"And he'd easily be able to grab that security camera tape."

"Yes."

Her gaze shifted back to him. "Then we've got him?"

He shook his head. "It's going to take more than a fuzzy newspaper photo. But it's a good start."

Darien turned to look once more at the photograph. She stared at it for what seemed like a long time, but Colin knew by now that her mind was probably racing. And then she spoke, and proved him right.

"A Gardner wouldn't wear cheap jewelry, right?"

"Not likely."

She swiveled in the chair and looked up at him. "Then wouldn't it be likely that that ring is insured somewhere?"

His brows furrowed. "Probably. It would—" He stopped abruptly as what she was thinking hit him. "And insurance means photographs!"

"Detailed closeups, I'd expect. Is the name of the insurance company anywhere in the reports, for the items reported stolen?"

"Should be, it's pretty routine." He grinned at her. "Next time anybody hassles you about how you got this job, you send them to me."

"I'll do that."

The look she gave him then made him feel as if he'd done a whole lot more than simply acknowledged that she had what it took to do this job. It also made him feel downright warm inside, a sensation he didn't even bother to try and shrug off this time. At this point, he wasn't sure he cared if he was on a runaway train.

"So Lyle Gardner is suspect number one," he said after a moment.

"His own brother," she said, shaking her head.

"He must have found out about the prostitution ring."

"You think he confronted Franklin about it?"

Colin nodded. "He seems the type who would want to protect the family name."

"And they fought over it. Maybe he never meant to kill him at all."

"That would make sense," Colin agreed. "And it would fit with the fall injury being the cause of death."

"So the rest, the ice picks and the stolen property, was just a cover-up, to make it look like a burglary."

"It's all circumstantial," Colin warned.

"But it explains what Stephen said, and Cecelia's protective reaction. It fits."

"Yeah. It fits."

"So now what?"

"Nothing, until morning when we can get the photos of the ring. Then we'll get them over to Maggie Sutter and see if the ring matches those bruises on the body."

"And if they do?"

"Then we call in the D.A., and Mr. Lyle Gardner goes to jail."

"I could get used to this," Darien said with an exaggerated yawn and stretch after she'd finished her last forkful of pasta and sip of wine. "Somebody else cooking is a novelty."

She got up and strolled over to the sofa, then turned to give him a sideways grin, and added, "Heck, somebody cooking in here is a novelty. I've become a takeout queen, much to my mother's shame.''

"Don't get your hopes up," he said wryly as he followed her to the living room. "You've just had my entire repertoire."

"Good thing I love spaghetti, then."

She colored suddenly, looking as if she'd just realized how what she'd said sounded, as if she were planning many more nights like this one.

"Don't tempt me," he said softly. He'd been thinking about it a lot himself, and the appeal of an endless string of nights like this was growing rapidly. He could even, if he worked at it, put a kid or two into the picture.

She had the grace not to deny it. "Sorry." She lowered her gaze. Then, after a moment, she added in a near whisper, "I think."

It was that little whisper that undid him. "Damn, Darien. That kiss was…almost an accident. This would be with full intent. Do you realize what we could get ourselves into?"

She looked up at him then. "Oh, yes," she said, her voice husky now.

Heat flashed through him with the speed of an explosion. He'd been keeping himself on a short leash for what felt like an eon now, although it had, amazingly, only been a short time. He took a step toward her, reached out, then froze. When he spoke, his voice was thick and harsh.

"If you want to stop this, you'd better say so now, because once I touch you, there's no turning back for me."

"There was no turning back for me once you took that first step," she whispered.

He groaned, then reached for her again. But instead of pulling her up to him as he'd planned, he found himself sinking down beside her. His mouth sought hers hungrily, and the soft warmth of her lips somehow had more kick than his .357 Magnum. His gut knotted as if he'd taken one of those rounds, and he couldn't have pulled away had someone drawn that gun on him.

"Colin," she said breathlessly, "I forgot. I…we… I'm not prepared for this."

He had to wait a moment for the hot, pleasurable haze to clear enough so that he could think. He mentally inventoried his wallet, remembered one of Sam's parting gifts—with the accompanying suggestion that he get a life—then said roughly, "I'll handle it."

She breathed a sigh of relief that made his body clench.

He traced the line of her jaw with his mouth, marveling at the smoothness of her skin. His fingers tangled in the soft silk of her hair, and he did what he'd been longing to do forever, planted a long, lingering kiss at the nape of her neck bared by the impossibly sexy haircut. When she shivered in reaction, he felt it as if it had begun inside him.

She moved, and only when he felt the sinuous caress of her hips against his aroused body did he realize he'd pulled her beneath him. She moved again, and he nearly gasped. Again, and he forgot to breathe at all.

This train is definitely in trouble, he thought. He'd never been derailed like this. Ever.

It was the last rational thought he had. He didn't listen to it anyway.

Darien had the fleeting thought that this was insane, that she was long past the age when she should be rapidly heading for a very intimate encounter on the couch in her living room. Yet here she was, half-undressed, and without hesitation helping a man she hadn't even met a month ago shed his own clothes. A man she'd known from the first instant meant trouble. She'd thought she'd loved Tony, but this...

And then he came back to her, his body hot, hard and ready, his hands moving over her with an eagerness that thrilled her and a tenderness that melted her. A delicious anticipation welled up inside her. When he slid into her she welcomed him with a matching eagerness, and a low groan of pure pleasure rumbled up from deep in his chest. She felt an answering ripple as her body strained to accept him, felt a glorious stretching fullness that made her cry out her own pleasure.

Suddenly it didn't matter where they were, or how long they'd known each other. The only thing that mattered was this glorious sensation, this building, tightening, rising tension that nearly made her scream.

And then he moved one last time, driving hard and deep into her, and the tension shattered, flinging her in what seemed a thousand directions at once.

And she did scream. His name.

Colin hung up the phone and turned to Darien with a wide smile on his face. "It's a match. Maggie says the ring in the photograph is a perfect match for the bruises on the body."

Darien smiled back, and potent memories of last night flashed through his mind in a hot, vivid stream.

"Is it enough?" she asked.

Never, he thought, then realized she was talking about the ring.

"For a conviction? Probably not, we'll have to keep searching for the thing. Stone'll need all the help he can get, including that ring and any trace DNA evidence on it. But for an arrest, definitely. The warrant's already in the works."

She let out a long breath. "What if we're wrong?"

"We're the good guys," he teased. "We're never wrong."

She laughed, and he couldn't resist reaching out to brush the backs of his fingers over her cheek. She blushed and lowered her gaze, but she also nuzzled his hand. And instantly he was again awash in those intense images. He didn't know what she'd done, had a strange feeling it was more what she hadn't done, such as throw herself at him, but somehow she'd blasted through every reservation he'd had.

"Ho, ho, ho, I smell fraternization!"

Colin stifled a groan as Palmer's voice told him he'd been caught. Served him right for succumbing to the urge to touch her here in the office.

"Isn't this sweet?" Palmer drawled. "Together at last. How convenient."

Colin summoned up an air of unconcern.

"Don't mind us," he said with a creditable laugh. "We're just celebrating the fact that in a minute we're going to pick up a warrant and make an arrest."

"In fact," Darien said, getting up, "we're going right now, aren't we?"

"Indeed we are," he agreed, and they left so quickly Palmer was left with nothing to do but gape after them.

They both breathed a sigh of relief that Mrs. Gardner wasn't at home. They hadn't looked forward to dealing with her when, after the murder of her younger son, they were about to cart off the eldest.

Lyle Gardner was his usual haughty self when they arrived. He demanded to know if they had made any progress. Darien kept her eyes on Gardner's face as Colin answered.

"Yes, we have. In fact, we're about to make an arrest. We've discovered a key piece of evidence."

Darien was sure she saw Gardner draw back infinitesimally.

"Did you think we wouldn't find out about it?" Darien asked softly. "It's pretty distinctive, after all. All Gardner jewelry would be."

Lyle paled visibly. "I lost that ring. Long ago. You can't prove otherwise."

Gotcha! Darien exulted silently.

"Did you?" Colin asked.

"Yes."

"So there will be a claim on file with your insurance company?" Darien put in sweetly, already knowing perfectly well there hadn't been.

Gardner suddenly seemed to realize he was digging himself into a hole. "I'm through with your questions. My attorney will speak for me from now on."

"Fine. We'll call him for you from the station," she said.

"I'm not going anywhere with you."

Colin reached into his pocket and took out some folded papers. "I'm afraid you are, Mr. Gardner. This arrest warrant says so."

"Whatever judge you got to sign that won't be on the bench for long."

"Amazingly enough, there is a judge in Chicago who doesn't owe the Gardners a thing," Colin said.

Fuming, Gardner swore indelicately. "I'm calling my attorney *now*."

Colin shrugged. "Doesn't matter. We won't be needing to ask you any questions now anyway."

He spoke as if the case was open-and-shut, as if he were utterly confident that nothing Gardner could do would make any difference. It rattled the man, Darien could see it in his face.

"Oh, wait," Colin said. "I was wrong, there is one more question."

"I won't answer anything."

"That's okay. I already know the answer, anyway."

Darien could see he was struggling not to ask. And saw the moment when he gave up. "The answer to what?"

Colin smiled. "To how you knew we were talking about your ring. We never mentioned it."

The man visibly blanched.

"Lyle Gardner, you are under arrest for the murder of Franklin Gardner," Colin said with satisfaction.

* * *

Darien typed the last line on the jail booking form, hit the enter key with a flourish.

"Voilà," she said. "The end. Mr. Lyle Gardner is officially booked."

"Too bad the investigation hasn't ended. We've still got to find that ring."

Darien sighed. "Don't rain on my parade just yet, will you? Give me an hour or so to feel some job satisfaction."

Colin grinned. "Well, since it's your first time…"

She took a swipe at him, but she was grinning back. It did feel good, even he had to admit it. The case wasn't a lock, not by a long shot, but he knew in his gut they had the right guy. Not that that would be worth a thing in court.

"Do you need to go back to the office?" he asked.

"No." She wrinkled her nose. "Besides, I don't want Palmer to ruin my mood."

"He was right about one thing."

"Palmer? Hard to believe. What?"

"The convenience."

She blinked. "What?" she repeated.

"It's convenient. If you were to marry me, you wouldn't have to change your initial."

Her breath caught audibly, but she recovered

quickly. As she always did. "What makes you think I'd change my name anyway?"

"Then I won't have to change my initial," he said with a lopsided grin.

She laughed then, warming him anew. Mostly because she hadn't shut him down outright. He still felt a little bit like he was on an out-of-control train, but to his own surprise, he didn't want to jump off.

Not as long as his new partner was on board.

* * * * *

VERDICT: MARRIAGE

Joan Elliott Pickart

* * *

With thanks to our editor, Ann Leslie Tuttle,
who was buried in e-mail during this
challenging project

Dear Reader,

It was a privilege to work with two such talented authors on this project, and the three of us were e-mailing back and forth in a frenzy to be certain that our descriptions and details matched.

As Evan and Jennifer became living, breathing people to me, I could feel Evan's frustration as he waited, and hoped, for the evidence that would convict Lyle Gardner. But despite Evan's dedication to his career, Jennifer staked a claim on his heart. Beautiful, spunky Jennifer, with her precious secret she feared to share with Evan, and who was also dedicated to her unique career, had the womanly wisdom to know there was room for so much more in her life.

While writing this book, I learned so much about what goes on behind the scenes as each step is taken to ensure that justice will be the victor when a horrendous crime has been committed.

We all owe a heartfelt thanks to the men and women in every area of law enforcement who make these troubled times in our world safer for all of us.

I hope you enjoy reading this book as much as I did writing it. I am very eager to read the first two stories in the collection now that they are completed. As you are curled up in the corner of your sofa turning the pages, know I'm doing the same right along with you.

Once again, I want to thank all of you for your continued support through the years and for the wonderful letters you take the time to write to me.

Warmest regards,

Joan Elliott Pickart

Chapter 1

Jennifer Anderson stopped in the hallway on the top floor of the courthouse and turned to look up at the very tall young man who had a camera balanced on his shoulder.

"Take a break, Sticks," Jennifer said. "I'm going to attempt to make some sense of these notes of mine while I remember what the scribbling means. Meet me in the lounge down the hall in half an hour or so."

"Yep," Sticks said, then ambled away.

Jennifer entered the empty lounge and sank onto one of the chairs that surrounded a large rectangular table. She propped one elbow on the top of the table, rested her chin in her hand and closed her eyes.

Oh, gracious, she thought, she was sleepy. She'd like nothing better than to curl up on the lumpy-looking sofa on the back wall of the lounge and take a nap. If she allowed herself to relax for even three seconds she'd nod off. Just one…two…

Jennifer jerked and opened her eyes as she began to drift off. She patted her cheeks, told herself she was wide-awake and looked at the notes.

Next on the agenda, she thought, was to film the final footage of the documentary, which meant it was time to glue herself to District Attorney Evan Stone.

Evan, Evan, Evan.

Dear heaven, what would Evan do, say, if he knew that she…

"Don't go there, Jennifer," she mumbled. "Not now."

Jennifer glanced at her watch, got to her feet, then smoothed the hem of her green sweater over the black slacks she wore with low-heeled, black shoes.

Okay, here I go, she thought. She'd put this meeting with Evan off for as long as she could, had filmed so much footage of police detectives, and secretaries and assistant district attorneys it was ridiculous. She'd been gathering her courage to see Evan again and be able to act pleasant and professional.

"I can do this," she said, starting across the lounge.

"Do what?" Sticks said, appearing in the doorway.

"Oh. Listen, Sticks, just hang out in here for now. I need to find out if Evan Stone is available, then chat with him a bit about how we're going to do this."

"Whatever."

"Fine. Okay," she said. "I'm going down the hall to his office now. Yep, that's what I'm doing. Right now. Bye." Jennifer didn't move.

"You're acting weird."

"I am not," she said, indignantly. "I'm…mulling over how to begin my conversation with Evan. He wasn't exactly receptive to this idea of a documentary on the inner workings of the district attorney's office, said D.A. being him. We ironed out the wrinkles three months ago, but there's no telling how he might feel about it weeks later."

"Ah, go for it." Sticks set the camera on the table. "Charm the socks off the guy."

"Right," Jennifer said, then stepped out of the lounge and into the hallway.

At that exact moment the door to Evan's office at the end of the corridor opened and a plump young woman emerged, leaving Evan framed in the doorway as she walked away.

Oh, my, Jennifer thought, there he was. There was Evan about a hundred feet down the hall and it appeared as though he was staring directly at her.

Feet. She had to move her feet, put one in front of the other, and produce a nice friendly smile at the same time. She could do this. No, she couldn't. She was going to turn around and hightail it out of there, never to be seen again.

"Get a grip," she said, under her breath, and started forward.

There she was, Evan thought, as he watched Jennifer approach very slowly. His heart was beating like a bongo drum, damn it. And was that...? Yes, it was. There was a trickle of sweat running down his chest. Where in the hell was this nonsense coming from?

Evan cleared his throat, causing Belinda Morris, his fifty-two-year-old secretary, to turn and look at him questioningly, then shift her gaze to what he was staring at.

"Oh-h-h," Belinda said, smiling. "So the time has come. I've had the pleasure of speaking with Jennifer Anderson already. She's delightful. You could be a gentleman and meet her halfway, you know."

"What's gentlemanly about that?"

"Well, you're standing there like the king of the hill, or something. It would be a tad warmer, more friendly, if you at least gave the appearance of welcoming her to your office, indicate that you're delighted to see her again. You did tell me it had been three months since you made her acquaintance.''

''I'm not delighted to see her again,'' Evan said, in a loud whisper. ''I'm in the middle of a very important, high-profile case that is about to go to trial, if you'll recall, and I don't have time for this documentary stuff.''

But here comes Jennifer Anderson, he thought. She was getting closer, and closer and...

Jennifer covered the remaining twenty feet separating her from Evan, then stopped, immediately switching her gaze to his secretary.

''Hello, Belinda. How are you?''

''Fine, just fine. And you?''

I'm falling apart by inches, Belinda, Jennifer thought. *I didn't know it would be this difficult to see Evan again but...*

''Hello, Jennifer,'' Evan said quietly.

Jennifer drew a steadying breath that she hoped wasn't noticeable, then slowly turned her head to meet Evan's gaze.

''Evan,'' she said, hating the squeaky little noise that was passing itself off as her voice.

''Did you want to see me?''

''Yes, if you're free,'' she managed to say.

''Come in,'' he said, stepping back. ''Belinda, please hold my calls.''

''You betcha, boss. Just close that door and I'll

make certain that no one disturbs the two of you…sir.''

''You can be replaced, you know,'' Evan said, pointing a finger at her.

''Don't be silly. You couldn't run this office without me. Go right on in, Jennifer.''

Jennifer walked past Evan, catching the faint aroma of his woodsy aftershave. She heard him close the door behind him, the quiet click seeming more like an explosion. Sinking gratefully onto one of the chairs facing Evan's desk, she crossed her legs, squared her shoulders and lifted her chin.

Evan went around the desk and sat down on the butter-soft leather chair. His office was large, boasting a wall of floor-to-ceiling windows. Bookcases lined another wall and a grouping of a love seat and two easy chairs was off to one side.

How was it possible, he thought, that Jennifer was even more lovely now than she had been three months ago before she left for California on that assignment?

Her shoulder-length black hair seemed to glisten, those incredible green eyes were sparkling emeralds, and there was a radiance about her, a glow, or some such thing. *Oh, for crying out loud, Stone, knock it off.*

''I hear you've been busy around here,'' Evan said, breaking the heavy silence that had fallen.

''Yes. Yes, I have.'' Jennifer nodded. ''Sticks and

I...Sticks is my cameraman...have filmed a great deal of footage here in the courthouse and over at the police station. Everyone has been very cooperative, which certainly makes my job easier. Yes, it certainly does.

"We filmed the empty courtroom downstairs where the case you're taking to trial soon will be held. I thought that might have a dramatic effect. You know, show the empty jury seats, the judge's bench, the table where the defendant will sit, what have you, with an over-voice to emphasize that while that room is silent now it will soon hold many people and a man's future will be decided within those four walls.

"I must say, Evan, that you certainly granted my request and then some. Do you remember me saying it would add a real punch to my documentary if you were involved in a high-profile case by the time I got here? And bingo...they don't get bigger than the Gardner case. Chicago is buzzing about it. You can't pick up a newspaper or catch the news on television without hearing about...I think I'm babbling."

"I think you are, too. Are you uncomfortable seeing me again, Jennifer?"

"Are you uncomfortable seeing *me?*"

"I asked you first." Evan frowned and shook his head. "That sounded like something a kid in elementary school would say."

"All right, yes," Jennifer said, averting her gaze

and picking an imaginary thread from her slacks. "I'm a tad nervous about seeing you again, Evan, because there's no erasing what happened between us, what should *not* have happened. I just don't want you to think that I make a practice of... There's no point in discussing this."

"No, there isn't any point in discussing it. Except I want you to know that I certainly don't think less of you because of what took place. My behavior was out of character for me, too. Let's agree that our mutual respect is still intact."

"My, my," Jennifer said, an edge to her voice, "aren't we just so civilized and sophisticated? We made a mistake but, hey, it's old news so forget it."

Evan frowned. "What would you have me say?"

"I'm sorry." Jennifer sighed. "It's just not an easy subject for me to discuss. What you said was fine, very nice, and I appreciate it." She paused. "Let's get on with why I'm here, shall we?"

"Yes, here you are," Evan said, "and the fact that I *am* in the midst of a high-profile case prompts me to ask you to finish your documentary after the Gardner trial is completed."

"What?" Jennifer said, leaning forward. "You've got to be kidding."

"Look," Evan said, folding his arms on the top of the desk, "I'm putting in very long, high-stress days getting ready for this trial. The last thing I need is a camera in my face and you taking notes, or recording, every little thing I do and say.''

"But…"

"Let me finish," he said, raising one hand. "I know that you and I agreed that I had final approval on the documentary before it's aired. Dandy. But in the meantime you and this Sticks guy might hear something that could demolish my case if it got out. I don't want to run that kind of risk.''

"You don't trust me?" Jennifer said, splaying one hand on her chest, then slouching back in the chair. "That's insulting, it really is. I'm a professional, Evan, not some kid who has just been assigned her first story to cover. Give me some credit here.''

"I'm not saying I don't trust you," he said, his voice rising. "But slip-ups happen. You and your cameraman might be discussing something you filmed in this office and it could be overheard by the wrong person. I repeat…I don't want to run that kind of risk.''

"It's true, isn't it?" Jennifer said. "What the papers and anchormen are reporting. You have a shaky case against Lyle Gardner, circumstantial evidence that you somehow have to convince a jury is enough to convict him of killing his brother. If you had a heavy-duty, solid case against him, you wouldn't be so concerned about loose lips sinking ships, or however that goes.''

"Hell, what do you want from me?" Evan said. "Do you think I'm going to allow you to film me saying something like 'This is a weak case with a bunch of circumstantial evidence, but if I get lucky I can still send the bum up the river'? Give me a break. And for heaven's sake keep what I just said confidential. I'm going with 'no comment' with all reporters who snag me regarding the evidence I have against Lyle Gardner. I'm attempting to give the impression that I have more than I do, Jennifer.

"I can count on one hand the number of people who know the details of my case against Gardner. I sure as hell don't feel like adding a photojournalist and a cameraman to that list."

"Well, I'm afraid you don't have any choice in the matter, Mr. Stone," Jennifer said, narrowing her eyes. "I'm here to do my job and you'll just have to trust me, like it or not. If you think you can put me on the back burner until this trial is over, why don't you call the mayor and tell him that you're going to change a dynamite documentary into vanilla pudding.

"Go ahead. Pick up the telephone and call him. Maybe he'll order us to go out to dinner and settle our differences like he did three months ago and…" Jennifer's voice trailed off, and a warm flush crept onto her cheeks.

"And we not only settled our differences about the documentary," Evan said quietly, looking directly at her, "we ended the evening by making love."

"Yes. Well. We agreed not to discuss that further at this point."

"Meaning there will be a point that we'll discuss it further?" Evan said, raising his eyebrows.

"Don't push me, Evan. I am not going to postpone finishing this documentary until after the Gardner trial. That's it. Bottom line."

"You," Evan said, pointing a finger at her, "are a pain in the neck."

"And you," Jennifer shot back, "are being rude. Evan, you were hopping mad three months ago that any kind of documentary was going to be done about you and this office. The mayor wants this film for positive public relations.

"You and I compromised back then with my agreeing to allow you to give final approval on the film, and you agreed to cooperate when I returned from California and got rolling on this. You can't change your mind about the whole thing now." Jennifer paused. "We're not doing very well here."

Evan sighed and ran one hand over the back of his neck. "No, we're not, and you're holding all the cards. If I talk to the mayor about postponing your being here, he'll blow a fuse. I'm stuck with you."

"That," Jennifer said, jumping to her feet, "is the most demeaning thing I have ever heard and…

Whew.'' She pressed one hand to her forehead and sank back onto the chair.

''What's wrong?'' Evan said, rising and coming around the front of the desk. ''You're white as a sheet all of a sudden.''

''I just got up too fast, that's all. I was dizzy for a second there, but I'm fine now.''

''Do you want a glass of water? Some soda? Orange juice?''

''No, no,'' she said, waving one hand in the air. ''I'm okay. Really. You can go back and sit down in your chair now. I don't need you hovering over me like you are. So close…and…hovering…like that.''

''I suppose you know,'' Evan said, still hovering, ''that the sweater you're wearing matches your eyes to perfection.'' He nodded. ''Of course, you do.''

''Is that a crime?'' she said, glaring at him. ''Are you going to arrest me?''

''No, but you reap what you sow. Pick the sweater, pay the price.''

And with that, Evan gripped Jennifer's upper arms, hauled her to her feet and kissed her.

Jennifer's eyes widened in shock, then in the next instant her lashes drifted down and she wrapped her arms around Evan's back and returned the searing kiss in total abandonment.

Oh, dear heaven, she thought, she'd been waiting three long months for this. For Evan. She remembered every exquisite detail, every overwhelming sensation, of making love with Evan Stone. It had been like nothing she had ever experienced before and...

But it had been wrong, wrong, wrong, should not have taken place. They'd only known each other for a handful of hours back then and...

Evan raised his head a fraction of an inch to draw a rough breath, then slanted his mouth in the opposite direction and captured Jennifer's lips once again, drinking in the taste of her, savoring.

Three months, his mind hummed. An eternity, that's what it had been, waiting for this kiss. But he wanted more. He wanted to make love with Jennifer again. Now. Right now.

Ah, hell. They had been near-strangers when they'd made love, should never have let things go that far, so out of control, and here he was again, falling under Jennifer's spell and... No.

Evan broke the kiss, inched Jennifer away from his aroused body, then lowered her back onto her chair. She blinked, shook her head slightly, then took a wobbly breath.

''Oh...my...goodness,'' she said.

Evan marched around his desk, sank onto the chair, and dragged both hands down his face.

''That was dumb,'' he said, his voice gritty with passion. ''Really stupid. And it won't happen again.''

Well, phooey, Jennifer thought, rather hazily, why not? That kiss had been sensational, absolutely wonderful. Oh, Jennifer, get it together. It was wrong, wrong, wrong.

"We're going to be working very closely together during the next couple of weeks," Evan said, "and I can't afford to be distracted from having total concentration on this pending trial. Is that clear? Therefore, I'm going to do everything within my power to pretend you aren't there, close, next to me and... Are you getting this? As far as I'm concerned you'll be invisible."

"I..."

"And one other thing," he went on. "Don't wear that sweater again."

"Oh, for Pete's sake," Jennifer said, rolling her eyes heavenward. "This is ridiculous."

"No. This is dangerous. You took part in those kisses we just shared, Jennifer. Totally. This... whatever it is...between us didn't diminish in the time we've been apart. But I cannot, and will not, allow anything, or anyone, to keep me from concentrating fully on this case."

"No, of course, not. I understand." Jennifer nodded. "You really believe that Lyle Gardner is guilty of killing his brother, don't you? And you're worried that you won't be able to prove it with the evidence you have. This is me, Jennifer, asking you this, Evan, not Jennifer Anderson the film journalist.''

Evan hesitated a moment, then nodded. ''Yes, I'm worried that Gardner is going to get off.''

''But everyone I've interviewed for the film believes that he's guilty. I spoke with those two detectives who handled the case. Colin Waters and Darien Wilson, right? They are both adamant about Lyle Gardner's guilt.

''I also interviewed Maggie Sutter, who gathered forensic evidence at the scene for the investigation. She's convinced that Lyle killed his younger brother but…''

''But we're missing the last piece to the puzzle,'' Evan said wearily. ''The evidence that would make it possible for me to feel confident I can get a guilty verdict from the jury. We're not giving up. Waters and Wilson are putting in grueling days trying to find what we need, and I'm going over every shred of evidence we do have, time and again.''

''You all must be exhausted.''

''We are, but there's no getting around the fact that all the defense has to do is establish reasonable doubt, while I have to prove *without* a doubt that he did it. If I can't do that, he walks. Lyle Gardner will stroll out of that courtroom a free man and he's guilty as sin. I know it. I feel it. I'm just not certain that I can prove it.''

Chapter 2

That evening Jennifer sat curled up in the corner of the sofa in her apartment with a mug of hot tea. Her hair was still damp from a long, soothing shower and she was wearing her favorite old chenille robe that had once been a bright blue but was now a rather faded, dingy gray.

Her notebook was propped on the arm of the sofa and she was transferring her notes onto the legal pad on her lap, adding more details and impressions.

No wonder Evan was concerned about the outcome of the trial that was rapidly approaching, she thought, staring into space. The case was complex with a myriad of players in the drama.

And no wonder the press was everywhere, hoping

for any details they could add to their daily reports to the public. The Gardner family, one of the icons of Chicago, had been toppled in a wave of scandalous disgrace to the delight of the sensation-seeking citizens of the windy city.

The murdered man, Franklin Gardner, had been a highly visible member of the socially prominent and civic-minded family. Franklin, along with his brother Lyle and mother Cecelia, were continually lauded for their generous donations of time and money as they supported fund-raising events for a multitude of charities.

"The mighty have fallen," Jennifer said aloud.

And in disgrace, she mentally tacked on. The investigation of Franklin's murder had revealed a dark side to the man. He'd been involved in a horrendous operation that kidnapped pretty young girls and sold them to an overseas prostitution ring.

"Unbelievable," Jennifer whispered, then flipped to the next page in the notebook.

How diabolically slick the whole thing had been, she mused. Gardner money helped support halfway houses and shelters in the city that Franklin often and understandably visited on behalf of his family.

It was there that he selected his victims, then arranged for Desmond Reicher, a business associate, to proposition the girls and bring them to the buyer. Franklin made certain that he selected only runaways, which resulted in the belief that the girls had once again decided to disappear.

Reicher had been arrested, was considered a flight risk and was in jail with no bail granted as he awaited trial. He adamantly denied any guilt in the murder of Franklin Gardner, and the detectives on the case believed him. Why would Reicher kill the golden goose in the form of Franklin Gardner? Without Franklin, Reicher's steady stream of money would be cut off. No, Desmond Reicher had not killed Franklin Gardner.

The detectives had shifted their attention to Lyle, Franklin's older brother. His alibi at the time of the murder was flimsy…he was home alone watching television. Also, the medical examiner had determined that Franklin had been murdered by someone who was left-handed. Lyle was left-handed. Reicher was right-handed.

The detectives were also going on their gut instincts, feeling the smiling, albeit haughty facade that Lyle presented was phony, covering up the truth he refused to reveal.

They didn't believe for one second that Lyle was surprised and devastated by the brutal death of his brother and the truth of what Franklin had been involved in.

The autopsy of Franklin's body had shown that in addition to stab wounds, apparently from an ice pick, Franklin had also received blows to his face.

The bruises there indicated that he had been struck by a fist where a heavy signet ring was worn. His actual death had been caused by a blow to the back of his head when he'd fallen and struck it on the edge of a table.

It had come to light that Lyle Gardner wore such a signet ring. He claimed he must have lost it somewhere because he couldn't find it. Nor had a police search of his home and office turned up the ring.

The detectives believed that Lyle learned of his brother's activities, confronted him, and the pair came to blows. The wounds from the ice pick had been administered after Franklin was dead to give the impression that a botched burglary had taken place. Lyle had taken a few valuable items from the apartment to further that theory and had disposed of the incriminating ring.

"Oh, dear," Jennifer said to herself, shaking her head. "It really is very circumstantial evidence. No wonder Evan is so worried about proving that Lyle killed his brother."

Evan had a rough road to go, Jennifer thought as she set aside her work and sipped her tea. He looked so tired, thoroughly exhausted, and Belinda had told Jennifer that Evan was putting in very long days at the office as he prepared to go to trial.

Jennifer glanced at the cuckoo clock on the wall and saw that it was nearly ten o'clock.

Was Evan still in his office at the courthouse? she

wondered, poring over every scrap of evidence he had. What a lonely picture that painted in her mind. Evan would be in a small circle of light with total darkness and heavy silence beyond it. All alone. Thinking of nothing but the case he was determined to win. How stark, narrow and empty that was as it flitted across her mind's eye.

But that was *her* reaction to the scenario she was creating. It might seem bleak and lonely to her, but to Evan? His career was his world, the focus of his existence. If he *was* still at the office he was probably relieved that everyone else had gone home so he could work in peace with no chance of being interrupted.

The telephone on the end table shrilled, causing Jennifer to nearly jump off the sofa from the sudden noise.

Who on earth would be calling at this hour? she thought, staring at the phone that continued to ring. She snatched up the receiver.

"Hello?"

"Jennifer? Evan."

Jennifer's eyes widened. He'd read her mind. From wherever he was he'd peered into her brain, knew she'd been thinking about him. He… Oh, for Pete's sake, Jennifer, you're totally losing it.

"Jennifer?"

"What? Oh, yes, I'm here, Evan."

"I hope I didn't wake you."

"No, no, I was working on my notes and… Where are you?"

"At the office."

Of course he was, she thought. That was his favorite place to be. His home away from home, or some such depressing thing.

"And you called me because?"

"I'm going to stop off at Franklin Gardner's apartment tomorrow morning before I come in here to the office. Your cameraman…what's his name? Slates?"

"Sticks. He's very tall and thin and has long legs, and he goes by the name of Sticks."

"Whatever. Sticks can film the building from the outside, but the apartment itself is still considered a crime scene and he can't go in there. I'll take you inside with me, but no footage is to be filmed."

"All right. Sticks can go by there whenever and get what he needs from in front or across the street." She paused. "Why are you…we…going to the scene of the crime now?"

"I don't know," Evan said, sounding very weary. "I was called the night it happened because of the fact that a high-profile Gardner had been murdered, but I would have been in the way if I'd gone over then.

"I went the next morning so I would have a clear picture of things in my mind. Now? I'm just retracing my steps, going over everything again with a fine-tooth comb. I want to walk through those rooms once more. I figured I'd better include you in on this, or you'd pitch a fit.''

"My, my, how can I pass up such a warm fuzzy invitation to accompany you, Mr. Stone? I wouldn't miss it for the world.''

"I'm sorry,'' Evan said, then chuckled.

A funny little flutter whispered down Jennifer's spine as she heard that oh-so-sexy sound.

"I didn't phrase that very well, did I? Chalk it up to the fact that I'm so tired I'm punchy. But be honest, Jennifer, wouldn't you have pitched a fit if I went there in the morning and told you about it later?''

Jennifer laughed in spite of herself. "Yes, I certainly would have. I'm supposed to be documenting your every little move, you know.''

"Believe me, I'm aware of that. Do you know where Gardner's apartment building is?''

"Yes, I have the address in my notes.''

"Okay. Eight o'clock tomorrow morning. I'll meet you in the lobby of the building.'' Evan paused a moment. "What are you wearing right now?''

"Pardon me?'' Jennifer said, sitting up straighter.

"I'm sitting here having put in such a long day that I feel like I've been in this suit for three weeks. I just wondered what someone who is home, relaxing, probably about to go to bed…is wearing.''

Jennifer glanced down at her less-than-fashionable robe.

"Am I allowed to lie?"

"Nope."

"Well, darn. After a sinfully long shower I donned my favorite robe which is older than dirt and looks like it was given to me by a bag lady who decided it was too decrepit to be seen in."

"Sexy, huh?"

"To the max," Jennifer said, smiling.

"What color is this fashion statement?"

"I don't think this faded shade really has a name beyond blah."

"Got it. Okay, nice long, soothing shower, security-blanket type comfy robe and... Hmm... you're curled up in the corner of the sofa with a drink. Something warm on this chilly night. Coffee? Hot chocolate? No, tea, I think. Yes, you're having a cup of tea, maybe one of those fancy flavored kind."

"You're amazing," Jennifer said, smiling. "The tea is cinnamon. Caffeine-free. How did you know all that, Evan?"

"I'm not sure. I'm just picturing you in my mind and what I said fits. I guess I know you better than either of us realized. Where did you think I was when you asked me?"

"At the office."

"Bingo. I rest my case. It's rather interesting."

"Disconcerting is closer to the mark. We really *don't* know each other very well, but we just somehow knew... Definitely disconcerting."

"Oh, I don't know. I think it's kind of...nice. Very nice, in fact." Evan paused. "Well, I guess I'll call it day, or a night as the case may be, and head on home. It was nice...there's that word again...chatting with you, sweet Jenny. Sleep well and I'll meet up with you in the morning. Good night."

"Good night, Evan," Jennifer said softly.

She replaced the receiver, then smiled. "Very, *very* nice."

Evan continued to hold the receiver until a shrill buzzing noise emanated from it, announcing it had been off the hook too long. He slid it onto the base, then leaned back in his chair, laced his fingers behind his head and stared up at the ceiling.

Sweet, sweet Jenny, he thought. All he had intended to do when he telephoned her was set up the meeting in the morning at the apartment building where Gardner had been killed.

But once he'd started talking to Jennifer he hadn't wished to stop. The "what are you wearing" bit must have sounded corny as hell, but he'd sincerely wanted to know so he could complete the image of her in his mind's eye. At least he hadn't gone so far as to ask what she had on beneath the soft, old robe. That would have been *really* pushing it.

Evan glanced around, unable to see anything in the darkness beyond the circle of light cast by the lamp on his desk.

And there he sat, he mused, in a chilly office. He was attempting to begin the first draft of his opening statement to the jury for the Gardner trial.

He preferred to write his opening and closing arguments in longhand rather than on the computer, and his trash can was filled to overflowing with wadded-up sheets of paper, each holding a handful of words that he'd rejected the minute he'd written them.

"I've had it for today," he said aloud, getting to his feet. "Drag it on home, Stone."

Home, he thought, as he flicked off the lamp, then made his way cautiously toward the door in the inky darkness. Yeah, his expensive apartment was his home, he supposed, but it wasn't *homey* the way Jennifer's was. His was just *there*, a place to sleep, eat once in a while, shower, shave, change clothes. It wasn't warm and inviting, didn't wrap itself around him with comfort to ease his stress. It was just some walls, floors, ceilings that meant he didn't have to sleep in his vehicle.

Maybe it took a woman to add that homey touch, he thought as he locked his office door. Maybe the average man wasn't capable of doing such a thing. Or maybe it was just him who lacked that ability.

No, it was the fact that there weren't enough hours in the day to accomplish everything he might wish to do.

First priority was his role of district attorney and the responsibilities that title produced. He was determined to be the very best D.A. he was capable of being, even if it meant he had little else in his life, such as turning his apartment into a homey haven, or being in a relationship with a special woman.

But what would it be like, he wondered, as he rode down in the elevator, to know that someone like Jennifer... No, if Jennifer herself was waiting for him to come through the door? Fresh from her shower, clad in her funky robe, a smile would light up her face, she'd rush into his arms which would make him forget instantly that he was weary to the bone. He'd kiss her for a long, heart-stopping time, then...

"Shut up, Stone," he admonished himself, as he got into his vehicle in the parking garage. "Sleep, I need lots of sleep."

But first thing tomorrow morning, he mused, as he merged into the traffic, he'd meet up with sweet Jenny Anderson. And that was very...well...nice.

Hours later Jennifer tossed back the blankets on the bed and reached for her robe.

She couldn't stay in that bed a second longer, she thought, starting toward the bedroom door. She was doing nothing more than tossing and turning, and definitely not getting the sleep she needed. Hopefully a mug of hot milk would relax her and allow her to drift off into blissful slumber.

A short time later Jennifer was once again curled up in the corner of the sofa, her legs tucked next to her, the mug of steaming milk cradled in both hands. She blew on the hot liquid and took a sip.

Her insomnia was Evan Stone's fault, she decided. He had telephoned her just before she went to bed and, therefore, she'd taken the image of him and the sound of his voice right along with her as she'd snuggled under the blankets. Definitely his fault. And she sounded like a grumpy three-year-old in need of a nap.

Her whatever-it-was with Evan was so complicated and confusing. She was attracted to him, which was putting it mildly, melted like soupy ice cream on a summer day when he took her into his arms and kissed her. He was inching his way into her heart, staking a claim that he wasn't even interested in possessing.

Evan had referred to what they had shared three months ago on that fateful night as making love. Did he really feel that way about it, or was he just being polite and refraining from referring to it as one-night-stand sex, plain old tacky sex in its purest form?

No, it had been more than that. Their joining had been wondrous, exquisitely beautiful, so intense and meaningful and…and nothing could erase the fact that they'd gone to bed together after knowing each other for a few hours, the majority of which had been spent arguing like cats and dogs about the filming of the documentary.

She'd do well to just forget about that night as Evan apparently intended to do. Chalk it up as poor judgment, and a rather immature lack of control. Her behavior that night had been very, very out of character. That theory was just dandy, but there were extenuating circumstances that made it impossible to *ever* forget what she had shared with Evan Stone.

That night had changed her life for all time.

Because she was pregnant with Evan's baby.

Jennifer set the mug on the end table then put her hands on her stomach.

Oh, my, she thought, a baby. She was carrying Evan Stone's baby. She'd repeated that message so many times in her mind in the past few weeks until she really believed at last that it was true.

She was thrilled, so happy that she wept at the drop of a hat, which was partly due to wacky hormones at this point, she supposed.

But the daddy in this scenario? Oh, heavens, she didn't even want to think about what Evan's reaction to her baby bulletin would be. He was dedicated to his career, totally focused on his role of district attorney. No, Evan was not going to beam with delight when she told him she was pregnant.

Which was why, Jennifer thought, staring into space, she was going to keep this pregnancy a secret for as long as possible. Yes, a man had the right to know that he had a child on the way, but she wasn't prepared, not yet, to tarnish the pure joy she was feeling with what could be a very nasty and angry response on the part of Evan Stone.

She worked continually with men who put their careers first, was aware of the long hours they were away from home with little, or no, thought given to their wife and children waiting for them. Their families seemed very low on the list of what was important to them. No, Evan would not be happy when he heard her news.

"It takes two to get into this situation, buster," Jennifer said, narrowing her eyes.

That, no doubt, was what she'd fling at Evan if he accused her of being careless, for not considering birth control the night they had been together. Well, he hadn't brought up the dicey subject, either, by golly. He'd have to admit that, no matter how upset he might be.

But taking equal responsibility for the creation of this little one wouldn't make Evan want this baby, wouldn't send him racing off to buy cigars so he'd be ready for the big day that he was ecstatic about.

Evan might tell her that she would hear from his attorney regarding child support payments because he was an honorable man who would provide for his child, but he wanted no part of the role of father to their baby. He didn't have the time, nor the desire, to do so.

Oh, what a depressing thought.

"It's just you and me, kiddo," Jennifer said, patting her stomach, then sniffling. "And maybe a weekend father. But he might not even want to take on *that* role. I'm so sorry..." she sniffled again "...just so sorry, little darling. Your daddy is magnificent but he isn't mine, or ours. But we'll be fine, just the two of us. Fine and dandy. You'll see."

Jennifer picked up the mug of milk, then plunked it back down when she saw the scummy film on the top of the now-cool liquid. She took a wadded tissue from the pocket of her robe and dabbed at her nose.

She was *not* going to cry, she told herself. She was tired, so very tired, and she was on emotional overload from talking on the telephone with Evan earlier and from being with him in his office after not seeing him for three months. There she had sat, knowing she was carrying his child while he glared at her and grumpily said he guessed he was stuck with her for the duration of the filming of her documentary. What a crummy thing for him to have said, the rotten bum.

"And I think I'm falling in love with him," Jennifer wailed. "Oh, I'm a wreck, a complete wreck."

She got to her feet and stomped down the hall to her bedroom. Exhaustion claimed her, and she was asleep within moments of climbing into the beckoning bed.

The building where Franklin Gardner's penthouse apartment took up the entire thirty-fifth floor was in the prestigious Gold Coast area of Chicago. It was cream-colored stone with an expensive brown tint added to the windows that caused a golden hue to be reflected when the sun shone on the structure, as though it was constantly reminding the general public that it took wealth to live within its walls.

At eight o'clock the next morning Jennifer arrived at the building and Evan pushed open the door to the lushly decorated lobby to allow her to enter.

"Good morning, Evan," Jennifer said, smiling. "Gracious, I think this lobby is bigger than my entire apartment."

"Let's get upstairs," Evan said, then frowned. "You look pale, Jennifer."

You would, too, she thought, if you'd been tossing your cookies since 5:00 a.m. Her doctor had said that the morning sickness should end any time now.

As far as she, wobbly-tummy Jennifer was concerned, it couldn't happen quick enough to suit her.

"Pale? Me?" she said. "I had a little problem
with getting to sleep last night, but I'm fine."

"If you say so," Evan said, then started across
the lobby.

When they reached the elevators a uniformed police officer was standing by one elevator set apart
from the others. Evan nodded at him as he and Jennifer stepped into the elevator. There was only one
button on the panel and Evan pushed it.

"This is a private elevator for the penthouse?"
Jennifer said. "Impressive."

The doors swished closed and the elevator began
its ascent.

"Yep," Evan said. "This one only goes to the
penthouse. It normally requires a special key, but
we're making it accessible to our people with no
hassle."

The elevator bumped to a stop and the doors slid
silently open.

"Oh, my," Jennifer said, as she stepped forward.
"No wonder a private elevator is needed. We're actually standing in the foyer to the penthouse itself.
The elevator is the front door, per se. Mmm. So this
is how the other half lives in Chicago, the haves
versus us have-not working stiffs."

"Right," Evan said, frowning, "but the Gardner
family money wasn't enough for greedy Franklin.

He had to have more. So the slime sets up a racket of kidnapping girls no one would miss and selling them to prostitution rings in foreign countries. Unbelievable. The Gardner name has been held in high regard in this city for many, many years and now it's tarnished beyond repair.''

They entered the enormous living room, then Jennifer followed Evan across the richly furnished expanse to a room on the opposite side. A chalk outline of a body was visible on the carpet in what was obviously a study, or den, with floor-to-ceiling bookshelves.

''Well, Franklin paid the ultimate price for his greed,'' Jennifer said quietly, staring at the outline of the murdered man's body. ''It's probably terrible of me to say this, Evan, but with Franklin Gardner dead we can at least know that a great many young girls have been saved from a horrible existence.''

''That thought has occurred to me more than once.'' Evan nodded. ''Franklin paid the piper, big-time. But even though he was an evil, heartless man, his killer can't go unpunished. No one has the right to get away with what happened in this room, to take the life of another human being. Lyle is going to pay his dues, too.''

Jennifer placed one hand on Evan's arm. ''You'll get your conviction, Evan, I know you will.''

''Will I? I need more evidence than what I have, Jennifer. The detectives working this case and I are convinced that the bruises were caused by the signet ring that Lyle always wore. A ring, he claims, he lost. Damn, we need that ring, but it's nowhere to be found. The detectives are still looking for it but…'' He shook his head.

''Are you here this morning to search for it again?''

''No, this place has been gone over inch by inch. The ring isn't here. There's no real purpose to be served by my being here. I just wanted to connect with the whole event again, try to imagine it in my mind as it unfolded that night. I suppose you could put in your documentary that the district attorney wasted taxpayer money by returning to the scene of the crime for no plausible reason.''

''I wouldn't do that. If you feel the need to be here, then here you should be. It's sort of creepy though to be standing here realizing that a man was murdered by his own brother in this very room. It's too bad you can't bring the jury here, let them see this, feel the evil vibes in here.''

''The judge would never go for that.''

''I suppose not.'' Jennifer paused. ''Can you imagine what Cecelia Gardner must be going through? One of her sons is dead and the other one is accused of his murder. Her world as she knew it is destroyed. Her heart must be breaking.''

''I don't know about that,'' Evan said, starting to wander slowly around the room. ''From what I hear, there are mixed opinions about whether Cecelia Gardner even *has* a heart. Oh, she's considered the grande dame of Chicago society and makes certain her picture is in the newspaper whenever possible in connection with charity events she sponsors. But she's a tough old gal who is used to having her own way.

"She went all the way to the top, to the governor, to attempt to get Lyle released on bail. He refused but Cecelia managed to rattle some cages, get some very pithy quotes in the paper about the need for a new governor, new mayor, a new district attorney, and a complete overhaul of the police department."

"She wanted you fired?"

"Oh, yeah," Evan said, smiling. "I said we had enough evidence against Lyle to go to trial. The lady is after my hide. Belinda knows to never put through any call to me from Cecelia Gardner. I have neither the time, nor the patience to deal with her."

"It's probably the first time in her life that her money and social standing haven't gotten her what she wants. She doesn't sound like a pleasant person, but a part of me can't help but think about the fact that she's a mother who might very well lose *both* of her sons. What a chilling thought."

Evan turned to look at Jennifer. "You *sound* like a mother right now. You're taking Cecelia's actions to a place I hadn't even thought of, but one that a mother would understand. It doesn't make me particularly like the uppity woman any more than I did before, but it does show me another layer to her that I hadn't considered. It doesn't have anything to do with Lyle's trial though, if you stop and think about it.''

"I realize that."

"Strange. You haven't even met the woman, yet you immediately jumped to her role of mother and what she might be feeling in that arena."

Because I'm going to *be* a mother, Evan, Jennifer's mind yelled. She was already so fiercely protective of the baby she carried that it startled her at times. Well, she wasn't going to open her mouth and announce that little tidbit to Evan Stone.

"It's a woman thing," Jennifer said breezily.

"Oh," Evan said, chuckling, "I see. There are a whole bunch of those woman things that men can give up on ever understanding. Women are very complicated creatures."

Jennifer smiled. "Give me one example of what you perceive to be a woman thing."

"Okay, but let's get out of this study. You're right about the nasty vibes in this room."

Back in the living room Evan commented on the fantastic view of Lake Michigan and Lincoln Park from the wall of windows on the far side of the room.

"Postcard-perfect picture, and you're stalling," Jennifer said, folding her arms beneath her breasts.

"You're right." Evan laughed. "Okay, okay, give me a minute here." He ran one hand over his chin. "A woman thing. I got one. When I was in high school I walked into the room just as my mother asked my father if he still loved her. He lowered the newspaper he was reading in his favorite chair, looked at my mom like she was nuts and said 'I'm still here, aren't I?' I can remember nodding and heading for my room, but my mother burst into tears."

"Well, of course, she did," Jennifer said, shifting her hands to her hips. "She needed to hear the actual words right then, at that very moment. She needed to hear your father say that he loved her."

"He thought he had," Evan said, shrugging, "with the answer he gave her."

"Oh-h-h...men," Jennifer said, rolling her eyes heavenward.

"That," Evan said, pointing one finger in the air, "was a fine example of a woman thing."

"You're right." Jennifer laughed. "You're absolutely right. You'd do well to remember that incident, Evan, because you may need that data at some point in your life. 'I'm still here, aren't I?' does not cut it when your wife asks if you still love her."

Evan closed the distance between them and looked directly into Jennifer's green eyes.

"I doubt that I'll ever need that information.

Maybe I will, someday, but I…'' He shook his head. ''With the hours I put in with this job I wouldn't even be in a position to blow it by saying that because I'd probably not be there the majority of the time.''

''It would depend on how badly you wanted a wife and family, I guess,'' Jennifer said, hardly above a whisper. ''Whether or not you loved someone enough to make changes, learn to delegate some of the workload and…. If the president of the United States can find time for his wife and children, then…I'm sorry. I'm overstepping. This is none of my business.''

''Isn't it?'' Evan said, still pinning her in place with his intense gaze. ''Aren't you as focused on your career as I am on mine?''

''Yes, at the moment I am.''

But things were going to be different once their baby was born, she thought. She had no intention of traveling all the time, or dragging in so exhausted late at night that she fell across her bed fully clothed and went to sleep. She'd find the proper balance between her role of mother and career woman. And wife? No, she wouldn't be a wife. Without even realizing he was doing it, Evan was making that fact crystal clear.

''What do you mean 'at the moment'?'' Evan said, pulling Jennifer from her thoughts.

"Nothing," she said, averting her eyes from his. "Could we leave? I don't like being in this place."

Evan glanced around. "Yes, I'm finished here without having accomplished a damn thing to help my case."

"You mustn't give up, Evan."

"I don't intend to. When I want something, sweet Jenny, I fight for it until the last bell rings. I don't admit defeat until it's popping me in the chops. When I really want something I hang in very tough to get it."

Well said, Jennifer thought, as they started across the room. If only Evan wanted to discover with that intensity what they might have together. If only he would be thrilled beyond measure when told she was carrying his baby. Pipe dreams, Jennifer. That's all that those are.

Chapter 3

Late that afternoon Evan sat in the leather chair behind the desk in his office and stared into space. For the umpteenth time since being in Franklin's penthouse the question he had asked Jennifer and the answer she had given echoed in his mind.

If a woman who appeared to be totally dedicated to her career implied that that was the status of her life now, *at the moment,* didn't that mean she might very well have a different focus planned for the future somewhere in her "it's a woman thing" mind?

Like…perhaps…maybe…Jennifer might, just might, wish to fall in love, marry, have a family? It made sense to him that that was what she had meant. And every time he centered on that thought, he was suffused with a strange and foreign warmth that started somewhere in the vicinity of his heart then traveled throughout him.

Evan shook his head in self-disgust.

He was really going off the deep end. He was rewriting the future script of Jennifer's life based on a statement she had made, then refused to elaborate on. For all he knew, she was saying she was tired of working so hard, planned to have more leisure time for herself between assignments to relax, party, date a multitude of men.

A cold knot tightened in Evan's stomach at the mental image he was painting of Jennifer dancing at a nightclub with a faceless man who was the recipient of Jennifer's sunshine smile. A man who would take her home, be invited in for coffee, then...

"If he touches her I'll..." Evan said, lunging to his feet, then glanced quickly at the door to be certain it was tightly closed.

He sank back onto his chair and sighed. It was a sigh that came from the very depths of his soul and took his heart along for the ride. It was a sigh of defeat, of having nowhere to hide from the truth.

He was slowly but surely falling in love with Jennifer Anderson.

And it was, without a doubt, the dumbest thing he had ever done in his entire life.

He didn't have *time* to be in love, to be half of a

whole, to do his part to nurture a relationship that would hopefully lead to marriage and babies. And there was no hint from her that she was in love with him, would consider making room in her life for a husband and children.

Yeah, sure, she cared for him, was attracted to him, responded to his kisses with no hesitation, and when they made love? Oh, man, when they made love….

"Don't go there, Stone," he said, as heat rocketed through his body.

He leaned his head on the top of the chair and closed his eyes.

What a mess, he thought. He was falling in love for the first time in his life and was losing his heart to a woman who was as dedicated to her career as he was to his. A woman who might very well take off for parts unknown to film her next documentary when she was finished with this one without a backward glance. A woman who cared for him, but wasn't in love with him, and who would have no problem walking out of his life and dismissing him from her mind.

While she was *dismissing* him, he would be *missing* her. Aching for her. Scrambling around to find the pieces of his shattered heart so he could hopefully glue it back together.

Damn it, why couldn't she be falling in love with him, just as he was with her?

"Oh, that's good," he muttered, not opening his eyes. "So mature. Make it all her fault that you're a miserable wreck, Stone."

Now that he thought about it, why would Jennifer fall in love with him? He'd made it clear to her that he had no room in his existence for a serious relationship. Someday, maybe, sure he might want a wife and kids, but now? Hey, he was the district attorney, worked twenty-four seven, which was exactly the way he liked it. He hadn't exactly presented himself as the catch of the year.

But he didn't have to put in the long, long hours he did to excel at this job. He had a top-notch staff of assistant district attorneys, paralegals, secretaries, research people, investigators. He could delegate so much of what he did on his own and not diminish one iota his dedication and purpose.

He could do that, *would* do that, if Jennifer actually loved him.

And that, he thought gloomily, was a pipe dream.

A knock at the door caused Evan to jerk upward in his chair.

"What!" he yelled.

The door was opened and Jennifer poked her head around the edge.

"Is it safe to come in? Or should I just throw you some raw meat? Belinda isn't at her desk, but she told Sticks earlier that you wanted to see me."

"Sorry I barked at you," Evan said, getting to his feet. "Yes, I do want to see you."

And hold you, Evan thought, and kiss you senseless, and make love to you for hours. There, walking toward him right now, was the only woman he had ever inched toward falling in love with. She was coming closer and closer, but she might as well be on the opposite side of the world for all the good her close proximity would do him. Ah, Jenny.

Jennifer sat down in one of the chairs opposite Evan's desk. He remained standing, looking at her intently.

"Do I have a ladybug on my nose?" she said. "Why are you staring and glaring at me?"

Evan sank onto his chair. "Sorry. My mind was off and running somewhere."

"You wanted to see me?" Jennifer prompted.

"I did?" Evan said, frowning. "Oh. Yes. I did. I do. And here you are. Good."

"Evan, for Pete's sake, what's wrong?" she said, matching his frown. "You're acting very strangely."

"Tired. I'm very, very tired, that's all." Evan cleared his throat. "Okay, here's the deal. We're running out of time as far as lightning striking, or some such thing, and producing some solid evidence against Lyle.

"To be more precise, we need the damnable ring he claims he lost and a way to prove he was wearing it when Franklin was murdered. That ring isn't suddenly going to drop into our laps so I'm going to have to go to trial next week with what I have."

"You'll get your conviction, Evan."

"I wish I had your confidence," he said, shaking his head. "Anyway, I'm going to spend the next two or three days reviewing information with the people who are going to testify for the prosecution. In all fairness to them I don't want you filming them coming in and out of here. Granted, the reporters will see that their pictures are splashed across the newspapers, but I don't think it's fair to expose them to further scrutiny in the documentary."

"I understand." Jennifer nodded.

"And it goes without saying, I'm sure, that a D.A. going over testimony with his witnesses is not meant for public review. So, what I'm saying here is that beyond maybe showing my closed office door and stating what is taking place in this office, there's nothing for you to do around here until the trial commences."

"Oh. Well. Yes, I guess you're right. Sticks and I will spend the time back at the studio viewing what we have so far and starting to edit the film."

"That sounds very…productive," Evan said, leaning forward and fiddling with a pen. "Because the mayor is so high on this documentary, you'll be allowed to film in the courtroom while the reporters are stuck taking notes and making do with artist drawings of various witnesses. You're not going to be very popular among the press, you know. Jealousy will rear its ugly head.''

Jennifer shrugged. ''I've been through that before. You wouldn't believe who I've been accused of sleeping with to get my coveted up close and personal coverage of various events.''

''The reporters might think you slept with the mayor?'' Evan said, his voice rising.

''Sure. Or the governor. Or…'' a warm flush crept over Jennifer's cheeks ''…you. Don't worry about it, Evan. I can handle whatever remarks the press may fling at me.''

''Not on my watch,'' Evan said, his jaw tightening. ''If any one of them hassles you, you let me know and I'll straighten them out, believe me.''

''And say what? That, yes, I slept with you, but it was the mayor who decreed that I should film the trial? That ought to make page one of the tabloids, if nothing else. Just stay out of it, Evan, and let me take care of it if it happens. You're supposed to be concentrating on the trial, not on me and whatever slings and arrows the press might decide to shoot my way.''

''It's not that easy. I care about you, for you. I can't stand the idea that you might be harassed because the mayor is calling the shots and…I want to protect you from that garbage, stand between you and harm's way and... Ah, hell.'' He tossed the pen to one side.

Damn it, Jennifer, he thought fiercely. *Don't you get it? Can't you see it? I'm falling in love with you.*

"That's...that's very sweet,'' she said, blinking back sudden and very unwelcomed tears. "And while it isn't necessary, I appreciate it, I really do.''

And it just makes me realize that I'm falling deeper and deeper in love with you, Evan, she thought miserably, so stop saying such beautiful things to me *please* before I dissolve into a puddle of tears.

Jennifer cleared her throat. "So, the witnesses you're seeing in the next few days will sit in this chair where I am now and you're there behind your desk and...I just want to be certain I have the details right. I might decide to shoot your office with no one in it, then explain what will transpire behind the closed door that would be shown next.''

"Actually, no. I use the conference room for this type of thing. I don't want to make my witnesses feel like they're in the principal's office with me looming over them from behind my desk.''

Jennifer frowned. "What conference room?''

"Follow me, ma'am,'' Evan said, getting to his feet.

They crossed the large room to a door on the far wall and entered an even bigger room that held a long table surrounded by chairs, a sofa and easy chair grouping, a small refrigerator and a multitude of filing cabinets and bookcases filled to overflowing. The table had a row of neatly stacked papers as well as several accordion files.

"This is impressive," Jennifer said, walking forward. "I didn't even know this room was here."

"This is where I get organized before a trial. Plus we have department meetings in here on a regular basis so the A.D.A.'s can bring me up to date on their cases. I go over testimony with witnesses in here because we can sit on the sofa and chairs, or whatever, and it's less intimidating."

Jennifer nodded. "Sticks and I will film this room with no one in it, then show the closed door. Okay?"

"That's fine." Evan paused. "You know, Jennifer, the first days of the trial will be spent on jury selection. Again, I'd like to protect the jurors' identities as far as the documentary goes, even though the press will be hovering around with cameras outside the courtroom."

"In other words, you don't want me filming during jury selection."

"No, and no footage of the jury once the trial begins."

"I have no problem with that, Evan," she said, turning to meet his gaze.

"Well, there is one problem with it."

"Such as?" she asked, raising her eyebrows.

Evan closed the distance between them and looked directly into her eyes.

"Well, if I'm tied up with witnesses for the next several days, including through the weekend, then the trial starts next week and jury selection takes place, that's a whole lot of time during which I won't see you. That's not good. Not good at all."

"It's not?" She smiled up at him.

"No, it's not," he said, matching her smile. "I've gotten used to you hanging around, so to speak. I'll be looking over my shoulder wondering where you are, which would be hazardous to my concentration."

"I see." Jennifer laughed. "Well, is there a solution to this dilemma?"

"Why don't we go out to dinner tonight and discuss it?"

"Well, I certainly want to do everything I possibly can to assist you, sir."

"Good. I'll pick you up at seven. Dress casually. I know a restaurant that serves the best steaks in town, but it's rustic. You know, wooden tables and benches, that sort of thing."

"Sounds like fun. Oh. Maybe we're not supposed to have fun while we're discussing details of this and that regarding this case."

"I won't tell, if you won't."

"My lips are sealed."

Evan's expression became serious and he drew

one thumb over Jennifer's lips, causing her to shiver at the sensual foray.

"Your lips," he said, his voice very deep and very rumbly, "are so kissable they should be declared against the law."

"So, arrest me," she said, hardly above a whisper.

"No, I'd rather..." he lowered his head toward Jennifer's "...much rather kiss those lips that are so..."

The hazy mist that was settling over them was shattered by the sound of Belinda's voice in Evan's office beyond the conference room.

"You don't have an appointment," Belinda said. "You can't just barge in here and..."

"I can and I am," a woman said. "Now where is Evan Stone? I don't intend to leave until I've spoken with him."

"What the hell..." Evan muttered, striding toward the door leading to his office.

Jennifer was right behind him.

"I'm sorry, Evan," Belinda said, throwing up her hands, "but she wouldn't listen to me and..."

"It's not your fault, Belinda. I'll take it from here."

"Thank goodness," Belinda said, stomping from the room and closing the door behind her.

"Mrs. Gardner," Evan said, "won't you have a seat?"

So this is Cecelia Gardner, Jennifer thought, the grande dame of Chicago society. Or she was until this scandal broke. This was Franklin and Lyle Gardner's mother. She was definitely an intimidating figure. Tall, thin, white hair swept up and couture clothes that suited her perfectly.

"You've been refusing to accept my calls," Cecelia said, sitting down opposite Evan's desk, "so I came in person." She swept her haughty gaze over Jennifer. "I'd prefer to speak with you privately, Mr. Stone."

Evan stepped forward and moved the second chair from in front of the desk to the side and away from Cecelia.

"I'm afraid that won't be possible. Ms. Anderson is filming a documentary on the inner workings of the D.A.'s office, per strict instructions from His Honor the mayor. Anything you say to me will be said in front of Jennifer." He looked at Jennifer. "Jenny? Your chair?"

Jennifer sank onto a chair, her eyes darting back and forth between Evan and Cecelia. The tension in the room was a nearly palpable entity. She studied Cecelia more intently, looking for the sorrow, the mother who had lost one son and had another facing charges of murdering his own brother. All she could see was anger flashing in Cecelia Gardner's icy blue eyes.

Evan sat down in the leather chair behind his

desk. "Now then, Mrs. Gardner, what can I do for you?"

"You can drop the charges against my son Lyle," she said, lifting her chin. "This trial is a travesty, part of a conspiracy carefully planned by those who are jealous of the social standing, wealth and power that my family possesses. The lies being told about Franklin now that he's no longer alive to defend himself are further proof of the evil forces who wish to diminish us. I won't stand for it."

Evan leaned back in his chair, crossed his arms over his chest, but didn't speak.

"The story in the newspapers," Cecelia went on, "relating that Franklin was involved in some sordid nonsense about young girls being sold into prostitution is ridiculous, and I plan to sue for slander, believe me. And as if that isn't enough, you have all gone on to accuse Lyle of murdering his own brother."

Evan nodded.

"Do you know, Mr. Stone," Cecelia said, her voice quivering with fury, "that I have been asked to resign from the governing board of six charities that I have helped establish and run for many years? Do you know that the name Gardner is to be removed from the shelters and halfway houses I worked tirelessly to put into operation? Do you have any idea what you have done to my reputation in this town?

"You will pay with your job, as will the mayor and governor. Yes, you will pay for what you've done. But you will first petition the court to drop all charges against Lyle so I can begin to reestablish my name and status to its proper place. Is that clear?"

"Dear heaven," Jennifer said, speaking aloud before she even realized she had done it, "where are your tears? Where is your grief for your dead son and for the other son who faces charges of taking his brother's life? What kind of mother are you, Mrs. Gardner? All you can think about is you, your wants and needs." She slid one hand protectively across her stomach. "Your...your baby boys, your babies are... Don't you care?"

"You have no concept of what is important in my level of society, young woman." Cecelia glared at Jennifer. "Respect for me, my name, my power and wealth must be reestablished before more damage is done.

"Once I have regained my proper standing, I will see to the clearing of Franklin's name and, in the meantime, Mr. Stone will drop the charges against Lyle so I don't have to be concerned about that. I *will* have the respect due me. That is first and foremost on my mind."

"Incredible," Jennifer whispered, as she stared at Cecelia.

"I trust we understand each other, Mr. Stone?"

Cecelia said, getting to her feet. "I doubt seriously that you intend to see your career destroyed over this nonsense. I expect Lyle to be released from jail before this day ends. I will also be looking for a public apology from you. A brief press conference should take care of that nicely. I will, in fact, be making a list of everyone who owes me an apology and I will see to it that they are forthcoming. I assume you have no questions regarding this matter?"

"Just one," Evan said, a steely edge to his voice.

"Yes?" Cecelia said.

"Do you plan to attend Lyle's trial," Evan said, "or just catch the highlights in the evening paper since you'll be so busy attempting to repair your status in Chicago's Gold Coast society? Can you fit witnessing your son convicted of murdering his only brother into your schedule, Mrs. Gardner?"

Cecelia Gardner narrowed her eyes. "You are finished in this town, Stone, and I will see to it that no one, *no one,* across the entire United States will hire you. You don't seem to comprehend who I am."

"I understand perfectly who *and* what you are," Evan said, "and I think it's very, very sad."

Cecelia squared her shoulders, then turned and crossed the room, leaving the door open as she left the office.

"If I hadn't seen it, heard it," Jennifer said, her voice quivering, "I wouldn't believe it. She's not a mother. She's not. How can a woman give birth to two sons and not be a mother?'' Two tears spilled onto her pale cheeks. ''She's horrible, Evan. Didn't she hold her babies in her arms, nurture them, sing to them, read them stories and...'' She shook her head. ''I'm sorry. I just...I'm sorry.''

''Hey,'' Evan said, getting to his feet and hunkering down next to Jennifer's chair. ''Ah, man, she really upset you, didn't she? I'm the one who is sorry, Jenny. I shouldn't have subjected you to that despicable woman.''

''No, no, it's not your fault. I'm overreacting,'' she said, swiping the tears from her cheeks, ''because...I'm...tired. Yes, that's it. I'm just tired.''

Evan slammed his hands onto his thighs, pushed himself to his feet and began to pace around the office. He dragged one hand through his thick, dark hair, a deep scowl on his face.

''Damn that Cecelia Gardner. I should have just called security and had her hauled out of here instead of allowing her to sound off.

''No, no, she's not a mother, not really. You're right about that, Jennifer. She might have gained the title by giving birth but she doesn't have a clue as to what it really means. She is the most selfish, self-centered...

''I'll tell you this, Jenny,'' Evan ranted on, as he continued his trek. ''I don't have one iota of experience in the role of father, parent, but I don't have to even think twice about how I would feel about my child, how I'd move heaven and earth to protect him, her, whatever. I'd put my life on the line for my son or daughter if it came to that. I would. Do you understand what I'm saying?''

Evan stopped in front of Jennifer and met her wide-eyed gaze.

''Yes, I'm listening, hearing, everything you're saying, Evan,'' she said, her voice still wobbly as fresh tears filled her eyes. ''I didn't realize you felt so passionately about being a father.''

''I didn't either until that witch came in here and did a fine job of show-and-tell of what a lousy parent is.'' Evan shook his head. ''That woman is...''

''Hello,'' Belinda said, rapping on the open door, then coming into the office. ''I was stuck on the phone when Cecelia Gardner stormed out of here. She was one furious lady, that's for sure.

''Jennifer? Oh, my dear, what's wrong? Why are you crying? And Evan? You look like you're ready to chew nails. Oh, gracious, Cecelia upset both of you, didn't she? What an awful person she is.''

''I should never have let her get on her rip,'' Evan said, taking a steadying breath.

''I overreacted to her, I guess,'' Jennifer said, then sniffled. ''I just assumed that Cecelia Gardner was a...a mother who was in pain, who was heartbroken over losing one son and standing helplessly by as she faced the truth that her other son killed his brother. I was wrong. Giving birth doesn't make a woman a mother. That title is earned, comes from the heart, from the love, from…'' Her voice trailed off and she shook her head.

"Damn straight it does," Evan said. "Cecelia Gardner isn't a mother, she's a social-climbing, power-hungry…"

"Watch your mouth now, Evan," Belinda said. "We get the point. Let's back up to why I came in here, besides wanting to know what happened with Cecelia, of course.

"This envelope was just delivered by a uniformed police officer, who actually ran down the hall to give it to me. It's from Detectives Waters and Wilson." She extended the interoffice envelope to Evan.

Evan took it and opened it so quickly he tore the flap off, then pulled out the contents, reading the enclosed note, then looking at the other piece beneath it.

"Yes!" he said, punching one fist in the air.

"What is it?" Belinda and Jennifer said in unison.

"Waters and Wilson are good, they are very, very good at what they do," Evan said. "All we had to go on as far as the description of the ring that Lyle wore when he beat up his brother was a rather blurry print from a newspaper photograph that showed Lyle wearing the ring.

"Then Maggie Sutter, a forensics detective, did an absolutely brilliant job of lifting an impression of what caused the bruises on Franklin Gardner's face. She determined that it was, indeed, a heavy signet ring with the letter *G* engraved on it.

"Now? Waters and Wilson contacted the Gardners' insurance company on the off chance that since the ring is valuable there was a picture of it on file there."

"And?" Belinda said.

"Here it is," Evan said, turning a photograph around to show Belinda and Jennifer. "A crystal-clear picture of that ring. This has got to help in locating the damn thing. It just has to." He reached for the telephone receiver. "I'm going to call those detectives and tell them what a fantastic job they did getting this."

"Evan, wait just one second, please. I know I said I'd go out to dinner with you this evening, but I'm going to take a rain check. I have a headache and I'm exhausted. The best place for me is home and early to bed."

"Are you sure?" he said, frowning as he released his hold on the telephone receiver. "You have to eat. We can make an early evening of it."

"No, I'll have some soup and toast. I'll come by tomorrow afternoon and see how things went with your witnesses. I must go. Bye."

Jennifer got to her feet, took one step forward, then gasped as a wave of dizziness swept over her.

She reached out blindly for the chair as black dots danced before her eyes.

"Evan, quick," Belinda said, "catch her. I think she's going to faint."

Evan closed the distance between himself and Jennifer and swept her into his arms just as she began to crumble.

"I'm...I'm fine," she said, blinking several times. "Evan, put me down. I'm fine. Just...just a little...dizzy and..."

"Take a deep breath, honey," Belinda said. "Slow and easy. I fainted a few times at the beginning of my first pregnancy, too. It's nothing serious, but you should tell your doctor about it. Your body is going through a great many changes right now and sometimes it just blinks out from the overload. Deep breath."

"What...did...you...say?" Evan said, looking at Belinda, Jennifer, then back to Belinda.

"I really don't want to be here right now," Jennifer said, then slumped against Evan's chest as everything went black.

Chapter 4

Jennifer wondered hazily why she was standing in the shower allowing icy cold water to cover her forehead and dribble down her face and along her neck. She frowned, opened her eyes, and found herself almost nose to nose with Belinda, who was pressing a wet paper towel to Jennifer's forehead.

"What…"

"Easy now," Belinda said, removing the soggy wad of paper. "You're all right. You fainted, but you were only out for a little bitsy time. Evan carried you in here to the conference room and you're on the sofa. Are you with me so far?

"I sent Evan off to bring his vehicle around to the front of the building so you won't have to traipse all the way through the parking garage before he can take you home.''

''Oh, but...'' Jennifer said, struggling to sit up.

''Stay,'' Belinda said, pushing her back gently to a prone position.

Belinda got to her feet, pulled a chair next to the sofa and settled onto it.

''I...'' Jennifer's eyes widened as she stared at Belinda. ''Oh, dear heaven, Belinda. I heard you say that you had fainted during your first pregnancy, *too,* meaning just the way I was fainting during my first pregnancy and...'' She covered her face with her hands. ''Oh-h-h, this is terrible. How did you know that I... Oh-h-h.''

Belinda lifted Jennifer's hands and placed them on her stomach.

''How did I know that you're pregnant?'' Belinda said. ''It's just a silly knack I've had forever. I can just...tell. You're going to have Evan's baby.''

''Your strange powers announce who the father is, too?'' Jennifer asked, frowning.

''No, of course not.'' Belinda laughed. ''That's just simple logic, for mercy sake. The sparks between you and Evan are enough to start my backyard grill. What I want to know is when you intended to tell him he's going to be a daddy?''

''That's a rather moot point, isn't it? You already told him, Belinda. I wanted to postpone it for as long as possible because I knew he'd be upset, probably angry and... What kind of mood was he in when you shuffled him off to get ready to play taxi?''

''I'm not sure. I couldn't read his expression like I usually can. I think he was sort of shellshocked.''

''Dandy.'' Jennifer paused. ''I'm going to sit up and see if the room will stay still.''

Belinda helped Jennifer upward, then she shifted so her feet were on the floor.

''So far, so good,'' Jennifer said, then sighed. ''Everything is in such a mess. I'm just not...not ready for Evan to know about this baby. I'm so thrilled about being pregnant, I really am, and I wanted to enjoy the very thought of it, the...

''But it's definitely reality check time. Evan knows. *He* certainly won't be thrilled about this news. Oh, I'm not saying he'd turn his back on us, refuse to support us monetarily, but I have to face the truth of how dedicated he is to his career. He doesn't have room for anything, or anyone else, in his life.''

''Would you like my opinion?'' Belinda said.

''Do I have a choice?''

''Nope. So listen up. I believe you're selling Evan short. Did it ever occur to you that he devotes himself to his career because there isn't an important woman in his life? He probably figures that working long hours here is better than sitting at home alone watching television.''

''Mmm,'' Jennifer said, frowning.

"Are you in love with Evan, Jennifer?"

"I...I'm not sure. I just don't know. I care for him, about him, but...I think I'm falling in love with him, slowly, step by step, but...I've been attempting to deal with the fact that I'm pregnant, plus sift and sort through my feelings for Evan and I'm exhausted. Emotionally and physically drained."

"That makes sense." Belinda nodded. "I wouldn't be surprised if Evan wasn't struggling to understand his feelings toward you right now, too. Love is a very simple, yet complicated thing."

"If he is in love with me, or even thinks he might be falling in love with me," Jennifer said, lifting her chin, "why hasn't he told me?"

"Have *you* told *him* that your feelings for him are steadily growing? Tit for tat, you know. He could very well think that *you're* so focused on *your* career you have no room in your life for him."

"But that's not true. When I have this baby I'll cut back on the number of assignments I take, I wouldn't travel so much and..."

"What we have here," Belinda said, pointing one finger in the air, "is a basic lack of communication. You two need to talk to each other, for crying out loud."

"Oh?" Jennifer said, raising her eyebrows. "Something like 'Evan, my sweet patootie, you don't happen to be kind of falling in love with me, are you? Because I think I'm falling in love with

you, you know what I mean? Oh, and by the way,
how do you feel about the little news flash that Belinda let out of the bag? Isn't that a kicker? You're
going to be a daddy.' How's that, Belinda?''

''It's definitely lacking something,'' she said,
shaking her head.

''No joke. I just want to go home and curl up in
bed with the covers over my head.'' She sighed. ''I
wish I had at least a clue as to how Evan reacted
when he heard you say…''

''Uh-oh,'' Belinda said softly, as Evan strode into
the room.

Jennifer's heart thundered as she stared at Evan
as he approached. His eyes were narrowed slightly
and his teeth were clenched so tightly she could see
a muscle ticking in his jaw.

This was not, she thought miserably, a happy
man.

''Can you walk, or should I carry you?'' Evan
said, looking at a spot just above Jennifer's head.

''I'm perfectly capable of walking, thank you,''
she said coolly, getting to her feet slowly and carefully. ''Yes, I'm fine. Steady as a rock. In fact, I'm
going to drive myself home.''

''No, you are not,'' he said, a steely edge to his
voice as he finally met her gaze. ''Give me your
keys and I'll make arrangements for a couple of police officers to deliver your car to your apartment
building.''

"I..."

"Don't argue with me, Jennifer, not now. Come on." Evan spun around and started back across the room.

"Hey, wait just a minute here," Jennifer said indignantly.

"Go, go," Belinda said, flapping her hands at Jennifer. "You can't talk to each other if you're not in the same place."

"He's not in the mood to talk. He's barking orders like a drill sergeant."

"Jennifer!" Evan said from the doorway.

"Oh, geez," Jennifer said, hurrying toward him. "Goodbye, Belinda. If you never hear from me again you can have my half-dead Christmas cactus."

The drive to Jennifer's apartment was made in total silence. The ride up in the elevator in her apartment building was made in total silence. By the time Evan and Jennifer entered her living room that ominous, tension-filled silence was nearly crackling through the air.

The atmosphere in here, Jennifer thought, was certainly a world apart from the first time she and Evan had been in her home, the night their baby was conceived.

She sank onto the sofa and clutched her hands tightly in her lap, her gaze riveted on Evan. He swept back his suit coat and shoved his hands into the pockets of his trousers as he began to wander restlessly around the spacious room.

It was decorated with white wicker furniture with bright-colored cushions and an oak coffee table and end tables. A home entertainment center contained a television, VCR, stereo and a multitude of CDs and videos. An oak bookcase was filled to overflowing with books.

Evan stopped his trek, stared unseeing at the books for a long moment, then turned to meet Jennifer's gaze.

"When did you intend to tell me that you're pregnant with my baby, Jennifer?" he said, a definite edge to his voice. "Or didn't you think it was something I needed to know?"

"What makes you believe this is *your* baby I'm carrying? I've been on the coast for three months. There *are* men in California, you know." Jennifer sighed and shook her head. "Erase that. I have no intention of playing that kind of game. This *is* your child and you're aware of exactly when he, or she, was conceived."

"So, I repeat," he said, still standing across the room, "when did you intend to tell me, if at all?"

"Of course, I was going to tell you," she said, her voice rising, "because a man has the right to know that he's going to be a father. But as to when I was going to share this news with you? I don't know, Evan, I really don't. I was afraid it would result in an ugly scene and I was right, wasn't I? Because here we are locking horns, or whatever cliché you want to use. Bottom line? You're mad as hell.''

Evan nodded. ''I'm angry. I admit that. But it's due to the fact that I found out about this baby by accident, by hearing what my secretary was saying, for God's sake. If it hadn't been for Belinda blithering on and on I still wouldn't know.''

''I just said I would have told you...eventually. But why rush it? I know you don't want this baby, Evan. You have the focus you want in your life...your career as the district attorney. This baby is a glitch in your program, a nuisance you'll have to deal with somehow. Why would I be in a hurry to hear that you don't want this baby or...or me in your future? Try to see this from my point of view for a second.''

''Who in the hell are you to tell me how I feel, what I want, what my focus in life is?'' Evan said, none too quietly. ''You're capable of looking into people's minds, hearts, souls? That's a good trick, Jennifer. You ought to take it on the road and see if it will play in Peoria.''

''Don't yell at me,'' Jennifer yelled. ''I've been dealing with the existence of this baby for weeks, coming to grips with it. I struggled to find an inner peace about the way it was conceived, move past the fact that what happened between us that night was wrong because we'd only known each other for a few hours and...

"But I found that peace and centered on the baby. *My* baby. Mine. Because *I* want it more than I can ever express to you. I've been savoring the very existence of this little miracle," she rushed on, one hand on her stomach, "daydreaming about seeing her, him, for the first time, holding him, watching him grow, smile that first smile, take his first step."

Tears filled Jennifer's eyes and she blinked them away, angry at herself for losing control of her emotions.

"I didn't want you to intrude in my bubble of happiness, Evan," she said, "break it, that bubble, and now you have and we're yelling at each other and...I don't want anything from you. Nothing. I don't intend to make demands on you because I'm having your baby. You can set up a college fund for him if you want to, if that will ease your conscience, but you don't have to pretend that you're thrilled to pieces to have found out you're going to be a father."

Evan felt as though he'd been punched...hard...in the solar plexus, making it difficult to breathe.

I don't want any anything from you. Nothing.

Jennifer's words beat against his mind like physical blows. He sank onto an easy chair and dragged both hands down his face.

Jennifer didn't want anything from him, he thought. Not his love, not a future with him, not...not anything. He had been falling in love with her, losing his heart to her a little at a time. How did he stop his emotions from going further? Or how did he reverse them? Could a man do that? Just...just stop falling in love with a woman who had staked a claim on his heart and who was carrying his baby?

He had to, somehow, before the very essence of who he was was shattered into a million pieces. Jennifer sure as hell didn't love him, not even close. *She didn't want anything from him. Not anything.*

But what about his child? His son, or daughter? Dear God, he was going to be a father, wanted to be there for the same things Jennifer had spoken of so wistfully...holding his baby, seeing that first smile, witnessing those wobbly first steps and...

"I can't...I can't take this all in at once," Evan said, leaning his head on the top of the chair and staring at the ceiling. "It's a lot to digest, to get used to."

"Oh, believe me, I know that. When I first discovered I was pregnant, I told the doctor I went to in California four times that she had made a mistake. I was in complete denial, then I moved to terrified, then angry at myself, and you, for what we did that night, then finally...finally it came. The peace, the joy, the anticipation, the bubble of pure happiness."

"That I just burst."

"Well, it was going to happen eventually." Jennifer sighed. "Please believe me when I say I would never have kept the existence of your child from you, Evan. I wouldn't have done that."

"I know," he said, his voice hushed. "I'm sorry I lashed out at you before, asked you if you intended to ever tell me."

"Evan, look," Jennifer said, leaning forward. "You need time to adjust to this just as I did. I'm not telling you what to do, but I'd like to suggest that you try to put this on hold until after the Gardner trial. You're on mental overload already with that pending, hanging over you the way it is.

"I realize that it would be easier for you if I wasn't around all the time, but I have to continue to be with you to film the documentary. We're going to have to work together until the trial is over.

"It will be difficult, maybe even impossible, but do you think we could just put the existence of the baby in a special place and not address the issue, not discuss it or anything until after the trial? I don't want this pregnancy to be the cause of your not being able to concentrate fully on what you must do to be victorious in that courtroom, or be unable to have a clear mind when you focus on the baby."

"I could try, I suppose," he said, lifting his head. "Heaven knows I need every ounce of mental energy I have to present the prosecution's case." He nodded. "What you're saying is logical and wise. Whether or not I can do it remains to be seen."

"I understand."

"I care about you, Jenny. I'm worried about the fact that you fainted. You scared the hell out of me. Will you promise me that you'll make an appointment with your doctor and tell him what happened? Then let me know what he says about it? I need to know that you're all right, that the baby is all right. Will you go to the doctor as soon as possible?"

"Yes," she whispered, feeling the ache of fresh tears in her throat.

Evan was being so kind, she thought. Kind. What a bland word. People were kind to old ladies who needed help crossing the street, kind to a puppy with a burr in its paw, kind to the person who needed a door opened for them because their arms were full of packages.

But they didn't love that old lady, that puppy, that person. They were just there, allowing a momentary surge of kindness to rise to the fore. That's what Evan had to offer her...kindness. It was better than his earlier anger, but still...

What was she to do with her feelings for *him?* The kernel of love for him within her that was steadily growing? How did she snuff it out, make certain that it no longer existed, didn't have the power to cause her pain beyond measure? How did a woman stop falling in love with a man such as this one?

She didn't know.

But somehow, *somehow,* that's exactly what she was going to have to do.

"Jennifer?" Evan said, bringing her from her jumbled thoughts.

"Yes?"

"Will you be all right if I leave you here on your own?" Evan said, getting to his feet. "I…um…I need some time alone to… But I'll stay if you feel dizzy or—"

"No, I'm fine," Jennifer interrupted. "Really. I'm as good as new. I'm sorry I caused such a scene with my dramatic… Well, maybe it's just as well that everything is out in the open. I just don't want this to keep you from having total concentration on the trial."

"And I want you to go to the doctor."

"I will. I promise."

"And I promise you that I'll work very hard at focusing on the Gardner case…for now." Evan paused. "Well, if you're sure you're okay, I'll shove off. Don't get up. I'll let myself out." He strode across the room to the door.

"Evan," Jennifer said quickly, shifting on the sofa so she could see him.

Don't go, her mind screamed. *Don't leave me alone. I want you here, with me. I need you, Evan.*

If you love me even a little bit, and I allowed the love I have for you to grow, nurtured it, we could have it all, don't you see? A future together. You, me, our baby. We'd be a family. Husband, wife, child... Oh, Evan, please? I...

"Yes?" Evan said. "What is it, Jennifer?"

She drew a shaky breath, then dashed away an errant tear that spilled onto one cheek.

"Nothing," she said.

Evan stared at her for a long moment, then left the apartment, closing the door behind him with a quiet click.

Chapter 5

Late the next afternoon Jennifer approached Evan's office and saw that Belinda had already left for the day. The door to Evan's office was open and Jennifer stopped three feet away, gathering her courage to go farther.

Maybe she'd wait until tomorrow, she thought, to put the ''we're going to have to work together until the trial is over'' bit into motion. Yes, that was a good idea. She and Evan had had a very emotional confrontation yesterday and a little time and distance would…

No, she was just postponing the inevitable and the longer she put it off, the more nervous she would become. It would be better to just march right in there and ask Evan if anything had transpired during his day that she needed to know about for the film.

Right, Jennifer thought, squaring her shoulders and lifting her chin. She was a mature woman and she could handle this. She was a mature, *pregnant* woman and her child's mother was not a wuss.

Jennifer walked slowly, very slowly, toward the doorway of Evan's office. She peered inside just as a loud sneeze echoed through the open door of the conference room beyond.

"Evan?" Jennifer called as she made her way toward the large room.

"In here, Jennifer," he yelled.

Just as Jennifer entered the conference room, thunder rumbled and a bright flash of lightning zig-zagged across the darkening sky beyond the bank of windows. The lights flickered, then steadied. Evan sneezed again.

"Bless you," Jennifer said. "Did you get caught in that cold rain that's been whipping about out there all day?" She glanced at the ceiling. "And is picking up force even as we speak?"

"Yes, I did," Evan said. "I went out to lunch with the mayor and got drenched. I've been slogging around in a wet suit ever since." He frowned. "We forgot the greetings. Hello, Jennifer, how are you? You should have gone on home where it's dry and warm."

"Hello, Evan. I'm dry and warm standing here

because some of us have the good sense to carry an umbrella on a day like this. Please excuse my casual attire, but jeans and a sweatshirt are my fashion statement when I'm editing.''

"You look comfortable.'' Evan rolled up the sleeves on his shirt, his damp suit coat already draped on a chair to dry. "Have you had dinner?''

"No, I came straight here from the studio. I'm eager to know how things went with your witnesses.''

"Why don't I get a pizza delivered up here?'' Evan said. "The witnesses I dealt with today are as prepared as they are going to be. What I'm going to tackle now is examining the jury pool applications. If you're willing to keep it off the record, I'd appreciate your input. If you don't mind. Of course, if you'd rather not, that's fine, too.''

"Sounds like a plan,'' Jennifer said, then sighed. "Oh, for heaven's sake, we sound like people reading lines in a play. I guess our working together is going to be more difficult than I thought, but it's necessary. We've got to attempt to relax, just be ourselves.''

"That's a tough assignment,'' Evan said gruffly, "when there are so many unresolved issues between us.''

"Which will be addressed *after* the trial,'' Jennifer said. "Except... Oh, dear.''

"Oh, dear...what?''

"Well, I promised you I'd go to the doctor and I did, but I also said it would be best if we didn't discuss the baby until the trial was over and…"

Evan sat down at the conference table and pointed to the chair opposite him.

"Sit," he said. "Tell me everything the doctor said. Why did you faint? People don't faint for no reason. There has to be an explanation for it. What did he say was wrong with you that made you conk out like that?"

"Whoa," Jennifer said, raising one hand palm out. "Give me a chance to speak. The doctor said my blood pressure was a bit low but he'd keep an eye on it and it should straighten out once my body adjusts to being pregnant.

"Low blood pressure is better than blood pressure that is too high. Get it? I should…hopefully…be finishing up my tour of duty with morning sickness and that will help settle things down. He said I was doing just fine."

"Fainting is not doing fine," Evan said, shaking his head.

"Fainting when you're pregnant is doing fine. Are we going to argue about this?"

"No. No, of course not. I was worried, that's all. So, okay. You're doing fine."

"Yes." Jennifer paused. "Evan, there's one other thing I need to tell you about my visit to the doctor today."

Evan sat bolt upward in the chair. "What? What else? What is it?"

"I had an ultrasound and, oh, it was amazing. The printer wasn't working so I didn't get a picture to take home but…. Anyway, I thought you might like to know…well, maybe it doesn't matter that much to you but…"

"Damn it, Jennifer," Evan interrupted, "cut to the chase. You're scaring me to death here."

"Okay, okay." Jennifer drew a deep breath and let it out slowly. "The baby…our baby…Evan, it's a boy. I'm…you're…we're…going to have a…a son."

Evan got to his feet, opened his mouth to speak, then snapped it closed again when nothing came out. He plunked back onto the chair and leaned toward Jennifer.

"A son?" he said, awe ringing in his voice. "It's a boy? A…a son? Are you sure?"

Jennifer laughed, the musical sound seeming to fill the room to overflowing.

"Pictures don't lie," she said, still smiling. "The ultrasound was so clear it just took my breath away and, yes, believe me, it was very obvious that our baby has certain equipment, shall we say, that baby girls don't have.

"My doctor looked at the screen and said, 'Well, hello, young man.' I saw him, Evan. I saw his little heart beating and…" She laughed again. "Of course, I wept buckets, but I swear I'll never forget that moment when I saw…'' She flapped one hand in the air. "Don't get me started."

Evan sank back in the chair. "A son. Whew. Add that to the stack of 'I need time to adjust to this' stuff. Are you disappointed? I mean, don't women usually want a girl they dress in frilly, pink things, and put bows in their hair and on their socks and…"

"Bows on their socks?"

Evan shrugged. "I saw a little girl in a restaurant once who had bows on her socks. She was in a highchair and kept lifting her feet so she could see those bows. Her mother finally took off her shoes and socks so the kid would eat some dinner." He paused. "So, are you? Disappointed that it's a boy?"

"Not in a million years," Jennifer said, smiling.

Evan matched her smile and their gazes met across the table. The room seemed to disappear into a mist, leaving a private place where awareness was heightened and desire began to hum, gain force and heat within them. Jennifer was the first to break the sensuous spell.

"The jury applications," she said, tearing her gaze from Evan's. "We need to get to work, Evan."

"What? Oh, right. Work. Yeah." Evan got to his feet. "I'll order a pizza first, then we'll start tackling these things. You don't have to do this, you know.

I mean, if you're rather go on home I'll understand.''

"Do you want me to leave?" she said, looking up at him.

"No," he said quietly. "No, Jenny, I don't want you to leave."

"Then I'll stay."

"Thank you." Evan smiled. "Let's see how much of an argument we can make out of what toppings we want on this pizza I'm going to order."

"You're on," Jennifer said, laughing.

Four hours later Jennifer yawned, then stretched out on the sofa instead of being curled up in the corner of it with her shoes off.

"I like that one," she said. "The fact that she's a single woman with no children is excellent. She won't get caught up in the mental scenario that I did about Cecelia Gardner having lost one son and now here is the other on trial and blah, blah, blah.

"Boy, I sure was wrong on that score. Cecelia isn't a mother, she's a walking, talking social machine." Jennifer yawned again. "Anyway, I vote that you try to get that woman on the jury. I don't think she'd declare Lyle innocent out of sympathy for Cecelia."

"Mmm." Evan nodded, then wrote a note on the top of the paper.

Rain beat against the windows with a frenzy, the

hunder continued to roar and lightning followed closely behind each rumble.

"That's enough of this stuff for one night," Evan said, rotating his neck. "These people on the applications are all starting to sound the same to me. I think we should... Jennifer?"

Evan got to his feet and moved around the long table to stand next to the sofa where Jennifer had drifted off to sleep. She had shifted to her side, one hand tucked beneath her cheek, the other splayed on her sweatshirt-covered stomach.

So beautiful, he thought, his heart quickening as he drank in the sight of her. In the future he might work late one night...not often, but occasionally...then come home and move quietly through their home so as not to waken her. Then he'd stand next to their bed and gaze at her, just as he was now. He could find a way, he *could,* to cut back on the long hours he worked. He could. He would.

He'd shed his clothes and slip beneath the blankets and... No, no, wait a minute. He'd forgotten something. On the way to his and Jennifer's bedroom, he would have stopped first in the nursery down the hall to check on their baby, *their son,* to watch the little miracle they had created together sleep the sleep of the innocent.

An explosion of thunder jerked Evan from his thoughts. In the next instant the lightning lit up the room with an eerie glow, then the lights went out,

cloaking the room and the city beyond the windows
in inky darkness.

Evan reached blindly for a chair, connected with
one, then turned it around so he could sit next to the
sofa. He settled onto it and stretched out his legs,
crossing them at the ankles.

He'd stay right here, he thought, in case Jennifer
woke up and was momentarily frightened by the
darkness. Oh, yes, he'd stay right here next to his
sweet Jenny.

Evan slouched lower in the chair so he could rest
his head on the top and allowed himself the luxury
of being aware of nothing but Jennifer.

She'd been a tremendous help to him as he'd gone
over the jury applications, he mused. Her input had
been intelligent, and she'd often thought of details
about the person that hadn't occurred to him. He
couldn't think of even one woman he'd dated who
was remotely interested in the inner workings of his
career. He and Jennifer were good together, a team,
like two pieces of a puzzle that fit perfectly.

Just as they would as wife and husband.

Just as they would as mother and father.

Just as they would…forever.

"Ah, man," Evan said wearily, dragging his
hands down his face.

He couldn't go on like this.

Once this trial was over he was going to sit down
with Jennifer, start at the top of the list of issues

they needed to address and hit them, one after another, until solutions were found and questions answered.

Yes, once he won this trial for Jennifer so her documentary would have the power and punch he knew she needed and wanted, he...

Evan straightened in the chair, his mind racing and the sudden wild tempo of his heart echoing in his ears.

What? he thought. Repeat that one, Stone. Once he won this trial for *Jennifer?* Not for the feather in *his* cap? Not for the very basics of justice being served? Not for the satisfaction of knowing that Lyle would pay the price for killing his brother?

Those things were probably there somewhere in his beleaguered mind, but first and foremost was the deep and heartfelt desire to not disappoint Jennifer, not fall short in her eyes, or cause her problems with her project which her boss might decide to chuck altogether if it had a dud of an ending where the profiled D.A. lost the big case in question.

Damn it, he had to get a conviction. He had to win...for Jennifer.

His eyes having become adjusted to the darkness, Evan looked at Jennifer as she slept, a smile forming on his lips.

For Jennifer, his mind echoed. And there it was. The truth. He was, indeed, deeply in love with Jennifer Anderson.

How strange and complex was this thing called love. It brought to the fore aspects of himself he didn't even know he possessed, a whole section of his inner being that had been hidden from him. It made him complete, whole, filled with awe, and a wondrous sense of excitement and joy that was intertwined somehow with a soothing warmth of peace, of knowing he'd journeyed far and had finally arrived where he was meant to be.

Oh, he liked being in love with Jennifer. She brought out the best in him, made him put her first in importance, yet it somehow didn't diminish his sense of self. The very thought of being the one to make her smile, laugh right out loud, be the cause of her incredible green eyes changing to a smoky hue of desire for him, *him,* made him feel ten feet tall.

Evan leaned forward and gently brushed a silky strand of hair from Jennifer's cheek.

"I love you, sweet Jenny," he whispered.

And now there was more. She brought so much into his life and now there was more. A son. Their son. Their baby boy. He wanted to win this trial for his son, too, so that someday when he told his boy what had been going on when his parents fell in love, he'd be able to announce that he had won the trial in question and justice had been served.

He had to win in that courtroom.

For Jennifer.

For their son.

For himself.

And when the trial was over he was going to tell Jennifer how he felt about her, ask her to marry him, and wait to see if he was to become the happiest man in the world, or one who was sliced and diced.

Yes, a momentous question had been answered tonight…he was irrevocably in love with his sweet Jenny, but a great many questions remained.

The lights suddenly came back on, startling Evan so much that he jumped to his feet and bumped the sofa. Jennifer's eyes popped open.

"What?" She struggled to sit up, then blinked and shook her head. "Did I fall asleep? Well, that's mortifying. Big help I am." She laughed. "I'm sorry, Evan. I feel like a three-year-old who needed a nap and just conked out."

"Which means you're a very exhausted lady, who is calling it quits for today and heading home," he said, extending one hand toward her. "Up. Out." He glanced at the ceiling. "The storm is even co-operating, and it's not raining so hard."

Jennifer placed one hand in Evan's and allowed him to assist her to her feet. She made no effort to resist when he wrapped his arms around her and pulled her close, nestling her to his rugged body.

"Could I interest you in the last slice of cold pizza?" he said, his voice gritty.

"No, thank you," she said, her arms floating up to encircle his neck.

"Well, how about the last couple of inches of your soda, which is now flat and warm?"

"No, thank you."

"I can offer you about three or four hours more work examining jury applications?"

"No, thank you," she said, smiling. "I'm brain dead. They'd all sound the same at this point."

"Well, shucks and darn, ma'am," he said, "I guess I don't have one thing to give to you that you'd be interested in."

"Oh, I wouldn't say that, Mr. Stone," she said, shifting to tiptoes and brushing her lips over his once, then twice, then gaining courage to do it one more time as she felt a tremor sweep through him. "I think you have exactly what I want and need right now."

"Oh?"

"Kiss me, Evan," she whispered.

"I live to serve," he said, then his mouth melted over hers.

It was an explosion of senses. The kiss was as wild and intense and raging as out of control as the storm outside had been. The thunder of nature's fury was now the pounding tempo of their hearts. The brilliant lightning was the razor-sharp awareness of the marvelous differences between a body soft and a body hard and muscled that made them perfect counterparts. The swirling, beating rain was transformed into churning, pulsing desire deep within them.

But while the storm beyond the windows had been cold, what was consuming them was hot, burning flames that licked throughout them. The kiss intensified and breathing became labored as passions soared.

Evan lifted his head a fraction of an inch and spoke close to Jennifer's moist lips.

"I want you so damn much," he said, hardly recognizing the raspy tone of his own voice. "Ah, Jenny, you have no idea how much..."

I love you, Evan's mind hammered. No, this was not the time or place to declare his love for her. The Gardner trial possessed too much of them now. He wanted that done, finished, the slate wiped clean so he could concentrate totally on the future. A future he could only hope and pray would be spent with Jennifer.

"I want you, too, Evan," she said softly.

"Jenny, I..." Evan started.

"Yo, in the room," a man yelled. "Cleaning service. Is anyone here?"

Jennifer and Evan jerked apart, then each took a step backward. Jennifer fluffed her hair, Evan dragged a hand through his.

"Yes," Evan hollered, then cleared his throat. "We were working in here, but we're finished for tonight. Come on in."

A man appeared in the doorway to the conference room, pulling a cart stacked with supplies.

"Howdy, folks," he said. "You public servant types sure do put in long hours."

"Your tax dollars at work," Evan said, "but we're gone. Please don't disturb any of the papers on the table. It might look like chaos, but it's organized chaos, believe it or not.''

''Got it,'' the man said, dragging the cart forward. ''You must be getting ready for that Gardner trial, huh? Man, you can't pick up a newspaper, or turn on the tube, without having it in front of your nose. It's the topic at our dinner table at home every night, too. Guess folks are waiting to see if the rich folks in Chicago get to play by different rules than us poor slaving stiffs.''

Evan frowned. ''Really? There's some question about that? Whether Lyle will get off because he comes from a wealthy, powerful family?''

''Well, sure,'' the man said.

''If I don't get a conviction,'' Evan said, ''won't people realize that I just didn't have enough evidence to convince the jury of Gardner's guilt beyond a reasonable doubt?''

''Doubt it,'' the man said, shaking his head.

''That's absurd,'' Jennifer said, planting her hands on her hips. ''Wealth, power, whatever, will have nothing whatsoever to do with the outcome of this trial. Gracious, people have no idea how many long days this man…'' she pointed at Evan, who was staring at her with wide eyes ''…their district attorney, has put in to prepare his case against Lyle Gardner.

''Well, guess what? When the documentary I'm working on about Evan Stone and his staff is aired on television, the citizens of Chicago and beyond are going to know the truth. The rich and famous get no special favors when they have broken the law. No, sir. Never. Have you got that? If you don't, then make sure you watch my film because…''

"Um…Jennifer?" Evan interrupted, chuckling softly. "I think you've made your point."

"Oh, yes, ma'am," the man said. "Whew. You sure do have a temper there, ma'am, when you get going. And I believe every word you said, by golly. I surely do. Mr. Stone, you'd better count your lucky stars this lady is on your side."

"Oh, I count those lucky stars every day," Evan said, smiling at Jennifer.

"I…I guess I got a little carried away," Jennifer said, feeling a warm flush of embarrassment stain her cheeks. "I'm sorry. It's just that… What I mean is…" She threw up her hands. "Never mind. I need some sleep."

And he needed to spend the rest of his life with this dynamite lady, Evan thought, his heart swelling with love for Jennifer.

Chapter 6

The next day was a study in frustration for Evan. Reporters were calling one after the next in response to Cecelia's accusation that the governor, the mayor and District Attorney Evan Stone had concocted a conspiracy against her family because they feared the power the Gardners possessed. The three men had manufactured phony evidence against her deceased son Franklin, who was unable to defend himself, and were attempting to convict her remaining son Lyle of killing his own brother with a flimsy case that should be thrown out of court.

Evan found it impossible to concentrate as the telephone rang constantly, knowing that Belinda was being harassed and growing weary of the ''no comment'' she repeated over and over again.

Jennifer telephoned Evan to say that she and Sticks would be working very late at the studio. Her producer wanted her to thread the new development into her documentary to illustrate the level of pressure the D.A. was operating under.

The next two days were more of the same, resulting in short tempers and frazzled nerves in the D.A.'s office, and the added frustration that both Jennifer and Evan felt, but didn't voice, of being unable to see each other, not even during the work-packed weekend.

Before it seemed possible Evan found himself entering the courtroom for the first day of the trial of Lyle Gardner, having shoved his way through the maze of reporters in the hallway, his stormy glare taking the place of anything he might have said.

Evan had managed to go over the remainder of the jury applications, acutely aware of how much he missed having Jennifer's assistance in the chore as well as simply missing Jennifer herself to the point that he ached to see, hold and kiss her.

He placed his briefcase on the table designated to be his during the trial, removed some files, pens and a legal pad, then glanced up to meet the gaze of Lyle Gardner who sat at the table across the courtroom with his attorney.

Lyle had straight, slicked-back black hair, blue eyes, and the puffy, heavy-set physique of someone who had indulged in too many lavish meals and very

little exercise. Lyle smirked and shook his head as
he looked at Evan with blatant disdain.

Oh, what he wouldn't give, Evan thought, as he
settled onto his chair, to walk across that room and
punch that smug expression off Lyle's face.

Evan forced himself to tear his gaze from Lyle's
and look at the packed rows of spectators, immediately seeing Cecelia sitting in the first row directly
behind her son. The remainder of the crowd was a
sea of faces that did not include Jennifer's. He knew
she wouldn't be there during the selection of the
jury, but…

He'd telephoned her late last night but had obviously wakened her, resulting in a rather short, foggy
conversation that did nothing more than emphasize
how exhausted they both were.

Get a grip, Stone, Evan ordered himself. He was
as prepared as he was going to get for this trial, and
it was going to require his total concentration and
expertise to win a conviction. His case was still built
on circumstantial evidence and he knew it. Detectives Waters and Wilson and their assigned team of
uniformed officers had made no progress in finding
the incriminating signet ring.

"All rise," a man bellowed.

Here we go, Evan thought, getting to his feet as
the judge entered the courtroom. *And heaven
help me.*

* * *

Despite Evan's attempts to slow things down to give the detectives and uniformed officers every possible minute to find the missing ring, the jury and alternates were selected by the end of the second day in court. The judge announced that the trial would begin the following morning with the opening statement from the district attorney.

Evan waited until the courtroom was empty with the hope that he could avoid another confrontation with the reporters, then moved around the table just as one of the double doors opened and Jennifer entered, wearing jeans and a pretty red sweater.

"Hi, stranger," she said, hurrying toward Evan.

Evan left his briefcase on the table and rushed to meet her, immediately pulling her into his arms and kissing her deeply.

"My goodness," Jennifer said, when Evan finally ended the searing kiss, "that was quite a greeting from a stranger."

"Indeed, it was," Evan said, not releasing his hold on her. "Think what I might have done if I knew who you were, ma'am."

"It boggles the mind." She smiled. "I'm glad I caught you because I have something of extreme importance to tell you."

"Oh?"

"Yes." Jennifer laughed. "I've missed you. How's that for a bulletin?"

"It warms the cockles of my heart, and I've

missed you, too. How are you feeling? How is our son? How is the editing of the film going?''

''Fine, fine, and slow, per usual. My boss is pushing us to finish editing what we have, then keeping up with it when we start filming again, which I understand from the clerk will be tomorrow because the trial is starting. My boss wants to air the documentary very soon after the trial ends and it's still fresh in the public's mind.''

''Whew.'' Evan stepped away from Jennifer and began to wander around the area in front of the judge's bench. ''Talk about putting the pressure on. What if...'' He stopped and looked at Jennifer who was now about three feet away from him. ''Jennifer, has it occurred to your boss that I might not win this case for you?''

Jennifer slid onto the edge of the table where Evan's briefcase still sat, allowing her feet to dangle above the floor. She cocked her head slightly to one side, a confused expression on her face.

''Win this case for *me?*''

Evan dragged a restless hand through his hair. ''Yes. You've worked so damn hard on this documentary, given it everything you have.

''If I lose this battle and Lyle walks, won't your boss reconsider even airing the film? I get a knot in my gut just thinking about the possibility that all your hours will have been for nothing, Jenny. I can't stand the thought of...of letting you down like that.

And I can't bear the thought of having to tell our son that I didn't come through for his mother when she really needed me to.''

Never, Jennifer thought, as tears misted her eyes, never in her entire life had she felt so...so loved, so cherished and special. Evan wasn't even considering the damage that might be done to his own reputation if he lost the case against Lyle Gardner. Fuel would be added to the fire of the smoldering idea the public had that the rich got a break in the Chicago justice system.

Evan was focused on what losing would mean to *her,* and later to their son.

Oh, Evan, she thought, dashing away a tear that spilled onto her cheek. He loved her. *He did.* What he had just said was like a precious gift he was giving her, a declaration of his love she would cherish forever.

Should she gather her courage and declare her love for him? Oh, how she yearned to tell him what was in her heart.

Jennifer glanced quickly around the courtroom.

But no, not now. The majority of his concentration and mental energies must be centered on the trial.

It wasn't fair to him to ask him to envision a future with her...and their baby...when he had to stay in the present and the enormous challenge he was facing.

"You look upset," Evan said, bringing Jennifer from her racing thoughts. "I guess you haven't considered the possibility that you would suffer from my defeat in this room. There's more at stake here than whether or not a guilty man goes free. Your career could be dealt a devastating blow if I don't get a conviction against Lyle Gardner."

"No, no, Evan. It's not like that. I've talked at length with my boss about this. We're prepared for whatever the outcome of the trial is. If Lyle Gardner is found guilty we take the approach that your detectives combined with your expertise in the courtroom made it possible for justice to be served.

"If Lyle gets off? We'll show that even the best efforts don't always bring the proper results, whether the defendant is rich or poor, but that you have to move on to the next case, continue to believe in the system, refuse to allow a defeat to diminish your dedication."

Evan nodded.

"But, Evan?" she said, a sob catching in her throat. "The fact that you were worried about me, about my career, what it might do to me if you lost this case, means more to me than I can ever begin to tell you. Thank you. Oh, that's too small, too insignificant to express..." Tears closed her throat and she stopped speaking as she shook her head.

Evan closed the distance between them and

planted his hands on either side of her bottom where she sat on the table, trapping her in place.

"You've got it covered? You'll be all right no matter what the outcome of this trial is?"

Jennifer nodded.

"Oh, thank God for that. You have no idea how I've worried about you and... Well, that's one less thing to keep me awake at night." He smiled. "But I have plenty left to guarantee the tossing and turning routine. I am so glad, though, that we had this conversation."

"I believe Belinda would call it communication," Jennifer said, managing to produce a wobbly smile.

"Yeah, I think you're right. Belinda is very big on communication. When this trial is over, Jenny, you and I are going to have a very serious session of communication about...things."

"I..." Jennifer started, then stopped for a moment. "Yes, we need to do that. Communicate, discuss in depth some very important...things."

Evan nodded, then straightened and swept his gaze over the courtroom.

"Do you realize," he said quietly, "how many lives are changed forever in rooms just like this one every day across this country? What an awesome responsibility it is for those of us who play a part in that. It's big. It's heavy. It can consume a person if they're not aware that it's happening."

Jennifer was hardly breathing as she listened intently to what Evan was saying.

"It consumed *me,*" he said, turning to face her again. "But I'm going to change that, get a healthier balance in my life. Delegate, delegate, delegate. I think that somewhere along the line I started to have a godlike complex of believing that *I* had to do it if it was going to be done right. That's crazy. My staff is the cream of the crop. I intend to make room in my life for more, much more than just my career, sweet Jenny."

Will that more include me, Evan? Jennifer thought. *Loving me? Wanting me to become your wife, not just the mother of your son? Oh, Jennifer, don't do this to yourself. Keep the daydreams separate from what might still be pipe dreams.*

"That's…good. I'm thinking along those lines myself. Once I have the baby I don't intend to travel so much. And I'm certainly entitled to some time off between assignments, too, and… Well, I want a healthier balance, to quote you, in my life, too. I… What's that noise?"

"I don't hear… Oh, cripe, it's my cell phone. I put it in my briefcase."

Evan hurried to the table, flipped the catches on the briefcase and retrieved the ringing phone, pushing the appropriate button.

"Stone," he said.

Jennifer watched with building concern as Evan

stiffened as he listened to what was being said, then the color drained from his face.

"Evan?" she whispered, sliding off the table. "What is it? What's wrong?"

He held up one hand to silence her and she pressed her lips together as she continued to stare at him, her heart racing.

"The statement is signed?" Evan said. "And he'll testify?... You did? You took it to Maggie and she's positive that it's... Do you realize what this means? What you've done...? Yes... Yes..."

"Yes, yes...what?" Jennifer whispered, clutching her hands beneath her chin.

"I don't know what to say," Evan continued, shaking his head. "You two deserve a raise? Steak dinners? Letters of commendation from the mayor? The governor? Hell, the president of the United States. Name it, it's yours... A vacation, huh? Sold... Yeah, fine. I'll connect with you back at my office." He laughed. "Do you like my office? Hell, I'll give you my office if you want it... No?... Okay. Later."

Evan pressed the button on the small phone, then set it in the briefcase with exacting care. The color began to return slowly to his face as he snapped the latches on the briefcase in seemingly slow motion.

"Evan Stone," Jennifer said, her voice trembling, "if you don't tell me what just happened I swear I'm going to... Oh!"

Jennifer gasped in shock as Evan turned, grabbed her waist and twirled her around and around until she yelled for mercy. He set her on her feet, steadied her as she staggered slightly, then framed her face in his hands.

"That call," he said, his voice choked with emotion, "was from Detective Extraordinaire Colin Waters, who had Detective Extraordinaire Darien Wilson standing at his elbow as he spoke to me."

"And?"

"Ah, Jenny, they did it. Those two found the signet ring."

"Oh, my God," Jennifer whispered.

"Lyle pawned it. I guess he figured it was tucked safely away in a seedy side of town across the state line in Michigan where no one would ever think to go looking. The ring is worth a bunch of bucks, and he was too greedy to just toss the thing in a Dumpster.

"Maggie has examined the ring, will testify that it's the one that made the marks on Franklin's face, and the pawnshop owner has positively identified Lyle from a picture as the man who brought in the ring, having signed a statement to that fact. We've got him, Jennifer. Lyle Gardner is going down."

"You're going to win," Jennifer said, awe ringing in her voice. "Oh, Evan, I'm so thrilled, so... I don't know what to say."

"I do," he said, suddenly very serious. "This trial

is over except for the shouting. Lyle has no defense left. It's over."

"Well, yes, I guess it is, isn't it? You'll tell the judge and Lyle's attorney that... Oh, my."

"So, yes, sweet Jenny," Evan said, dropping his hands from her face, and running a trembling hand down his tie in a nervous gesture, "I do know what to say now. It's time. It's time to...communicate."

"It is?" she said, looking up at him with wide eyes.

"Yes, it is." Evan drew a steadying breath. "Jennifer Anderson, I, Evan Stone, am deeply and forever and a day in love with you."

"I...I beg your pardon?"

"I love you, Jenny. I swear I do. You're my life, my other half, my soul mate, my...I love you. I love you, I love our baby. Please, oh, please, say that you love me, too. Say that you'll marry me and stay by my side as my partner until death parts us. Say that we'll raise our son together, be a family, and that you'll help me pick out a name for our dog and cat, create a home out of a house we'll buy and...I'll cut way back on my work hours and... Oh, God, Jennifer, do you love me as much as I love you?"

Tears filled Jennifer's eyes. "Yes. Oh, Evan, yes. I love you beyond measure. You make me complete, so glad that I'm a woman who can be a counterpart to you, my magnificent man, and...I hoped, I prayed, that you loved me in return and..."

"Will you marry me? Please?"

"Yes! Oh, yes, yes, yes, yes…"

Evan pulled her close and kissed her until they were both trembling with desire and emotions too deep and complex to give name to. When he broke the kiss, he made no attempt to hide the tears glistening in his eyes that matched those shimmering in Jennifer's.

"Thank you," he said, his voice husky. "Thank you for agreeing to be my wife, for making me the happiest man on this planet, for just being you. And, Jenny? Thank you for the greatest gift a woman can give a man. Our baby. Our miracle. I'm going to be a father. I love you and our son so very much."

"And I love you and our son so very much," she said, smiling through her tears.

"I don't want to leave you right now for anything, but I have to get things rolling about the ring being found. I have a feeling that Lyle, who will be not so smug, will be more than ready to plea bargain."

"I understand. I'll go to my apartment and wait for you there. Sticks and I will film the press conference later when you announce the wonderful news."

"This could take a while. I might be very late."

"Evan, I've waited a lifetime for you. A few more hours are fine. I'll be there…waiting for you to come home."

Evan smiled, brushed his lips over Jennifer's, then picked up his briefcase.

"I'll get there as soon as I possibly can," he said. "Let's get out of here."

"Yes, I... No, wait a minute," Jennifer said, pointing one finger in the air. "I have one teeny-tiny question first."

"Whip it on me."

"What dog and cat?"

Their mingled laughter echoed through the big, empty room as Evan encircled Jennifer's shoulders with one arm and they walked through the double doors, taking the first steps toward their future, their forever...together.

"I'll see you as soon as I can."

"Yes," Jennifer said, then watched her future husband stride out of view down the corridor.

It was nearly nine o'clock when Evan knocked on the door of Jennifer's apartment. She rushed to greet him, frowning when she saw the exhaustion etched on his rugged features.

"You're so tired," she said, as Evan sank onto the sofa.

"You should have called and told me you were going home to get some sleep."

"Not a chance," he said, tugging on her hand so she'd settle next to him, which Jennifer did willingly. "Today the woman I love agreed to marry me, spend the rest of her life with me. Sleep can wait. Seeing you tonight definitely could not.''

"That's sweet.'' She smiled at him warmly. "Now, tell me what happened.''

"His lawyer wasted a lot of time with bluster and blow,'' Evan said, yanking the knot of his tie down and undoing the two top buttons of his shirt. "You know, what does a ring prove? Anyone could have been wearing it the night Franklin Gardner was killed to frame Lyle and blah, blah, blah. But *anyone* didn't pawn it, Lyle did, and he finally confessed to the whole thing.

"To make a long story short, my Jenny, they copped a plea for manslaughter in the second degree due to the fact that Franklin actually died from whacking his head on the table, not from being beat up by Lyle, or stabbed with the ice pick.''

"Well, it's better than having the creep walking the streets.''

"True. Oh, Cecelia was there during the negotiations, which was interesting.''

"Why? What did she say?''

"Nothing. She… I don't know how to explain it…but she seemed to shrink, turn old before my eyes. I think it finally hit her that all the money in the world couldn't solve this problem. When we reached an agreement of fifteen years with no parole, she got up and walked out of the room. Lyle called to her, but she didn't even look at him. Lyle just put his head down on the table and started to cry.''

"My goodness.''

"Chalk up one for the good guys. We won. Justice has been served. But, Jenny? That isn't why this day will always be very special to me, why I'll see this date on the calendar in years to come and smile, remembering. Remembering that the classy lady who stole my heart, the wonderful woman, the mother of my son, agreed to be my wife on this day.''

"You're going to make me cry,'' Jennifer said, then sniffled.

"No, I'm going to make love to you, with you, if you're willing,'' Evan said, then brushed his lips over hers. "I love you, Jenny.''

"And I love you, Evan.''

Evan kissed Jennifer deeply, then with no more words spoken and none needed, they went down the hallway to her bedroom.

And it was magic.

Clothes seemed to float away with a mere thought, and the blankets on the bed were swept back by an invisible hand to reveal cool mint-green sheets that beckoned.

They tumbled onto the bed, then stilled, sweeping their gazes over each other in the golden glow of the small lamp on the nightstand. A body soft and womanly, with a tummy just beginning to show a gentle rise where a son was being nurtured. A body hard and masculine and taut with muscles. Perfect counterparts. And minds that matched with the knowledge that this was theirs to have, to rejoice in, because...

"We're in love for all time," Jennifer said, her voice ringing with awe and wonder. "That's where the magic comes from, Evan...our love. This is how it should be. This is the difference between when we made love the first time and now...the love, the commitment to forever, the pledge."

"We'll always have the magic, Jenny."

They kissed, caressed, explored and discovered anew the mysteries of each other, marveling, savoring, memorizing. The desire within them burned hotter, causing breathing to quicken and hearts to race.

When they could bear no more they joined, a soft sigh of pleasure escaping from Jennifer's lips as a groan rumbled deep in Evan's chest. He began to move within her, deep so deep, increasing the tempo, taking her with him as she matched him beat for beat. The heat coiled tighter, hotter. The moment of release neared. It was ecstasy. It was theirs.

And now...it was very, very right.

They were flung into oblivion seconds apart, each calling the name of the other, holding tightly through the wondrous journey, then drifting slowly back to lay close, not speaking, just feeling. Remembering. Tucking it all away in private chambers of hearts that wished to keep the memories of what they had just shared.

They slept. Heads resting on the same pillow and hands splayed on the other's moist, cooling skin. Neither dreamed because no fantasy produced by subconscious minds could be more glorious than the reality of what had transpired.

When fingers of sunlight inched beneath the curtains on the window at dawn and tiptoed across the bed to wake Jennifer, she opened her eyes, then turned her head on the pillow to see Evan sleeping peacefully beside her.

"That's your daddy, baby boy," she whispered, spreading one hand over her bare stomach. "That magnificent, warm, funny, intelligent, loving man is your daddy."

"Who is in love with your mommy, baby boy," Evan said, as he slowly opened his eyes, then smiled at Jennifer. "Forever."

Chapter 7

A week later Jennifer stood in front of her open closet door wearing a silky slip and a frown.

"I don't have a thing to wear," she said aloud.

A newspaper suddenly appeared inches before her nose and she gasped in surprise before smiling and tilting her head back to look up at Evan who stood behind her.

"You want me to wear a creation made of newspaper to this shindig?" she said.

"No," Evan said, chuckling. "I just thought you'd like to see yet another rave review about your documentary. It was aired three nights ago and the accolades are still pouring in." He dropped a kiss on the top of her freshly shampooed hair. "Congratulations...again. May I have your autograph?"

"I think I should ask for *your* autograph," she said. "After all, you were the star of the famous flick. Evan, move that paper before you get newsprint on my nose. Oh, I really don't have a thing to wear."

Evan tossed the paper onto the bed, then narrowed his eyes as he scrutinized the clothing choices on the hangers. He lifted the material of the full skirt of a silk, teal-blue dress with a pleated top and long sleeves.

"This is the dress you wore the night the mayor ordered us to have dinner together. I like it. It's very pretty. Simple but classy."

"You remember what I wore that night? That was several months ago."

"I remember," he said, looking directly into her eyes, "every detail of that night."

"Really? You're so sentimental. I don't remember that you wore a dark brown suit that did wonderful things for your thick brown hair and fudge-sauce eyes. Nor do I recall that you added a tan shirt, chocolate-colored tie with a matching handkerchief peeking above the pocket of your jacket."

Evan laughed. "Well, tonight I'm wearing a blue suit, pale blue shirt, as you can see, and a dark blue tie. In other words, I'm ready to go so pick something or we're going to be late for the mayor's party."

"Here we are again. Going out because the mayor has spoken."

"Yes, but this time we're not squabbling."

Jennifer wrapped her arms around Evan's neck.

"Definitely not squabbling," she said, then outlined his lips with the tip of her tongue.

"Oh, no, you don't," he said, pulling her arms free. "You start that and we'll never leave this bedroom, Ms. Anderson."

"That's the plan, Mr. Stone," she said, batting her eyelashes at him.

"We'll make an early night of it. I know you've put in some very long hours to get that documentary ready to be aired and you must still be tired, but we really do need to make an appearance at this party."

"Okay, okay. I guess I'll wear the teal-blue number that you remember so well. The top blouses a bit and since I'm getting a tad tubby in the tummy it will cover the evidence."

Evan patted the tummy in question. "How's our baby boy?"

"He's fine and dandy, and the morning sickness has stopped, thank heavens. Do you like the name Daniel? It just popped into my head today."

"No," Evan said firmly. "When I was in the fifth grade a kid named Daniel stole my Joe DiMaggio baseball card. I wonder if that's why I went into the prosecution side of the law?"

"Oh, good grief," Jennifer said, laughing.

"Okay, I'll remove Daniel from the list of baby boy names."

"You could add Joe DiMaggio to that list. Joe DiMaggio Stone. Now that has a nice ring to it, don't you think?"

"Forget it."

"That's what I figured."

The very well-attended party in the private room at the exclusive restaurant was in full swing when Jennifer and Evan entered, their arrival evoking a loud round of applause and shouts of congratulations to them both.

Lyle's confession had made the headlines in the newspapers and was the lead story in every newscast in the country.

Mayor Ned Jones made his way through the crowd to vigorously shake Evan's hand, then give Jennifer a peck on the cheek.

"Fantastic jobs, both of you," the mayor said, beaming. "You look good, I look good, we all look good. That counts at election time. I'm more than satisfied with the sentence Lyle got. Oh, in case any reporters ask, the tab for this party is coming out of my personal pocket. The taxpayers are not footing the bill for this celebration. I invited everyone who had anything to do with winning this case. We all deserve to celebrate.

"Jennifer, you are a vision of loveliness this evening, I must say. Your documentary is the talk of Chicago at the moment, since the hoopla about Gardner is fading. Any chance of your film being shown beyond this area?''

''My boss is negotiating for prime time with one of the national networks,'' she said. ''Apparently they're very interested.''

''Excellent. You deserve recognition for a fine, fine job.'' The mayor patted Evan on the arm. ''And our man here deserves every bit of credit he can get for the outcome of the Gardner case.''

''I appreciate your compliments,'' Evan said, ''but I really didn't do anything to win this case. All the credit goes to Detectives Waters and Wilson. I made that clear in my earlier statement to the press. If they hadn't found the ring in that pawnshop I'm not convinced I could have won the case with the circumstantial evidence I had to work with.''

''Nonsense,'' the mayor said. ''You'd have won. We're spreading out this victory so everyone gets a piece of the public relations pie.'' He paused. ''By the way, I hear that congratulations and best wishes are in order for you two as well as the other heroes and heroines involved in this case. Ah, yes, that *is* a sparkling diamond I see on your pretty finger, Jennifer. When is the wedding?''

''Soon,'' she said, smiling. ''The sooner the better, in fact.''

''Fantastic. Months ago when I ordered you two

go out to dinner and settle your differences you ertainly took me at my dictatorial word.''

"You have no idea how true that is," Jennifer aid, unable to curtail a bubble of laughter. "Yes, ir, we have a verdict in this case…marriage.''

"I must mingle," the mayor said. "Oh, did you ear the latest? Cecelia has resigned from the boards f every charity she was involved with that hadn't lready asked for her resignation. She's moving to Australia.''

"Australia?" Jennifer said incredulously. "She loesn't intend to visit her son in prison?''

"Apparently not. She's packing up and leaving he country, didn't even invite her grandson Stephen o go along. I must mingle, mingle," the mayor said, hen hurried away.

"And Cecelia Gardner calls herself a mother," ennifer muttered.

"Don't get started on that subject," Evan said, huckling. "Hey, there's Belinda and her husband t that table over there. Shall we join them?''

"Yes, that's perfect," Jennifer said.

They wove their way through the throng of peo-le, being stopped often to receive congratulations nd handshakes. Each time Jennifer replied with a imple thank-you, while Evan said the credit for the ourtroom victory was due to the detectives who efused to admit defeat over not having found the nissing ring. They spoke briefly with Josh and Maggie, then Colin and Darien exchanged best wishes for the future.

When they finally reached the table, Belinda introduced her husband Henry to Jennifer, then Evan and Henry exchanged handshakes and genuine smiles that reflected their long-standing friendship. Henry was a tall, distinguished-appearing man in his early sixties.

"So," Belinda said, once Jennifer and Evan were settled onto their chairs, "have you chosen a wedding dress yet, Jennifer?"

"No, I haven't," Jennifer said. "I've been a tad busy editing the film for the documentary. Besides, I don't need a fancy gown. I told you it's going to be a very small group of people at the ceremony, you and Henry included, of course."

"Are you starting a list of possible names for the baby?" Belinda said.

"Belinda, for crying out loud," Henry said, "Miss Manners would tar and feather you. You don't ask the bride-to-be about her wedding dress one minute, then inquire about names for the expected baby in the next second."

"Well, why not?" Belinda said. "Would it become proper if we discussed the weather between the two subjects? That's silly."

Jennifer laughed. "It's all right, Henry. To answer your question, Belinda, the name Daniel was rejected by the daddy-to-be about an hour ago."

"The name Joe DiMaggio didn't cut it with the mama, either," Evan said, smiling.

"I should hope not." Belinda frowned at Evan. "That's a ridiculous name."

"I liked it," Evan said, shrugging.

"I still say," Henry said, "that you don't ask about the wedding dress in the same breath as inquiring about the coming baby, for heaven's sake."

"This baby is no secret, Henry." Jennifer laughed. "I'm surprised that the mayor held himself back from mentioning our little bundle of joy. Of course, he may have missed Evan's statement that has been quoted in the newspapers ad nauseam in the twenty-four hours since he delivered his pearly words. Apparently you didn't see it, Henry."

"I guess I did miss that." Henry looked at Evan. "What did you say?"

"I missed it, too," Belinda said. "Evan, what have you gone and done?"

Evan frowned. "Well, hey, I could understand the press wanting details on the breaking news about the Gardner case, and how did I feel about the documentary, but they wouldn't stop there. They'd heard a rumor about Jennifer and me being involved with each other and pushed, and pushed, and pushed, until..."

"Uh-oh," Belinda said.

"Until," Jennifer said, then dissolved in a fit of laughter and shook her head.

"Evan Stone," Belinda said, narrowing her eyes, "spill it."

"Well, hell, is it any of their business? No. So decided to end the speculation, the questions and rumors, the whole nine yards. I said that yes, Jennifer Anderson and I were planning to be married and that baby boy Stone would be attending the wedding, much to our joyous delight."

Henry put his head back and roared with laughter, which set Jennifer off again. The sound was infectious and Belinda and Evan's laughter soon intertwined. People near the table glanced over, wondering enviously what joke they had missed. When the four finally settled down, Henry became quite serious.

"Humor me here, Evan," he said, "then I promise to change the subject to something more pleasant. I've been out of the country for weeks on business and just flew in this evening.

"I scanned the newspapers Belinda had saved for me for details of the Gardner case, but didn't have a chance to really digest it, then my beloved wife was bringing me up to date on family news during the drive from home to the party. Would you mind clearing up a question for me?"

"No, I don't mind. What has your brilliant brain baffled, Henry?"

"I know about the prostitution ring that Franklin Gardner was running, fine fella that he was," Henry aid. "Then, I take it, Lyle discovered the truth bout his younger brother and confronted him, reulting in the nasty fistfight between the two."

Evan nodded.

"Lyle panicked," Belinda said, "and tried to aake it look like Franklin interrupted a burglary of is fancy-dancy apartment. Lyle stabbed him with n ice pick after Franklin was already dead from vhopping his head on a table. Lyle might have gotn away with it if it hadn't been for the impression ft of Lyle's ring in the bruises on Franklin's face. hen Lyle stashed the ring in a pawnshop in Michzan and on the story goes. You know all that part, lenry."

"Yes, that much is clear," Henry said. "Those wo detectives did a heck of a fine job by finding hat ring. Incredible."

"Jennifer, tell the baby not to listen to this terrible ale about ice picks and dead bodies," Belinda said. 'The poor little darling will have nightmares in here."

"Oh, okay," Jennifer said, patting her stomach.

"What was your question, Henry?" Evan said, aising his eyebrows.

"It doesn't work for me, that's all. Here we have man…Lyle…who is so distraught about his rother…Franklin…destroying lives of innocent oung girls that he confronts his brother about the rostitution business."

"Mmm," Evan said.

"How can a man…and this is my question fi nally…who is that sensitive and sickened by th horror befalling those girls turn around and beat th pulp out of his brother, then stick him with an ic pick, for heaven's sake? Panicked or not, the tw sides of the man don't match up. They really don't."

Henry shook his head.

"Because you've assumed that Lyle was co cerned for the young girls, Henry," Jennifer sai "That's not why he confronted Franklin. Lyle w; worried that if what Franklin was doing was ev made public knowledge the Gardner name would b tarnished, leading to the Gardner power and soci status being diminished. He couldn't bear th thought of *that*." She nodded decisively. "Lyle de initely learned his attitude at his mother's knee."

"Oh, I see," Henry said. "Well, that makes sens then. Lyle was a scumball."

"Right." Jennifer turned to Evan. "You've bee so patient with everyone who has stopped you an blithered on about the case, and it was really nic of you to answer Henry's question, Evan, but this a party and I think we should go visit that yumm looking buffet over there."

"Hear, hear," Belinda said. "Jennifer is eatin for two now, and I'm going to do the same becaus I'm such a dedicated friend."

Jennifer and Belinda got to their feet and began o chat as Henry and Evan rose more slowly.

"You didn't answer my question, Evan," Henry aid, frowning. "It was Belinda and Jennifer who…"

"I know," Evan said, smiling, "and I doubt seriously that they realize it. Trust me, Henry, I understand this stuff. It's a woman thing. And as far as *my* woman goes? I intend to enjoy every crazy, wonderful, loving minute with Jennifer for the rest of my life."

*　*　*　*　*

MILLS & BOON®

Visit millsandboon.co.uk and discover your one-stop shop for romance!

Find out everything you want to know about romance novels in one place. Read about and buy our novels online anytime you want.

Choose and buy books from an extensive selection of Mills & Boon®, Silhouette® and MIRA® titles.

Receive 25% off the cover price of all special releases and MIRA® books.

Enjoy bestselling authors – from Penny Jordan and Diana Palmer to Meg O'Brien and Alex Kava!

Take advantage of our amazing **FREE** book offers.

In our Authors' area find titles currently available from all your favourite authors.

Get hooked on one of our fabulous online reads, with new chapters updated regulary.

Visit us online at
www.millsandboon.co.uk

…you'll want to come back again and again!!

/RS1 V2

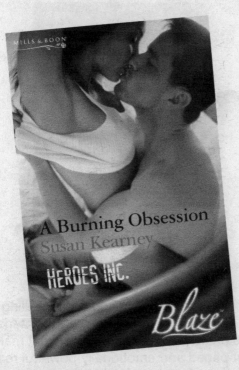

Escape into...
SPECIAL EDITION

Life, love and family.